JUST A LITTLE GAMBLE

MERRY FARMER

JUST A LITTLE GAMBLE

Copyright ©2021 by Merry Farmer

This book is licensed for your personal enjoyment only. This book may not be re-sold or given away to other people. If you would like to share this book with another person, please purchase an additional copy for each recipient. If you're reading this book and did not purchase it, or it was not purchased for your use only, then please return to your digital retailer and purchase your own copy. Thank you for respecting the hard work of this author.

This book is a work of fiction. Names, characters, places, and incidents are products of the author's imagination or are used fictitiously. Any resemblance to actual events or locales or persons, living or dead, is entirely coincidental.

Cover design by Erin Dameron-Hill (the miracle-worker)

ASIN: B08RY2WFD5

Paperback ISBN: 9798736937882

Click here for a complete list of other works by Merry Farmer.

If you'd like to be the first to learn about when the next books in the series come out and more, please sign up for my newsletter here: http://eepurl.com/RQ-KX

 Created with Vellum

CHAPTER 1

LONDON – FEBRUARY, 1891

The best suit that Cameron Oberlin owned was far from suitable enough for a concert at the Royal Albert Hall. Not even close. To begin with, he'd purchased it second-hand when John Dandie had hired him as a clerk at his law office. Not only was the style just out of date enough to be noticed, but the elbows and knees were embarrassingly threadbare. He stood in front of the warped and cracked mirror in the corner of his meager boarding house room and chewed his lip anxiously over the picture he made.

It wasn't good enough. Nothing about him was good enough. He was a shambles as a clerk, he looked more like a vagabond than a concert-goer as he adjusted his tie and smoothed his blond hair back, and he was a failure as a son, as the letter on the beat-up bureau behind him attested. He sighed at his reflection and tried once again to brush over the elbows of his suit jacket, hoping the fabric would somehow magically knit itself back together. But if he couldn't expect his life to knit itself back together, what could he expect from a suit?

Frowning, he turned away from the mirror and went to the bureau to fetch his pocket watch and hat. He checked the watch, relieved that he had enough time to make it to the concert hall so that he could meet up with John Dandie at the appointed hour, then slipped the fancy piece into his jacket pocket. He couldn't afford a watch fob, so there would be no wearing the watch as a display piece. He wasn't sure he wanted the thing on display anyhow, considering how he'd gotten it. He should have sold it and sent the money to his parents, but if they knew the source of that money, they would have sent it back, along with all his other letters.

Cameron let out a sigh as he touched the latest letter to his mother that had been returned. Inside the envelope she'd sent him was the letter he'd written to her two weeks ago, still sealed. His mother hadn't read a single one of his pleas for understanding and his insistence that he still loved her, even if she'd rejected him as perverted and broken. Strangely enough, she never had a problem opening the letters he sent home once a month with the lion's share of his salary from working for John Dandie.

He didn't fool himself to think anyone in his family actually read the sentiments in those letters, though. They only cared about the cash.

There was no point in dawdling in his room, eating his heart out over the past and the family he'd lost. He had an important job to do. John Dandie was relying on him to help discover the whereabouts of Lady Selby, wife of Blake Williamson, the Duke of Selby, who was now living openly with his lover, playwright Niall Cristofori. Well, openly to members of The Brotherhood—a discreet organization that provided a social life and protection for men in London who fancied other men. Cameron was a member of The Brotherhood at John Dandie's insistence. He doubted he'd have had the nerve to set foot in the same circles as most of the members on his own.

He headed out of his room, shutting the door carefully behind him so as to make as little noise as possible. For as long as he'd known the truth about himself, he'd found that being as quiet as possible and drawing no attention to himself was the only way to get by. He practically tip-toed down the hall and past the rooms of other boarders to the stairs, then walked as softly as he could down to the front hall, putting on his winter coat and hat as he did.

He'd almost made it to the door when the stern voice of his landlady, Mrs. Fielding, stopped him with, "Mr. Oberlin, just where are you going at this late hour?"

Cameron cringed and turned to face the stout, grey-haired woman as though he'd been caught doing far more than simply going to a concert for the night. He swept his bowler hat from his head, worried the brim through his fingers and said, "Good evening, Mrs. Fielding. I was just on my way out to a concert at the Royal Albert Hall."

Mrs. Fielding glared at him. "Do not toy with me, boy," she snapped. "Since when does a country rube like you attend events in high society?"

Cameron swallowed hard. "M-my employer, Mr. John Dandie, has requested I attend tonight. It's the premier of an associate of ours, you see. Mr. Samuel Percy. M-mr. Percy is part of an investigation Mr. Dandie is currently undertaking, and…and business will be discussed tonight."

It was a lame explanation. Cameron felt as though he'd said more than he should and not enough to make a lick of sense at the same time. And judging by the way Mrs. Fielding crossed her arms and narrowed her eyes at him, she didn't believe a word of it.

"How much is that Mr. Dandie paying you?" she asked, narrowing her eyes even more. "Because it strikes me as odd that a man as fancy as he is should have a clerk who can barely afford to pay his rent on time and who walks about looking like he stepped out of the rag bag."

Cameron chewed his lip and nearly crushed the brim of his hat. "I send a great deal of my earnings home," he mumbled.

"Earnings, you say?" Mrs. Fielding radiated disapproval. "Just you be sure you're not gaining those earnings in evil ways, Mr. Oberlin. I don't give lodgings to telegraph boys."

"Oh, no, Mrs. Fielding." Cameron feigned extreme shock. "How could you even think such a thing? I-I have a girl back in Derbyshire, you see." It was a blatant lie, and since Cameron was terrible at lying, his face went bright pink. But Cameron was masculine enough to pass as normal, in spite of being shy, and most people would rather have believed a soothing lie than a disturbing truth. And as it turned out, he had worked as a telegraph boy when he'd first come to London. With everything that implied.

Mrs. Fielding hummed suspiciously. "You just watch that company you keep, boy. Everyone knows that there's more dandy in that John Dandie than meets the eye. Your employer is likely to be arrested on charges of indecency one of these days, and then what will you do to pay your rent?"

Cameron had worried about the same thing himself for far longer than he wanted to admit. Not that John would ever do anything foolish enough to have himself arrested, but there was no guarantee he would employ Cameron forever. Particularly since Cameron considered himself rubbish with basic tasks, such as filing and using the new typing machines. He knew full well from past experience that, if it should come to it again, he could fetch a good price as a rent boy, but his heart would never be in that sort of activity. He wanted a calm, domestic life, like some of the couples living in Darlington

Gardens had. He wanted love and affection, not just pleasure and risk.

"Are you daft, boy?" Mrs. Fielding snapped, jerking him out of his thoughts. "Did you not hear me? It's high time you found another employer. One that won't threaten your immortal soul."

"Yes, Mrs. Fielding." Cameron nodded and bowed to her as he inched toward the door. He plunked his hat back on his head. "If you will excuse me, I really must be going."

He edged his way out the door and into the dreary, February evening as Mrs. Fielding snorted and shook her head in disapproval.

Cameron's boarding house in Clerkenwell was a long way from the Royal Albert Hall in Kensington, but John had provided him with fare for an omnibus to take him across town so that he wouldn't be late. Cameron was grateful for John's generosity, but it made him uncomfortable. He would never be able to pay John back. For anything. John had found him and taken him in when he'd landed in London the year before, after the scandal that had wrenched him from his home and everything he'd ever known. Cameron had known nothing about navigating life in a city, nothing about working as a clerk, and absolutely nothing about the underground society of men like him and all the ways they looked out for each other. He didn't know what would have become of him if not for the chance meeting with John when he delivered a telegram to his office.

Now here he was, wearing a suit and whizzing across London on a crowded omnibus with an evening among high society in front of him. That was all amazing in and of itself, but the true wonder of the evening was the company he would be keeping.

He spotted Mr. Samuel Percy nearly immediately after hopping off the omnibus and walking the rest of the way down the block to the Royal Albert Hall, and his heart and cock reacted to the sight of the man. John had introduced them at The Chameleon Club—the club on Park Lane reserved for members of The Brotherhood—months ago, and Cameron had been enthralled by the tall, handsome composer at once. Samuel was everything Cameron wasn't. He was bold, outspoken, and jovial. He interacted with people easily, laughed loudly, and could converse with anyone at all. Samuel was also black, with eyes like pools of midnight, broad shoulders, and long, muscular legs that his trousers did little to conceal the tempting shape of.

But it was the way Samuel treated him that had sent Cameron's thoughts into dangerous territory from the moment they'd first met.

"Look who's here at last," Samuel boomed, smiling broadly and holding out an arm to welcome Cameron into the circle of friends that consisted of him, John, and Niall. "And looking a treat, I might add."

Samuel swept Cameron with a look that said he wouldn't mind escorting him to a dark corner, bending him over, pulling down his trousers, and fucking him until they were both dizzy with pleasure. He was that obvious, in spite of the crowd of theater goers around them. And, Lord help him, Cameron would have willingly gone with the fascinating man and done anything he said just for the honor of basking in his presence.

"Cat got your tongue?" Samuel continued to tease him as Cameron stood awkwardly at the edge of the group.

"I...er...um...." Cameron couldn't think of a thing to say. He was in so far over his head that he couldn't see the light above the water. Not just where Samuel was concerned, but with society in general.

"You really need to stop teasing the poor lad," John admonished Samuel with a laugh. "He's shy."

Cameron was far more than just that, but he let John pretend he was simple so he wouldn't have to argue.

"We were just discussing how there has been no sign of Lady Selby or Lord Stanley for a week," John informed Cameron, switching to business. Lord Stanley was Blake Williamson's five-year-old son and heir, with whom Lady Selby had run off. Blake was desperate to get his son back. So much so that he'd exposed himself to ridicule and the possibility of arrest by appearing at a public ball just over a fortnight ago, even though news of his devotion to Niall had spread like wildfire through high society.

"The best lead we could possibly hope for is to discover the identity of the nurse who is caring for Alan,"

Niall said, his frown showing how frustrated he was with the situation.

"And no one has been able to discover the woman's identity yet?" John asked.

Niall shook his head. "She's evasive."

"I thought I'd figured out who she was two days ago," Cameron added, though he felt awkward talking about his most recent failure at work in front of Samuel. "But it turned out not to be her."

"I thought you had her," John said with a consoling smile.

"You'll figure her out yet," Samuel said, thumping Cameron's back.

Cameron went hot all over at the contact and turned his head away to hide his bashful grin.

"In the meantime," Samuel went on, as though he didn't notice Cameron at all, "I'm still making inquiries about my sister. If Ian Archibald is her prisoner in some way, she would tell me."

Ian Archibald was Lady Selby's lover and coconspirator in keeping Lord Stanley away from Blake. He'd been kidnapped from Hyde Park about a week ago—at least, that was what it had looked like to those who had witnessed Ian being dragged into Samuel's sister's carriage. They'd been able to determine that the woman who called herself The Black Widow was indeed Samuel's sister. Cameron had been the one to identify the carriage as belonging to the late Mr. Thorne—a wealthy and eccentric collector of the exotic who had an estate near where Cameron had grown up, in

Derby. Ian had apparently been working for Samantha Thorne to retrieve an Egyptian medallion to complete one of her collections, and because he owed her a great deal of money. But they hadn't worked out what for or why The Black Widow would still want to keep Ian a prisoner.

"I've invited Sammy to the concert tonight," Samuel went on. "If she's still in London, she won't be able to resist coming out to see her twin brother debut his latest symphony in a venue like this." He turned to nod up at the Royal Albert Hall as though it were an adversary he'd finally gotten the better of.

Indeed, Cameron was utterly amazed that a place as hoity-toity as the Royal Albert Hall would debut a work by a black composer. It gave him hope that the world was truly changing. Women were gaining more rights with every day, men like him were able to live quiet but respectable lives, provided they didn't draw attention to themselves, and a black man was being celebrated as a musical genius. The world was a hopeful place indeed.

"With any luck," John said, "we'll nab The Black Widow tonight, and by tomorrow we'll discover the identity of that nanny."

"I'm willing to do whatever it takes to reunite Alan with his family," Niall said with a wistful sigh. "You don't know how difficult it's been to watch Blake tie himself in knots of guilt and regret. All I want to do is make our family whole so that we can go on together and live in peace."

"I know, my friend, I know." John patted Niall's shoulder.

"If you want to find the people you're looking for, you should have hired an expert from the beginning," a new voice joined the conversation.

They all turned to find the short but powerful figure of Detective Arthur Gleason sidling up to their group. Gleason wore a sly smile that he directed immediately to John. John's back went up in an instant, and even though he glared at Gleason, Cameron was certain anyone for miles around could sense the sexual tension between the two men.

"This will be interesting," Samuel murmured close to Cameron's ear.

Cameron flushed even hotter at the whisper of Samuel's breath against him and nodded, giving his attention to Gleason and John.

John sighed. "What do you want, Gleason?" he snapped.

"The same things as ever," Gleason said with a half shrug, raking John from head to toe with a look that undressed him. The look was salacious enough that Cameron jerked his head this way and that, praying that no one was observing them. Fortunately, they didn't appear to be.

"You're not welcome here," John told Gleason with a frown. "You're not needed in this investigation."

"I think I am," Gleason said. "After all, you're a solicitor, not a detective. Shouldn't you be trying cases or helping men make their wills?"

"I'm not that kind of a solicitor," John said, crossing his arms and challenging Gleason with a stare. "But if you must know, I have a full caseload of exactly those sorts of wills and contracts and business dealings in addition to this case, which I have taken on for a friend."

"He's definitely on the back foot," Samuel muttered to Cameron again, sliding so close their arms nearly touched. "He wouldn't brag about his caseload if he wasn't trying to impress the bastard."

Cameron agreed. John wasn't exactly subtle in his feelings for Gleason—if lust could be considered a feeling.

"You need to find the nanny," Gleason went on, so confident that he didn't even bother saying whose nanny or why they needed to find her. He shrugged. "I can have her name, her family, where she grew up, her education, and her previous employment by tomorrow afternoon, if you'd let me in."

"I'm not letting you in anywhere," John said. "You have a tendency to back the wrong horse."

"Yes, and what exactly do you know about your former employer, my sister's, whereabouts, eh, Gleason?" Samuel challenged him, but with a cheeky grin instead of John's intense stare.

"I stopped working for your sister the moment I realized her intentions weren't pure," Gleason told Samuel with more respect than he was showing John. "Where she is now is her business."

"But you could have that information for us by tomorrow afternoon, and Ian Archibald's location as well, if you so choose," Samuel teased him. He nudged Cameron's arm, as if he were in on the joke too.

Cameron gently touched the spot Samuel had nudged, wondering if he would ever stop feeling excited every time Samuel so much as brushed against him.

"My money is on your sister already being back in Derby," Gleason said, then faced John again. "As for your little problem…."

He didn't have a chance to finish. The doors to the Royal Albert Hall were opened, and the concert-goers who were waiting around for entrance surged to the door.

"Gentlemen, shall we take our seats to bask in my glory?" Samuel asked them all with a gloating smile.

"I think that's a grand idea," John said. He spared a final glare for Gleason before turning his back on him and mounting the stairs to the front door with Cameron and the others.

Cameron's heart sped up. He'd never dreamed he'd be able to afford to step foot inside the Royal Albert Hall. Not once in his life had he thought he'd be permitted into a place so opulent. The closer they grew to the entrance, the more he was convinced they would take one look at his shabby suit and battered hat and throw him back into the gutter.

Indeed, when they reached the door and the usher

stepped into their path with a glare, Cameron was certain the moment of humiliation had come.

"He can't come in here," the usher said with a sneer.

"I beg your pardon?" John said, affronted.

"His kind aren't allowed in decent company." The usher sniffed, curled his lip, and stared down his nose.

But it wasn't Cameron he looked disgusted with; it was Samuel.

CHAPTER 2

Few things were as exciting as having one's composition premiered at the Royal Albert Hall. Particularly when one's mother worked on the Caribbean sugar plantation where one's great-grandparents had been enslaved. Samuel was ridiculously proud of himself for achieving such an honor after years of hard work, and rejection—not because of any lack of talent, but because of the color of his skin—rankled him. He'd made the right friends—including his late father's family—and shook the right hands to get where he was, and he fully intended to bask in the accomplishment, even if it made him seem like an arrogant prick.

He also fully intended to bask in the enjoyment of having the gorgeous, timorous, virile presence of Cameron Oberlin at his side in his moment of triumph. Cameron was a tasty morsel that he'd been wanting to take a bite of for months. He was everything Samuel loved—reserved, yet masculine, fit as any dancer, yet youthful in appearance, and unsure of himself, but brimming with potential. Samuel wanted to bring the young man out of his shell, and out of his trousers, and out of his skin with pleasure, if he were being honest.

He could tell that Cameron was nervous to be so close to him as they stood side-by-side, watching John and Gleason spar with each other. That was another amusement Samuel could have watched for hours. As far as he could see, John and Gleason were involved in the longest stretch of foreplay he'd ever seen two people engage in.

He wouldn't have minded a bit of teasing and foreplay with Cameron himself. As they mounted the stairs to make their way into the Royal Albert Hall, he devised at least half a dozen different scenarios whereby he could coax Cameron into indulging in a bit of an afterparty, once the concert was done, so that he could make the night the most triumphant of his life.

His thoughts were absorbed in indulgent bliss so much that he didn't see the crushing blow coming until the hammer had already fallen.

"Excuse me, young man," Samuel addressed the usher, even though the man was of an age with him. "You seem to be ignorant of whom you are speaking to." He wasn't certain he'd spoken entirely correctly, but the more important he sounded, the more the usher was likely to back down.

Except that instead of being intimidated by Samuel's confidence and booming voice, the usher appeared to dig in his heels. He crossed his arms and said, "No negroes allowed."

"This particular negro is the composer of one of tonight's works," Samuel informed the louse, pulling himself up to his full height.

The usher snorted. "A likely story. A negro? Composing music? This isn't a third-rate music hall." He sniffed again, then made a shooing gesture. "Run along now, boy."

Samuel saw red. It took every ounce of restraint and dignity he had not to punch the supercilious usher in his stubby nose. Doing that would only end with him being the one arrested, unfair though it would be. But there was something about being challenged with Cameron standing right by him that embarrassed Samuel more than a simple dismissal ever could.

"I demand to see your manager," he told the usher in as even a voice as he could manage.

The usher merely sneered at him.

"He's telling the truth," Niall said, stepping forward. "Do you know who I am?"

"No," the usher said firmly, arms crossed.

"That's Niall Cristofori, the playwright," a patron passing behind the usher said.

Samuel was grateful for the interruption, but not so much when the smug man stood back to watch the confrontation, as if getting a show before the show. In fact, several people had gathered around to see what was going on.

"I don't care if he's Prince Albert himself," the usher said. "No negroes are getting in this vaulted establishment while I'm on duty."

The man must have intended to say "vaunted" establishment. Samuel would have rolled his eyes at the man's manner if it weren't so humiliating for him.

"I'll give you one last chance to pull out that stick that you so obviously have up your arse and give me admittance," Samuel said in as threatening a voice as he could.

He peeked at Cameron, hoping and praying that the younger man would be impressed by his boldness and not embarrassed to be seen with him. Cameron most certainly looked embarrassed, but no more than he usually did, bless the man.

"Call for the manager, or the conductor, or the concert master," Gleason suggested, stepping up on Samuel's other side. "Call for anyone with more authority than this dolt. Either that, or we'll call for the police to sort it out."

"Here, now, that won't be necessary," the usher said, starting to look nervous.

It irritated Samuel to no end that the man wasn't intimidated by his size and presence, but the color of Gleason's skin made the usher doubt himself.

They were saved from even more embarrassment when an older gentleman in a suit that was nicer than the usher's uniform, but not as nice as the patrons attending the concert, stepped up behind the usher. "What seems to be the problem, Jenkins?"

"This negro, sir," the usher said. "Says he's the composer of tonight's concert." He laughed as though it were a lark.

Samuel stepped closer to the older man. "Samuel Percy, at your service," he said, extending a hand.

"Oh!" The older man adjusted the glasses he wore, sweeping Samuel with an assessing look. "And do you have any proof of that?"

The usher suddenly looked uncertain. Samuel seethed with indignation.

"We're proof of that," Niall said. "We all vouch for him."

"And who are you?" the older man—who Samuel was beginning to suspect was the manager—asked.

"Niall Cristofori, the playwright," Niall growled.

"John Dandie, solicitor," John answered.

"Detective Arthur Gleason," Gleason put in.

The manager turned to Cameron. Cameron mumbled, "I'm nobody."

Samuel's anger flashed suddenly to sentiment. He wanted to reach out and take Cameron's hand, but knew that would only complicate things.

"And do you have tickets?" the manager asked.

Samuel huffed impatiently and reached into his pocket. John, Niall, and Gleason did the same. The manager scrutinized the tickets they held, pursed his lips, looked uncertainly from Samuel to John to the others, then back at Samuel.

"All right. I'll allow you to enter. But I will be

checking with the conductor of tonight's work, and if he cannot identify you as genuine, I will call the police."

Samuel was livid, but at least the manager and the usher stepped aside and let him in. His spirits, which had been soaring high just moments before, felt as though they'd been struck by an arrow in mid-flight and plummeted to the ground. He stormed through the lobby of the theater, too frustrated to speak with the others, and searched for the correct door that would take him to the box that had been set aside for him and his friends for the evening.

"I'm sorry you had to go through that," Cameron mumbled once they found the correct stairway and started up. "People treat me like that all the time."

Samuel laughed bitterly and pulled away from him. "And why would they do that? You're a handsome, blond-haired, blue-eyed Adonis with a mouth made for sin. Who would ever turn you away as if you were a mangy dog in the street?"

Cameron nearly missed a step, his shapely mouth dropping open in shock. Samuel felt too much bitterness in his heart to stop for the lad, even though a strong burst of guilt hit him as he marched on and around the corner once he made it to the top of the stairs. He stomped down the hallway to the entrance to their box, not in a mood to speak to anyone.

To make matters worse, once he climbed down the stairs in the box to look out over the house to see how well-attended the concert would be, he spotted the manager having a word with one of the violinists tuning up on the stage. The violinist turned to squint at Samuel in the box, then nodded to the manager and said something, evidently confirming his identity. The manager scowled up at Samuel—who drew himself to his full height, hoping he looked like a king surveying his kingdom—then asked fully three other musicians to confirm who he was before dropping his shoulders and marching off the stage.

It was too much for Samuel. What should have been a moment of triumph had been spoiled beyond recognition. He moved to one of the back corners of the box, taking a seat and eschewing the conversation of his friends as more of them arrived. Instead, he occupied himself scanning the other boxes, hoping he'd see Sammy in one of them.

He hadn't just invited his sister to brag about his accomplishments to her. Sammy had enough accomplishments under her belt to match his when it came to infiltrating high society. She'd married an astoundingly wealthy man with homes in Derby, London, and the Isle of Wight. She'd managed to hold the reins of her husband's power once he passed. And she'd done it all while maintaining a place in society. To a degree, at least. She would never be accepted in some circles, but she'd fully conquered others.

He, on the other hand, despised the same people who should have been falling all over themselves to befriend a composer of his renown. None of them deserved the esteem they held. The only thing they'd done to earn it was to be born to the right family. Those people would never accept him, so he had made it his mission to live his life however he wanted, especially in ways they wouldn't have approved of, loving whomever he wanted to, whenever he wanted to, and thumbing his nose at so-called morality.

The burst of energy those thoughts brought with them died down quickly, leaving Samuel to feel like a lost child as he searched through the growing crowd in the theater for his sister. He didn't see her among the sea of the nobility as they crowded into boxes, though. And Sammy most definitely would have stood out.

Eventually, his gaze shifted from the other boxes to his own. More specifically, it shifted to watching Cameron. The young man was out of his depth. He sat uneasily in his chair, two rows down from the seat Samuel had taken. His suit was a disgrace, but at least he wore it well. The anxiety in Cameron's eyes was enough to break Samuel's heart, which calmed his fury a bit. Even when some of Samuel's musical friends attempted to speak to the lad—friends who were about as intimidating as bunnies on the moors in spring—Cameron stammered and shied away from them. It was a terrible shame too. As far as Samuel could see, Cameron was everything a man could want in a companion and a friend. He suspected that Cameron could be everything a man would want in a lover as well.

The orchestra began to tune, and the lights were

brought down in the house just at that convenient moment—a relatively new innovation in theaters across Europe that Samuel approved of. If he wasn't going to be able to enjoy the victory of his premier, at least he could enjoy the way his trousers grew tight as he studied Cameron's profile in the dimming theater light. The man truly did have the most alluring mouth. Samuel could just imagine what it would feel like stretched over his cock.

He shifted in his seat, spreading his legs a bit to give his prick and his imagination room to grow, as the audience applauded the conductor, as he took the stage. Carnal thoughts might have been inconvenient and inappropriate in a concert hall, but they were a damn sight better than wallowing in the sting of prejudice. The opening bars of his symphony might have been new, and hopefully magical, to the audience, but the music was familiar to him. As familiar as the feeling of need that pulsed through him. If he'd thought he could get away with it, he would have unfastened his trousers and treated himself to a sinful wank while watching Cameron's reaction to his music.

As the first movement gave way to the second, Samuel wasn't certain what Cameron thought. The man's eyes remained round, but he wriggled in distress, glancing around uncomfortably. Samuel wondered if the man had ever attended a concert of any sort before. He knew from John that Cameron was a country boy, and that he'd only come to the city recently. He was unrefined, but eager. And Samuel was a fanatic about eagerness.

When the second movement advanced to the third, Cameron surprised him by getting up and scurrying clumsily up through the box to the door. He made a quiet exit, but it still felt like a defeat of some sort to Samuel. Unless the exit was meant for something else entirely.

Heart racing with danger and arousal, Samuel got up and subtly followed Cameron out of the box. The hall running behind the boxes was empty. Cameron was already near the far end of the hall, searching for something, and trying various doors. Samuel followed him with a grin, charmed by the realization that Cameron was looking for a toilet. The adorable young man must have forgotten to go before departing for the concert, like any green child would. And as far as Samuel was concerned, that was the perfect opportunity for him.

He walked to the toilet's door, then checked up and down the hallway to make certain no one was observing before stepping in. The room was small, but designed for multiple occupants. It also had a lock for the door, which Samuel turned so he and Cameron wouldn't be disturbed. And sure enough, the sound of pissing came from behind a partition. Samuel moved to lean against a counter with a washbasin, crossing his arms and waiting.

Cameron was still fastening his trousers when he stepped out from behind the partition.

"I don't think you need to bother with that," Samuel

told him with a rakish grin. "They'll just be undone again in a few minutes anyhow."

Cameron jumped and gasped, grabbing onto the partition as though he would fall over in shock if he didn't. "You frightened me," he gulped, pulling himself straight.

"Yes, I suspect I've frightened you all along," Samuel said, raking him with a heated glance. "But you've no need to be frightened of me, Cameron. I'm very nice, I promise."

He was being unforgivable and aggressive, he knew, but it was a gamble he was willing to make. Cameron clearly didn't have the experience to know what to think of his overt sensuality. But after the evening he'd had, after the humiliation he'd experienced, Samuel wanted something to make him feel good. He wanted something wicked and wild that represented making a rude gesture at society. And what better way to spit in the eye of the so-called upright and proper set than to commit buggery in what could be considered a temple to the ruling class.

"Come here and give us a kiss, love," he teased Cameron, beckoning to him with a crooked finger.

Cameron's sinful mouth dropped open, and he glanced to the door. "We…we can't," he whispered.

"I've locked the door," Samuel said. "No one can get in and no one can see us. You know you've been wanting to be in this situation with me for ages."

"Um…I…." Cameron inched forward, a spark of

temptation in his eyes. He neither confirmed nor denied Samuel's bold statement.

Samuel pushed away from the counter. "Wouldn't you like a kiss and a fumble?" he asked, moving steadily toward Cameron. "Aren't you curious?"

"Er...well...um...I am a little curious, yes," Cameron said, his voice shaking.

"We've been doing this dance for months." Samuel reached him, and when Cameron didn't back away, he slipped his arms around Cameron's trim waist, dropping his hands to caress Cameron's firm backside. It was delicious too. Samuel wanted full, unfettered access to it as soon as possible. "Do you like that?" he asked in a purr, meeting Cameron's eyes.

Cameron swallowed hard, his Adam's apple bouncing. He didn't answer with words, but he did nod tightly.

"I bet you'd like to know what a black man's cock tastes like too," Samuel went on, blood racing, trousers so tight he couldn't wait to unbutton them as soon as Cameron was on his knees.

Instead of rushing into the position, Cameron's eyes went wide, and he looked a little hurt. "You're only propositioning me because you feel bad about being snubbed."

Samuel's throat constricted, and his heart stung in his chest. He opened his mouth to make a sly, suggestive retort, but found he couldn't. He couldn't, because Cameron was right. The young man had seen through him as though he were glass.

"Yes," he went on, massaging Cameron's arse and pressing their hips together so Cameron could feel his erection. "I do feel bad. But you could make me feel good." He brought his mouth closer to Cameron's.

"But how would that make me feel?" Cameron asked in a whisper, avoiding his mouth.

The second blow was even harder than the first. How *would* it make Cameron feel? Like he was just a convenient mouth to suck him off because he felt morose? Samuel had spent months flirting with Cameron and fantasizing about him while beating himself off before bed at night. Did he really want to ruin it all now by demanding something Cameron might not be ready to give?

Although, what if the lad *were* ready, but he needed a little coaxing along to let him know it was allowed?

"I would hope it'd make you feel good too," Samuel cooed, raising one of his hands to caress Cameron's face. "Wouldn't you like to feel good with me?"

He took a risk and slanted his mouth over Cameron's, stealing the kiss he'd been dreaming about for months. Cameron made a sound of surprise and pleasure in the back of his throat, but his body remained tense. It stayed tense, even when Cameron slid his arms over Samuel's shoulders, giving in and letting himself be kissed into oblivion. And Samuel did just that. He'd waited too long not to explore Cameron's mouth fully or to thrust his tongue alongside Cameron's.

It wasn't nearly enough. He reached a hand between

them, fumbling with the half-done fastenings of Cameron's trousers so he could slip his hand in to caress the lad's cock. Cameron let out a cry of pleasure, and when he tilted his head back, Samuel switched to kissing and licking his neck. The tension in Cameron's body was beautiful, and Samuel caught himself wondering how Cameron would feel once all that tension was released and he was satisfied.

He had just started to stroke Cameron's cock in earnest when the handle on the door rattled, as if someone were trying to enter. Cameron cried out with far more fear than lust and yanked away from Samuel, flushed and shaking. Samuel turned to the door as well, praying that the lock did what it was supposed to do.

CHAPTER 3

A handful of seconds. That was all it had taken for Cameron to land himself back in the same situation that had driven him from Derby. He'd been tempted by Samuel—more than tempted, if he were honest—he'd let his guard down and given in to pleasure for just a few seconds, and he'd ended up a heartbeat away from disaster. He could only thank God that Samuel had thought to lock the door before advancing on him.

The door handle rattled again, and Cameron held his breath. He backpedaled away from the door, glancing anxiously to the partition, wondering if it would be enough for him to hide behind. He couldn't be caught again, he just couldn't. London was the last resort for men like him. If he were shamed away from London, where would he go?

The door handle rattled a third time, and a muffled curse sounded from the other side.

"Occupied," Samuel called to the door in his booming voice. "And believe me, you truly do not wish to come in here at the moment."

The voice from the hall exclaimed something muffled, then whoever it was walked away.

Samuel chuckled, then turned back to Cameron. "Works every time," he said with a cunning grin. "We'll let the man's imagination come up with all the reasons he doesn't want to enter." He started back toward Cameron, his grin turning seductive once more. "Now, where were we?"

Cameron let Samuel come close enough to slide an arm around his waist and slant his mouth over his. Samuel was an accomplished kisser, as Cameron had somehow guessed he would be. He was tender, but demanding, and under different circumstances, Cameron might have been convinced to let the kissing go on for much longer and lead to something more. But the near miss of almost being caught was too much.

With a whimper, he pulled away from Samuel and marched across the room to the door. "No, we can't," he said, tucking himself fully back into his trousers and fastening them with shaking hands. It was devilishly uncomfortable, considering he was still hard.

"Who says we can't?" Samuel pursued him across the room. "I've seen the way you've watched me these past few months, Cameron. I know you want me."

"I do," Cameron said before he could think better of it.

"And I've wanted you right from the start too," Samuel said, striding up to him until Cameron was forced to turn and press his back against the door. "So why not act on all that desire?" He brushed his hand along Cameron's hot cheek.

"We're in a public place." Cameron scrambled to find reasons that would contradict his caution and allow him to do what, if he were honest with himself, he really wanted to do.

Samuel shrugged. "Hasn't stopped me before."

Cameron gaped at him. "It hasn't?"

"Why would it?" Samuel leaned closer to him, brushing his lips across Cameron's neck. Cameron sucked in a breath and leaned his head back, giving Samuel better access. "Don't you love the thrill of danger involved in the whole thing?" he asked. "Doesn't the possibility of being caught excite you?"

The lust pounding through Cameron deflated a bit. "No, actually," he said, managing to squirm away from Samuel and the door. "Getting caught is what landed me in gallons of hot water to begin with."

Samuel blinked in surprise, then frowned. "You won't be caught this time," he said. "I can promise you that."

Cameron's mouth pulled into a lopsided half-smile. "If you can guarantee we won't be caught, then where is the danger in wondering if we *will* be caught?"

Samuel's mouth hung open for a moment as though he were puzzling out that riddle.

Cameron didn't wait for him to come up with an answer. "I'm sorry. You're very lovely, and maybe some other time I'd like to...." He flailed his hand, hoping Samuel would understand what that meant. "But not at the Royal Albert Hall, and not tonight. I'm very sorry."

He took a breath to help him work up the gumption to march past Samuel, unlock the door, and step out into the hall.

"Cameron, wait," Samuel called after him. Cameron picked up his pace, more worried than ever that any scene Samuel caused would land them both in jail for the night, or worse. "It doesn't have to be here. We could go—"

Samuel stopped abruptly, and when Cameron sensed that he'd stopped following him, he turned to see why. They had just passed one of the stairways leading down to the lobby. Samuel stared at the back of a woman who was retreating down the stairs at a fast clip. Cameron could guess in an instant what had him so interested. The woman leaving the concert was black.

"Sammy?" Samuel called after her, then headed down the stairs.

Cameron looked up and down the hall, panicking for a moment as he wondered what he should do, then jumping after Samuel. He caught up to Samuel in just a few steps, and together, the two of them chased the woman through the lobby.

"Sammy," Samuel called again.

The woman didn't turn around, but she picked up her pace as she dashed through the theater's doors and out into the night.

"Is that your sister?" Cameron asked, even though he thought it was a foolish question.

"It has to be," Samuel said. "If we catch her, we can make her tell us where Ian Archibald is."

Cameron's pulse kicked up at the prospect. It would be lovely to be able to do something right in his work for John for a change. "Shouldn't we go back to the box and get our coats and hats first?" he asked all the same as they dashed out into the cold night.

"Not unless we want her to get away," Samuel said.

It was more difficult to see which way the woman was going in the darkness outside the theater, even though quite a few streetlamps illuminated the square around the hall. Samuel's sister seemed to know precisely where she was headed and dodged the carriages parked along the side of the concert hall, waiting to take some of the wealthier patrons home at the end of the concert, no doubt. Cameron thought for certain they would catch up to her once they made it past the first row of carriages, but as soon as they stepped out into a clearer part of the road, the woman was gone.

"How did she do that?" Cameron asked in a baffled voice.

"Sammy has her tricks," Samuel said. "She probably got into one of these carriages, probably had it waiting."

Cameron searched for the large, black carriage that they'd seen The Black Widow drive through Hyde Park a few weeks earlier. It was the same carriage Mr. Thorne used to drive through the Derbyshire countryside near his home to terrorize locals. That carriage was noticeable under any circumstances, and Cameron could tell right away it wasn't nearby.

"There." Samuel grabbed his arm suddenly, pointing to a nondescript carriage pulling away from the others. "That has to be her."

They jogged down the street a bit, and Cameron craned his neck, trying to get a look in one of the windows to see if Samuel's sister was, indeed, the passenger. He couldn't tell, but Samuel seemed certain.

"We're not going to catch her on foot," he said. "We'll have to hire a hack of our own to follow her." He continued down the road, waving at the line of carriages parked slightly farther from the concert hall.

As Cameron suspected, none of them seemed particularly willing to break ranks to take a black man as a passenger. He felt guilty doing it, but he stepped in front of Samuel and waved in his stead. Sure enough—although it took a moment—one of the carriages eventually did roll into motion, taking its time to pull out and swing around to pick them up.

"It'll never work," Cameron said, glancing down the street where Samuel's sister's carriage had disappeared. "She has too much of a head start. We'll never be able to follow her."

"Then it's a good thing I know my sister's London address," Samuel told him with a teasing grin.

Cameron felt his face heat with sheepishness. Of course, Samuel would know where his sister lived. It was the same sort of miscalculation he always seemed to make while working with John. Although, to be fair, when John had made inquiries earlier, he'd learned Mrs. Thorne wasn't in town. It looked as though that had changed, though.

He kept his mouth shut as the driver leaned down from the carriage and asked him, "Where to?"

Cameron glanced to Samuel, who answered, "Number Twelve, Mount Street, Mayfair."

The driver frowned and said, "A likely story." But when Samuel produced a large bill from his inside jacket pocket and handed it to the man, he changed his tune. "Get in."

"That was far too much money for so short a trip," Cameron told Samuel, in awe, as they piled into the carriage.

"That's the price of taking a black man to a fashionable neighborhood," Samuel growled.

Cameron felt horrible for mentioning it and sank back into the seat as the carriage lurched forward. Every which way he turned, someone or another was looking down their nose at him for being poor or queer, but it had to be much worse for Samuel. It didn't matter what Samuel did or how he dressed or what he said. Samuel was proud and masculine, and no one would have guessed that he had the sort of inclinations he did. But one look at his skin, and people far lesser than him would automatically assume the very worst.

He kept those thoughts to himself as the carriage charged on. Samuel didn't seem to be in much of a mood to talk either. He kept glancing out the window and searching for something, presumably any sign of his sister's carriage. Cameron didn't want to disturb his thoughts. He admired Samuel too much to bother him.

The carriage slowed to a stop within a relatively short time. Samuel didn't wait for the driver to open the door to disembark. Cameron followed him, nearly falling as he stumbled down to the street. They were in a far fancier neighborhood than he had any right to be in. He waved to the driver in thanks, but the man was already pulling the carriage back out to the street and didn't acknowledge them.

"There she is," Samuel said in an excited voice, breaking into a jog.

Cameron saw the carriage that had pulled away from the Royal Albert Hall entering what he presumed were mews that serviced the row of fine houses. He hurried to keep up with Samuel, and the two of them darted into the mews in time to follow the carriage to its stopping point.

But when the door opened and the woman they'd been chasing stepped down, it wasn't the same woman who had called herself The Black Widow in Hyde Park.

John must have been right about her leaving town after all.

"Where is my sister?" Samuel demanded of her.

"She's not here," the woman said with a triumphant grin. "But she sends her best regards."

"This isn't funny Clarisse," Samuel growled at the woman, approaching her with long strides. "Where is she?"

"Clarisse?" Cameron asked, thoroughly confused.

"She's one of Sammy's maids," Samuel explained as they followed the woman—who walked ahead to what must have been a kitchen door to Samuel's sister's house. "They bear a passing resemblance, so sometimes Sammy has Clarisse pretend to be her when she doesn't want to be seen. Tell her I'm coming up to talk to her, whether she wants me to or not," Samuel called after Clarisse.

Clarisse stopped before the kitchen door and turned to face Samuel with an indignant look. "I told you, she's not here."

"Not in London?" Samuel asked.

Clarisse kept her mouth pressed shut and lowered her eyes.

Samuel stepped toward her. "Tell me where she's gone and if she still has Ian Archibald with her."

Clarisse snapped her gaze up to meet Samuel's, worry in her eyes. Cameron was no expert at reading people, but he would have sworn based on that look that The Black Widow did indeed still have Ian Archibald with her.

"This is a matter of life and death, Charisse," Samuel continued to hound the woman. "My sister is playing games with the life of a child, Lord Selby's heir."

Clarisse looked even more surprised and guilty. "Mrs. Thorne has nothing to do with Lord Selby or his runaway wife. Her only concerns are her own concerns."

Samuel huffed a humorless laugh. "That's certainly true. Sammy never did care for anyone but herself. Has she gone to Derby or the Isle of Wight?"

Clarisse looked downright murderous at what she must have perceived as an insult to her mistress. "I'm not telling you. She doesn't want you to know."

"I'm her family, God help us," Samuel growled. "The only family she has."

"And we all know how important that is to the both of you," Clarisse said, tilting her chin up defiantly.

Cameron shuffled on his spot, feeling as though he'd stepped into someone else's concerns that were none of his. He rubbed his arms to ward off the chill and glanced around. The mews were fairly simple for being in such a fine neighborhood. Several carriages were parked under a sturdy shelter. The one carriage he didn't see, however, was Mr. Thorne's black monstrosity.

Which told him immediately where Samuel's sister was.

"She's gone to Derby," he whispered in Samuel's ear.

Samuel snapped to face him. "How do you know?"

Cameron nodded to the mews. "The carriage is gone.

It's too large to put on a ferry to the Isle of Wight, so she's gone to Derby. Also, that's John's theory."

Samuel glanced back to Clarisse with a triumphant grin.

"If you don't leave right now, I'll scream," she said. "I'll cry rape, murder, anything. You know they'll come and string you up for it."

"Have a pleasant evening, Clarisse," Samuel said with a wink, turning and walking out of the mews.

Cameron followed him.

"It seems John was right to speculate Sammy would head north, to Derby," Samuel said as they rounded the corner and headed back to the street. He turned to flash a sultry smile at Cameron. "I guess this means you and I will be traveling to Derby together after all."

"I don't...he didn't...I'm not certain...." Cameron flailed for words.

Samuel stopped when they were still in the shadows of the alley leading to the mews and stepped dangerously close to Cameron. "Why don't you and I get a jump on the game. I live only a short way from here. Come up to my flat and we can continue what we started at the Royal Albert Hall." He backed Cameron against the brick wall and closed a hand over the front of his trousers.

Cameron responded instantly, and for a moment, a part of him was ready to throw caution to the wind and go to Samuel's flat. "I can't," he replied all the same. "It's just...I can't." He pulled away from Samuel and fussed with the bottom of his jacket, hoping it hid things.

Even in the dark, Cameron could see Samuel's frown of frustration. "I think you can, but you won't," Samuel said.

"That's a fair assessment," Cameron said, squirming with discomfort and glancing around to make certain they weren't being overheard.

"Why is that?" Samuel asked in clipped tones. "Because I'm black? Because I'm not good enough for you?"

"No!" Cameron nearly shouted, then blanched and lowered his voice. "No, not at all. In fact, I think you're a great deal *too* good for me."

"And I say I'm not," Samuel said. "Let me prove it to you." He advanced on Cameron again.

"This isn't what I want," Cameron blurted, holding up his hands and backing away. "I want more than a nice fumble in a toilet or a night of debauchery at your flat."

Samuel stopped, his frown deepening. "And what's wrong with any of that?"

"Nothing," Cameron said, frustrated that he wasn't getting his point across. "There's no problem at all with you craving danger, or wanting to make up for the sting of being snubbed the way you were tonight. There's nothing wrong with a little friendly buggery between friends either." He lowered his voice even more, glancing anxiously around, terrified that someone who shouldn't would hear what he was saying. "But that's not what I want."

"So what do you want?" Samuel asked, crossing his arms and bristling with impatience.

"I want," Cameron started, then blew out a breath and rubbed a hand over his face. "I want a quiet, domestic life. I want a sweetheart."

Samuel rolled his eyes. "You probably want a flat in Darlington Gardens, along with all of the other bearded lions, eh?"

"Yes," Cameron said with more energy. Finally, Samuel grasped the point. "I want love and affection, pretty things, soft things. Things I've never had."

Samuel snorted. "Well, I want a good, stout fuck in the back room of The Cock and Bear before I go home and sleep off a night's drinking."

Deep disappointment twisted in Cameron's gut. It felt as though someone had died. The fantasy he'd been harboring for months turned out to be just that, a fantasy.

"Then I'm sorry," he said in a small voice. "It isn't going to work between us. We want different things."

Samuel snorted, rubbing a hand over his face. "We certainly do." He paced in an agitated circle, then walked past Cameron toward the street. "I'm sorry I wasted your time, then."

"And I'm sorry I'm not what you want," Cameron called after him.

Samuel turned and walked backward for a few steps, saying, "You're what I want, all right. But it seems like you're not what I'm going to have."

"No," Cameron sighed, shoulders sagging. "You're not."

That seemed to be the end of that. Samuel walked away, disappearing around the darkened corner. Cameron stood where he was for a few more minutes, rubbing his arms against the cold. And it was a cold that went far deeper than the February chill. He'd loved his fantasies about Samuel. They were wild and wicked and had kept him up at night, stroking himself off and smiling. It felt horrible to see the truth about the man now. He didn't think less of Samuel, not exactly, but it was plain as day that there would never be anything between them. That stung more than he wanted it to and made every step he took as he dragged himself home miserable.

CHAPTER 4

The most frustrating night of Samuel's life ended with an even greater frustration, one he could hardly believe. He stormed his way to The Cock and Bear—a pub near the west end that catered to his and Cameron's sort—intending to do exactly what he'd told Cameron he wanted and to find a willing bum to ease his tension. But for whatever reason, he didn't like the look of any of the usual candidates, and even when he found a likely lad he'd idled away a sweet hour with before, he couldn't summon the vigor to do anything about it. Quite literally. He'd never had a problem in that respect before. He blamed it on the miserable evening and the dozen or so insults he'd been lashed with along the way.

He'd gone home and spent the night tossing and turning, alone in his bed, unable to get Cameron's sweet, naïve words out of his head. What sort of man like them wanted nothing more than to mimic the domesticity of a society that would never accept them? Wouldn't it be far more satisfying to live life on the razor's edge of that society, flaunting everything that made dull society folks call them perverted and aberrant? *That* was the sort of life he wanted—taking pleasure where he wanted it just to spite the people who told him he was going straight to hell for it. Cameron's ideal of a domestic life was childish and unrealistic.

But a part of him could see the appeal of coming home to Cameron's sweet, innocent face every evening. He could see how lovely it might be to always know who would be in his bed at night, to never have to worry about the police—in as much as any of them could ever afford not to worry about the police—and to have his heart taken care of as well as his cock.

By morning, he'd rejected the idea thoroughly, though. It simply wasn't who he was. He would forever be an outsider, living on the fringe of society, never fully accepted. It didn't matter how well his music was received—and since he had left the performance early, he had no idea how the audience had reacted or what the papers might say that morning—his skin would always keep him out of the inner circles of London, and whom he liked to take to bed would forever make him a pariah. Even if the truth of that never came out.

All the same, he found himself walking through the streets of the city later that morning, heading to John Dandie's office with a splitting headache from lack of sleep and a sore chest from the gaping hole of rejection in his heart. He told himself it was nothing, that he merely had indigestion, and that his trip to John's office was for the sole purpose of conveying what he'd discovered about Sammy. It had nothing to do with his desire to see Cameron again and the hope that perhaps, just perhaps, the lovely young lad had changed his mind about that tumble he'd offered.

He knew the moment he stepped into John's office that he shouldn't have come at all. Niall and Blake were already there. Blake was pale and paced the length of the small office with a hand pressed to his forehead. John was clearly trying to calm him. All of that would have been inconsequential, if it weren't for Cameron lurking in the corner of the room, making a hash of preparing tea. The poor thing had dark circles under his eyes and a wan look that hinted he hadn't slept a wink more than Samuel had. And damn him, but Samuel wanted to fly straight toward him, take the sweet thing in his arms, and soothe away the troubled thoughts and feelings that Cameron obviously had.

"Ah, Samuel," John greeted him, breaking away from where Blake paced. "I was hoping you'd come by. I was about to send Cameron to your flat to fetch you."

A clatter from the corner betrayed that Cameron had dropped the teacup he'd been holding. Samuel glanced in his direction to find Cameron frantically cleaning up freshly spilled tea.

"Did Cameron tell you we pursued who we thought was my sister to her townhouse last night?" Samuel said, pretending to the others that nothing was at all out of the ordinary. The last thing he wanted was to lose face and look like a soppy fool in front of his friends.

"He did," Niall said.

"I brought your things from the concert hall, by the way," John said, gesturing to Samuel's formal coat and hat on the hat stand by the office door.

"Thanks," Samuel said, then brushed right on to, "The woman wasn't Sammy, but as Cameron has probably told you, she tipped her hand and more or less let us know that Sammy has indeed retreated to Derby."

"Which was what you suspected she would do in the first place," Blake said in a troubled voice as he paced.

"Darling, you need to stop fretting so," Niall said, stepping into Blake's path so that Blake walked right into his arms. "It's interfering with your digestion and your sleep."

Blake let himself be embraced and glanced at Niall with a sheepish look. "You're the one interfering with my sleep."

Niall's cheeks went pink, and he grinned at Blake with an outpouring of love that Samuel felt in his gut. "No, I'm the only reason you *can* sleep at the moment," he said, then lowered his voice so that Samuel almost didn't hear, "You never could stay awake after a good, strong orgasm."

Blake snorted with laughter, hiding his face against the side of Niall's head for a moment and whispering in his ear. Samuel turned away, finding the whole thing far too intimate and precious for his tastes. In the process, he caught sight of Cameron, staring longingly at the couple. Samuel's gut clenched with regret that he would never be able to give the poor thing the sort of affection he wanted.

John cleared his throat, and Niall and Blake stepped apart. "Do we have any indication that Ian is with Samantha in Derby?" he asked. "And has anyone been able to track down that nanny Lady Selby is using for Alan?"

"Clarisse wasn't specific about whether Ian is with Sammy or not," Samuel said, startled that his voice was hoarse enough after the display of emotion in the room that he had to clear his throat. "I, for one, think it's entirely likely Sammy still has Ian with her."

"He still owes her money, I presume," John said. "And if that's so, she wouldn't just let him waltz away to board the next ship for America."

"Thank God," Blake said, rubbing his forehead. "I can only hope that if Ian is still The Black Widow's prisoner, Annamarie will think twice about embarking on the next ship for New York to hide Alan with her father."

"They're still in London, I know it," Niall said.

"If they are, then you'd better find them soon."

The statement came from none of them, but rather from Arthur Gleason as he let himself boldly into the office. Immediately, the tension in the room trebled. John glared at Gleason with the sort of hate that could only be managed by a man stuck deep in the throes of lust.

Samuel knew the feeling a little too well. He couldn't help but steal another peek at Cameron.

It was just his luck that Cameron was watching him covertly. As soon as their eyes met, Cameron's face colored precipitously, and he snapped away, continuing to sop up the tea he'd spilled. Samuel found the gesture and Cameron's evasiveness entirely too delightful for his own good. They'd already established that nothing could happen between the two of them. So why did he feel as though the chase were still on?

"Gleason," John growled. "What are you doing here?"

"I've come to offer my services," Gleason said with a shrug, stepping farther into the room and raking John with a glance. "I hear you could use them. All of them."

Samuel couldn't help but grin, though for John's sake, he hid that grin with one hand. Gleason was a brazen strumpet, and judging by the flash that came to John's eyes, he liked it.

"Your help isn't wanted in this case, or any case," John said dismissively. "Please leave."

"Oh?" Gleason blinked innocently. "Then I suppose you don't want to know why Samantha Thorne left London or who she owes four hundred thousand pounds to, thanks to a gamble gone wrong?"

Gleason suddenly had everyone's attention, even Samuel's. "My sister is not a gambler," he said.

"Isn't she?" Gleason chuckled as though he were the only intelligent one in the room. "She certainly did something to need the money that Ian Archibald owes her. Which is why she is now employing him to comb through her messy finances to find a way to conjure four hundred thousand pounds and more out of nowhere."

"The Black Widow is *employing* Ian?" Niall asked incredulously.

"Why would she do that when she already has him by the balls, so to speak, with all of the money he owes her?" John asked, narrowing his eyes at Gleason as though he didn't believe the man.

"Because she needs someone who owes her to dig her out of the mess she's made for herself," Gleason said. "Just because Ian owes her doesn't mean Mrs. Thorne doesn't owe someone else. These things tend to set themselves up to fall like dominoes."

"Who does my sister owe money to, then?" Samuel asked, pulling himself to his full height and crossing his arms to appear as though he doubted Gleason's word, when really, he would have fallen all over himself to know what kind of trouble Sammy was in. She was a troublesome bitch and a thorn in his side, but she was still his sister.

"She owes a man in Derby who owns a great deal of property and who has political aspirations," Gleason said. "One Nathaniel Burberry."

Another clatter sounded from the corner of the room as Cameron dropped a spoon into the second cup of tea he'd been attempting to pour. The sound was enough to draw all of their attention.

"Cameron, perhaps you should put the tea aside for the moment and busy yourself with something else," John said with a teasing grin.

"Yes, sir," Cameron murmured, but set about cleaning up the new mess he'd made instead of going on to do something else.

Samuel stared at Cameron's back with narrowed eyes, wondering what it was about the name Nathaniel Burberry that had upset him. That was clearly what had caused the lad's reaction. Samuel burned with curiosity, far more than he should have. He'd made up his mind to have nothing more to do with Cameron. In a manner of speaking. Perhaps.

"It stands to reason that Mrs. Thorne has returned to Derby to sort out her financial situation and to find a way to repay this Mr. Burberry," John said, scowling as he spoke. Likely because Gleason was the one who had come up with the relevant information that he hadn't been able to find. "Which doesn't change what I have been suggesting all along," John said, making a point of it for Gleason, as if his help were secondary to the main plan. "Samuel, you and Cameron need to travel to Derby to visit your sister and get to the bottom of things." His lips twitched slightly with the last phrase, making Samuel think, once again, that John had been trying to push him and Cameron together on purpose.

Samuel heaved a sigh. "John, could I speak to you in private for a moment?"

John's mischievous look flattened a bit. "If you'd like," he said, starting for the door of his private office.

Samuel followed him, sending Cameron a brief, sideways look as he passed. Cameron seemed to deliberately not be looking at him, but judging by the deep flush that still painted his cheeks, he was highly aware of Samuel all the same.

As soon as they were in John's office, Samuel shut the door. John's brow lifted in surprise, but before he could say anything, Samuel said, "It's not going to work with me and Cameron."

"I cannot imagine what you mean by that," John said with false ignorance.

Samuel sent him an unimpressed look and crossed his arms. "Don't pretend you haven't been trying for months to toss me and Cameron into bed together, like we're a couple of dolls you're playing with."

"Whatever makes you think that?" John asked with even less convincing innocence.

"If anything was going to happen, it would have happened last night," Samuel confessed with a sigh, rubbing his throbbing temples.

"I noticed the two of you left the box right near the beginning of the performance," John said with a salacious lift of his eyebrows.

"It wasn't the beginning, it was in the third movement, but that's irrelevant," Samuel said. "And yes, I'll be honest, I cornered young Cameron in the toilet and took a gamble on him."

"And?" John looked hopeful.

"And in the first place, we were nearly interrupted, which frightened the poor dear half out of his skin." Samuel felt worse about it in the light of day than he had at the moment. Cameron must have been terrified, especially with the increasing number of men like them who were being nabbed by blackmailers in public toilets and brought up on charges of gross indecency.

"In the second place," he went on, "we stumbled across Clarisse, my sister's maid who often impersonates her. That's how we discovered what we know about Sammy departing for Derby."

"Yes, Cameron related the whole story," John said. "Well, not the whole story," he added with a grin. "He left out the part about the toilet."

"Then he likely left out the bit about the conversation that we had in the mews after," Samuel went on, trying not to sound bitter. "The one where he told me that he doesn't want a nice little bit of a suck and fuck, he wants a house and a garden and pretty maids all in a row." He couldn't keep the sarcasm or the resentment out of his tone.

John's clever look faltered, and he frowned at Samuel. "And that's not what you want?"

"God, no!" Samuel snorted. "Leave domestic tranquility to the breeders. We insult ourselves by pretending that their ideals are ours, and that if we imitate them perfectly enough, they'll accept us and let us go on our merry way."

John's look turned wary. "It is the natural state of man to crave love and acceptance."

"I'll take lust over love any day," Samuel snapped. "And I'm never going to find acceptance, so why should I bother?"

John's mouth hung open for a moment as he blinked at Samuel. "I had no idea you felt this way," he said at last.

"What choice do I have in the matter?" Samuel demanded, throwing his arms to his sides. "The rest of you can get away with pretending and hiding who you are to gain acceptance, but one look at me and even the chimney sweep turns his nose up."

"You're a celebrated composer, Samuel," John argued. "Didn't you see the rave reviews your symphony got in all of the papers this morning?"

"And did those papers mention the composer of the celebrated work is a black man whose mother labored on a sugar plantation?" Samuel snapped.

"Yes," John said with an incredulous laugh. "In fact, they did. One of the articles even heralded your success as the dawning of a new era."

Samuel pulled back, surprised by the news. He should have taken more time to read his own reviews. It didn't matter, though. He shook his head. "The dawning of a new era is not the era itself. I am not acceptable, and I never will be."

"Then why are you pushing away the help and comfort of the one group of people, perhaps the one man, who might be able to give you all the things you long for?" John said, taking a step toward him. "You're right, none of us are discriminated against for the color of our skin. But if you believe for one moment that we don't run the risk of being clapped in irons and sentenced to three years of hard labor if we are so much as seen holding hands with our lovers or kissing them in public, then you do us a disservice."

"It's not the same," Samuel argued.

"It isn't the same," John agreed, "but it is something."

He stopped there. The air between them crackled. Samuel found himself breathing hard, which came as a surprise to him. He tried to avoid emotion as much as possible, and there he was, wallowing in it. It must have been his lack of sleep. That and the fact that he hadn't had a good shag in months, not since setting his sights on Cameron. Fat lot of good that had done.

As if John could hear his thoughts, he said, "Take Cameron to Derby with you. It doesn't have to mean anything other than the two of you working to discover Ian Archibald's whereabouts and getting to the bottom of your sister's financial problems together."

Samuel huffed, crossed his arms, and shook his head.

"You'll find Cameron extraordinarily useful," John went on.

"At what, spilling tea?" Samuel said.

John frowned, clearly irritated with him. "That young man has more potential than anyone gives him credit for. Yes, he's quiet and a bit clumsy, but his mind is capable of extraordinary things, things I've not seen anyone else do."

Samuel doubted it. Then again, Cameron had deduced in an instant that Sammy must have gone to Derby due to the simple absence of a carriage.

"You don't know what that young man has been through," John went on in a quieter voice. "He's bound to face his family while he's up there, and after what he told me, I don't want him to have to face them alone."

"Why?" Samuel asked, heart beating for Cameron, whether he wanted it to or not. "What did they do to him?"

"That's Cameron's story to tell, not mine," John said. He was close enough to thump Samuel's arm. "Maybe he'll tell you on the train."

Samuel let out a long breath, rubbing a hand over his eyes. He wasn't going to be able to get out of going to Derby with Cameron. And if he were honest with himself, the thing that made him most anxious was being in forced proximity with the man after he'd made such an ass of himself the night before. But the fact remained that the two of them wanted different things.

"If I must, then I must," he sighed, admitting to himself that he'd lost the battle.

"Good," John said, walking past him and pulling open the office door. "Let's make arrangements, then."

"Arrangements?" Niall asked as they rejoined the others.

"For Samuel and Cameron to journey up to Derby to pursue The Black Widow," John said dramatically.

Samuel rolled his eyes. At least one of them was enjoying the situation.

"In the meantime," John continued, "we need to find that nursemaid."

Gleason sent John a gloating look. "I should have her location for you by tomorrow."

"No," John said, rounding on the man with a look of fire—though not, perhaps, the kind of fire John intended to send at him.

"We need all the help we can get," Blake said with a guilty look for John.

"Listen to the man," Gleason said, nodding to Blake. "It's his son."

John blew out a breath. "Very well, you can help. But I'm not paying you for your services."

"Oh, I'll receive my payment, all right," Gleason said. "Just you wait."

Samuel found himself grinning again in spite of himself. Better still, he peeked at Cameron and found the lad grinning as well. Their eyes met, and for one, beautiful moment, they were in accord. Then Cameron's smile dropped, and he looked away.

Samuel sighed and shook his head. The mission to Derby was going to be more of a challenge than he wanted it to be.

CHAPTER 5

The last thing Cameron wanted to do was travel home to Derbyshire. He'd left under the most ignominious circumstances, and had been surprised his family hadn't actually thrown rotten vegetables at his back as he'd slunk onto a third-class car on a train bound for London. He was willing to swallow his pride and make the journey for John Dandie's sake, and for the sake of Lord Selby, whom he both admired and pitied for the loss of his son.

But traveling all the way to Derby in a first-class compartment with Samuel was a unique kind of torture that Cameron hadn't known existed.

It had started at the station in London, when he'd stood anxiously near the departures board, chewing his lip and scanning the morning crowd for a sign of Samuel. Samuel had finally found him as he walked up behind

Cameron and snapped, "Well, hurry up, lad. We'll miss the train with you standing around looking like a rube."

Any pride Cameron had left sank into the dust under his feet with that greeting. "I...I don't have a ticket," he admitted, not quite able to meet Samuel's eyes. "John said he would take care of it, but he was called away to defend a client accused of gross indecency, so he never bought it."

"Then go to the ticket office and get one," Samuel said, blinking and shaking his head as though it were obvious.

Cameron shuffled his feet, face heating. "I haven't got the money for it," he admitted. "Maybe you should just go to your sister's house on your own."

Samuel let out an impatient breath and rubbed a hand over his face. "John should have made certain you were equipped before sending you on your way."

He tugged on Cameron's sleeve, nudging him toward the ticket office. Cameron couldn't tell if he was exasperated with John or with him. He bent to pick up his shabby, old suitcase, snapping the handle as he did.

Samuel turned back with a start. "Why did you bring that old thing?" he asked.

"It's all I have," Cameron mumbled, catching up to him and walking by his side to the ticket office.

"What is John paying you?" Samuel asked indignantly. "Can't he spare even enough for you to purchase a proper traveling bag for these sorts of journeys? Or a proper suit, for that matter."

They joined the queue at the ticket window, and Cameron answered, "I send most of my salary home to my mother."

Samuel huffed. "Your mother should be sewing you proper suits and sending them down to you with her deepest thanks."

Cameron let out a miserable breath. "My mother won't speak to me. Not since...." He couldn't speak the words in public, while they waited in line to purchase him a ticket, but he sent Samuel a significant look.

Samuel merely gaped at him. "Your mother won't speak to you, and yet you send your salary home to her and live like this in return?" He swept Cameron with a look.

Blessedly, Cameron didn't have a chance to answer. They reached the ticket window, and Samuel purchased a ticket for him. A first-class ticket. Cameron wanted to protest that the expense was too much, but the train was already boarding, and if they wanted to make it to the platform on time, they had to run without discussion.

Once on the platform, they endured the entirely expected hassle of the porter questioning whether a black man and a young man in a threadbare suit should really be traveling first-class. Samuel had to argue, bully, and eventually bribe the porter to let them into the compartment they'd paid for. Even then, once they were seated, Samuel pulled down all of the shades so that no one would know who occupied the compartment.

Cameron was so miserable once the entire process

was done that he sank into his seat, crossed his arms, and closed his eyes. He wanted to talk with Samuel, to ask him questions and find out more about his life and his sister. If he were honest with himself, he wanted to sit there and gaze at Samuel, take in the sight of how beautiful the man was and how powerful his physique.

But it was clear to him that Samuel had written him off as a failure. Samuel had made it clear the night of the concert that he didn't think much of Cameron's simple desires and sentimental views on things. And Cameron had to admit that he was furious with himself for being a coward and not going in for a night of debauchery. It wouldn't have hurt anyone. It would have made him feel good. And it wasn't as though he were completely innocent of those things to begin with. Far from it.

They were almost an hour outside of London before Samuel broke the silence in the compartment by saying, "How did you come to be employed by John?"

Cameron opened his eyes, blinked, then answered, "When I first came to London, about a year ago, I found employment working for the telegraph company." He hung his head, glanced out the window, and did whatever he could to avoid Samuel's stare.

"You were a telegraph boy?" Samuel asked incredulously.

Cameron nodded, knowing full well what that implied. Telegraph boys were notorious for delivering more than their prescribed telegraph message.

"Aren't you a little old for that job?" Samuel asked.

"No," Cameron said. "I needed the money, and I have a knack for memorizing addresses and things. Entire telegraphs, if I have to. And not every delivery was like…that."

But enough of them were that he'd made a tidy sum to send home to his family. He could only pray they never discovered how that money was made.

Samuel's look turned doubtful. "John Dandie would never hire a telegraph boy that way."

"I told you that not every delivery was like that," Cameron said defensively. "I delivered a telegram to him. I was tired, so he let me rest in the office for a moment. John was well aware of the other sort of work telegraph boys often do and took pity on me, saying he'd pay me a bit extra so I didn't have to make it up later. Then, when I couldn't find what happened to the telegram, I recited it to him. It was a long one, and John was impressed that I could remember it all word for word. He tested me with a few other things, and when he saw I memorize things easily, that I remember details, he hired me on the spot. I was so grateful not to have to…do that anymore, that I accepted the offer. And that was that."

Samuel gaped at him. "How long were you a telegraph boy?"

"Only two months, thank God." Cameron turned away, staring out the window. Samuel had lifted the shades once they were outside of London, when Cameron had his eyes closed.

Another long silence followed. Cameron didn't like

the feel of it. He didn't like the sizzle of pity that filled the compartment. He most certainly didn't like the way Samuel was looking at him with an almost pained expression when he peeked at the man again. Derision he could handle. He was used to it. Pity made him feel like his balls had been cut off.

"How did you and your sister get to be so—" he started to ask, hoping to turn Samuel's thoughts to something else. He didn't know how to finish the sentence without offending him, though.

"How did a black man end up as a famous composer and a black woman end up a wealthy widow with a reputation for menace, you mean?" Samuel asked with a teasing grin.

Cameron nodded, sitting stiffly and waiting for an answer.

Samuel shrugged, crossed his arms, and glanced out the window. "Our father was a British baron with a plantation in Barbados. He had more money than God. Of course, slavery was abolished in the Caribbean ages ago, but that didn't change much in terms of who does the actual work in the fields. Our mother had a mind of her own and a wicked streak, which Sammy inherited, and our father took a shine to her. We're not legitimate, of course, but we're the only children Father had."

"Was he married to someone else?" Cameron asked.

Samuel nodded. "He was, but she never bore him any children. Probably because she lived here, in Wiltshire, and Father and our mother lived in Barbados."

"But you and your sister both ended up here," Cameron said.

"Father was an eccentric, you see," Samuel explained. "And proud of his children. I rather liked the man and was sad when he passed. He made certain Sammy and I received the finest education Barbados could provide, and when that reached its limit, he sent us to live with his wife in Wiltshire."

Cameron's jaw dropped. "And what did she think of that?"

"She was charmed by us," Samuel said with a shrug. "It was Lady Alice who encouraged my skill with music, who introduced me to key figures in society, and who found Sammy Mr. Thorne as a husband. I was fond of Lady Alice."

Cameron couldn't believe a story like Samuel's was possible. But he'd seen stranger things among the upper classes. Queen Victoria herself had an Indian servant that she doted on, the Munshi, and had once had an African goddaughter. Where someone was born didn't necessarily determine their fate forever anymore.

"Sammy is and always has been a mischievous little chit," Samuel went on with a laugh that was both fond and vexed. "She would get into trouble at every turn, and drag me into the trouble with her. She hated being bored. Still hates it, I would assume. She will turn someone's world upside down for her own amusement, but she also has an uncanny knack for making others enjoy the trouble as much as she does."

"Do you suppose that's how she ended up in so much debt? Or why Ian Archibald is still with her?" Cameron asked.

"Probably," Samuel said with a sigh and a shrug. "I predict we'll reach her estate in Derby and find her and Archibald hosting tea for Cinderella and the Mad Hatter."

Cameron's brow shot up. "Truly?"

Samuel's expression flattened. "Yes, Cameron. My sister will be having tea with fictional characters. Probably out in her garden, with unicorns and fairies serving."

Cameron shrank back, stung by Samuel's irritation. He didn't deserve it. And while experience had taught him that Samuel was likely upset with something else, not him, it closed Cameron up. He crossed his arms, frowned, and returned to staring out the window once more.

It was a good fifteen minutes before Samuel blew out a breath and said, "I'm sorry. That was unkind of me. I'm frustrated because of my sister's behavior and put out that I have to chase her all the way up to Derbyshire when I would rather be in London, basking in the accolades of my symphony's premier."

"You mean you're frustrated that, in spite of having good reviews in the paper, you're not getting the praise you think you deserve," Cameron fired back.

He regretted his outburst instantly. Samuel looked as offended as Cameron felt. And though they'd traded wounds and been honest with each other, it didn't make Cameron feel better.

Another long silence followed. Cameron lost track of how much time passed. But the silence was eventually broken when Samuel said, "Tell me about this family of yours. The one who doesn't speak to you, but to whom you send all of your money."

Of all the topics Cameron could have picked to soothe the ruffled feelings between them, his family was not it.

"My father is a farmer," he said, unsure whether Samuel was trying to make peace or aggravate him more. "My mother rules the roost, though."

"Brothers and sisters?" Samuel asked.

"Yes," Cameron answered. "Too many of each."

"Do you get along with them?"

"Some of them." Cameron nodded, then lowered his chin. "At least, I did. After I was caught—" He cleared his throat, squirmed, and sank into his seat. "After that, they couldn't turn their backs on me fast enough. Except one sister."

Samuel's expression softened. "You were caught?"

"I don't want to talk about it," Cameron blurted, feeling his face and neck heat. "It was humiliating. And that was the end of that. Ma would have turned me out without any of my clothes or things, but she said she didn't even want those in the house, because they were probably all tainted with Satan's touch."

He sank even deeper into his seat, still feeling the

way he had then, as though he were tainted and unworthy.

"And yet, you still send those louses money." Samuel shook his head.

"They're my family," Cameron defended himself, and them, sitting a little taller. He gulped and went on with, "And if I didn't send them my salary so they can pay their rent, Mr. Burberry would turn them out. Father injured his leg a few years ago and can't work like he used to."

"Sounds to me like they deserve to be turned out," Samuel murmured. "Injured leg or no."

"And would you say that about your sister?" Cameron asked. "If she truly did lose a fortune gambling, if her debts are all called in, if Mr. Burberry turns her out, like I know he's capable of doing, would you let her end up on the street?"

Samuel's jaw went tense. "No," he admitted with a sigh. "I wouldn't. But Sammy would never turn me away either."

"Then you're fortunate and you should count your blessings," Cameron said.

Samuel laughed and opened his mouth as though he would say something, but he stopped. His sharp expression softened as he studied Cameron. Cameron could only imagine what he was thinking. It must have been that, at last, Samuel had found someone more wretched and reviled than he was.

They were spared having any further conversation on

the matter as the train pulled into the Derby station. Cameron stood and gathered his things, as did Samuel. A black man was even more of an unusual sight in the country than in London, and Cameron suspected the haste Samuel made to disembark from their compartment the moment the train screeched and whistled to a stop was so that they could leave the public area of the station and get to his sister's house as swiftly as possible.

That wasn't in the cards either, though, and it was Cameron's fault.

"Oy!"

They'd made it off the train and past the platform, almost to the station door, before the sharp cry stopped them cold. Cameron winced in misery, recognizing the voice too well, even though it was only one syllable. He stopped abruptly, hunched his shoulders, and turned to the uniformed porter who stormed toward him.

"And what in hell are you doing back here, you miserable piece of excrement?" Tony barked at him.

"Hello, Tony," Cameron said as patiently as he could. "I'm here for work. You don't need to pretend to know me."

Cameron started to move on, but Samuel had stopped as well and turned back, glaring at Tony.

"And who the hell are you to speak to this man in such a manner?" Samuel demanded, standing tall and speaking like a gentleman.

"I'm his brother. And who the hell are you?" Tony demanded.

"Cameron and I are working together on an investigation for the law offices of John Dandie in London," Samuel said, his eyes flaring with fury as he glanced over Tony with a sneer.

"Yeah?" Tony seemed to have no qualms at all about speaking to Samuel as though he were a street sweeper instead of a well-dressed man who had just made a trip from London in a first-class train compartment. "You know he's a bloody queer, right?"

Cameron wanted to sink into the ground in embarrassment. Far too many of the passengers rushing this way and that in the station had paused to watch the confrontation. They gaped at him as though he might be a plague carrier as well.

But Samuel took a step closer to Tony and said, "I'd be careful about throwing around that accusation, if I were you."

"Yeah?" Tony crossed his arms, sniffed, and looked down his nose at Samuel.

"People might start asking how you can be so sure this man is guilty of the crime you accuse him of," Samuel said. "They might see you as his accomplice."

"I never—you can't—I'm his brother," Tony blurted, his face going red.

"Do they know that?" Samuel asked, lowering his voice and glancing around.

Tony shrank in on himself for a moment. A second later, he came out fighting again. "And where's the money

Ma needs for this month's rent, eh, rent boy?" he hurled at Cameron.

"I sent it," Cameron said, brow furrowing with worry. He didn't know what might happen if the letter had been delayed or waylaid.

"Well, it wasn't enough," Tony said. "Old Burberry raised the rent again."

"Then why don't you give her some of your salary to make up the difference?" Samuel snapped, then gestured to Cameron. "Come along. We don't have time to waste with this wanker."

"Oy!" Tony shouted after Samuel in offense.

Samuel stormed on, Cameron following, out of the train station and into the busy, Derby street. It was deep in the afternoon, but plenty of hacks were lined up to take disembarking passengers to their final destination. Cameron felt like the very lowest worm under the heel of a beggar, but still found it necessary to flag down a cab in Samuel's place, since, once again, none of them seemed keen to give passage to a black man.

That tune changed as soon as Samuel told them where they wanted to go.

"You're Mrs. Thorne's brother, aren't you?" the driver who eventually pulled around for them asked.

"I am," Samuel answered.

The driver was satisfied, but it wasn't enough to put a smile on Samuel's face.

"I'm sorry you had to deal with that," Samuel said

once he and Cameron were settled in their seats. "No one deserves a brother like that."

"I have three brothers like that," Cameron muttered. He hadn't thought it was possible for him to feel worse than he had that morning, but there he was, shamed and humiliated once again.

"You handled yourself well," Samuel said with a hint of a sad smile. "I'm not sure I could have kept such a calm head if I'd been in the same situation."

"What choice do I have?" Cameron asked. "It's stay quiet and take the punishment or speak up and land in jail."

Samuel's face pinched. "I know," he said.

Cameron's heart squeezed and his stomach felt sour. Samuel *did* know, he was certain, but for an entirely different set of reasons.

For a moment, peace reigned. They smiled at each other. Whatever else they might have had that divided them, at least they had one thing that they could feel in common. It was a start, though Cameron knew it wouldn't be the start of what he wanted. He was a fool to be so flattered over the way Samuel had come to his defense. Samuel couldn't have meant anything particular by it. He was simply defending someone who had been downtrodden. But how lovely would it be if Samuel had told Tony off the way he had because he cared about him?

Those thoughts lasted about as long as it took for the cab to drive them up to the gates of Thorne Hall, the late

Mr. Thorne's palatial country estate. Cameron had seen it in passing more than a few times, but he had never been allowed through the gates, and certainly had never been permitted in the house. He was awed in an instant by the elaborate gardens, full of topiary and winding paths and patios. Cameron could just imagine what the place looked like in summer.

But it was the house itself that took his breath away the moment he and Samuel were allowed inside. It was as grand as any museum Cameron had ever seen, with gold leaf on the picture frames and taxidermy beasts from the farthest reaches of the globe arranged on stands to threaten visitors. Every rumor he'd ever heard about Mr. Thorne being a collector of the exotic came back to him as he stood in the grand, marble entryway, mouth hanging open, turning circles to take in the hodge-podge of paintings, sculptures, and artifacts that surrounded him, and that he could see in the rooms beyond the hall. Even the butler surprised him. The man was clearly from the Orient and had a long moustache, like the kind he'd seen in photographs from China. Everything around him came from a different world, and Cameron knew in an instant that he could never fit in with that world or, he feared, with Samuel.

CHAPTER 6

It was just a touch of a stomach ache, Samuel told himself. The uncomfortable, gnawing feeling in his gut was nothing more than the fact that he'd eaten a hurried breakfast, then no lunch at all during the journey. He hadn't wanted to risk drawing any attention to himself and Cameron in their first-class compartment by seeking out food on the train. The aching, hollow feeling that he couldn't shake as he and Cameron were let into the front hall of Sammy's, frankly, ridiculous house was hunger, not anything else.

It certainly wasn't regret for the way he'd been so curt and awkward with Cameron at St. Pancras Station in London. Really, John should have taken better care of the lad and made certain he had his ticket in advance of the journey. It wasn't the uncomfortable pull at his insides that Samuel had felt when he'd learned that Cameron's shabby appearance was because the man sent all of his money home to an ungrateful family. It couldn't possibly have been because of any feelings of remorse or sympathy over the way Cameron had had to make his living when he'd first arrived in London. And there was no possible way that he would find himself regretting the way he'd made such aggressive advances on Cameron, and then thought less of him for wanting love instead of just sex, after hearing how Cameron had been a telegraph boy. And on top of that, it couldn't be possible that the way his chest and stomach squeezed as Cameron glanced around Sammy's front hall was because of the sweetness of the wide-eyed wonder Cameron displayed at his sister's collection of eccentricities.

Samuel was absolutely certain that he didn't feel anything for Cameron other than a healthy dose of lust at the prospect of getting the man in his bed. He wasn't the sort to have feelings that could be described as tender in any way, and one train journey was not going to upend his entire outlook on life.

"What is this nonsense I hear about my brother darkening my doorstep?" Sammy's voice rang through the marble hall as she descended the grand, curving staircase that ran along the perimeter of the room.

"Sammy." Samuel grinned up at his sister with as much scolding in his eyes as fondness. Not only because of her recent behavior, but because it was the middle of the afternoon on a Thursday, and she wore a form-fitting gown in no fashionable style he'd ever heard of that seemed to be decorated with peacock feathers. "What in God's name are you wearing?"

"Do you like it?" Sammy said, reaching the bottom of the stairs and turning one way, then another. "Lord Hatteras is having a fancy-dress ball at the end of the month, and I'm determined to attend as a peacock."

"Peacocks are male," Samuel told her, striding close enough to kiss her cheek when she offered it.

"And peahens aren't pretty," she replied with a cheeky wink. "If you can bend genders to accommodate your tastes, then so can I."

Samuel shook his head. "You are a menace. I don't know why they haven't tossed you out of the country on your arse yet."

"Because I'm far too beautiful and entertaining," Sammy answered. She caught sight of Cameron, and her eyes widened in appreciation. "And who is this adorable bit of confection that you've brought me to play with?" she asked, sashaying through the hall toward him.

Cameron shrank from Sammy so abruptly that he nearly fell over backwards.

"Don't frighten the man, Sammy," Samuel followed his sister until he was close enough to whisper in her ear. "He's mine. And I would appreciate it if you could put us in those delightful, adjoining rooms you reserve for trysting guests."

"Consider it done," Sammy said before putting on a far less threatening smile and continuing across the hall toward Cameron, one hand outstretched. "It's a pleasure to meet you, mister...?"

"Oberlin," Cameron said, stumbling over his own name as he took Sammy's hand and shook it vigorously. "Cameron Oberlin."

Sammy's eyes went wide, and for a moment, Samuel prayed she wouldn't laugh. Clearly, she'd expected Cameron to take her hand and kiss it instead of shaking it like a fishwife. It was an amusing faux pas. But after the day they'd had, Samuel found himself thoroughly protective of Cameron's feelings, particularly since he feared he'd stomped all over them.

"Your young companion is very charming, Samuel," Sammy said, her hand still in Cameron's—because she wouldn't let it go, even though Cameron tried to pull back. "Wherever did you find him?"

"He works for the law office of John Dandie," Samuel said, rolling his eyes a bit as he came to stand beside his sister. He sent Cameron an apologetic look that turned into a smile. "We've been sent up here to determine what in God's name is going on with you and why you are holding Ian Archibald hostage, if you still are."

Sammy yanked her hand away from Cameron's and slapped it to her feathered chest, her dark eyes popping wide with offense. "I would never hold a man hostage," she said. "There is nothing whatsoever *going on*, as you put it."

Samuel crossed his arms. "Is Archibald here?"

"Yes, he is," Sammy said coyly. "He's been engaged to perform a very important task for me."

A rush of relief filled Samuel at the news Archibald was under Sammy's roof. Even if he couldn't persuade Sammy to let the man go, at least he might be able to pry the truth about Lady Selby's and Lord Stanley's location out of him.

But that didn't solve the other problem his sister presented.

"Is it true that you owe a great deal of money to one Nathaniel Burberry because you lost a gamble with the man?" Samuel asked.

"That is an egregious lie and a horrific falsehood," Sammy said, marching away from him and Cameron to one of the side hallways, "and I will not stand by and hear myself accused of such a thing as gambling." She glanced over her shoulder at Samuel with a withering look, then crooked her finger for him to follow.

"So it's true then," Samuel said. He sent a wry grin to Cameron, as if to say, "Do you see what I have to put up with?"

Cameron was too wide-eyed and pale with shock to do more than meet his eyes in return and follow down the hallway.

"It was only a small...challenge," Sammy said with a dismissive wave of her hand that had all the feathers on her gown fluttering. "Burberry is a rascal. And he cheated. He knew that the Canadian rail company I invested in would underperform the Australian one he threw his money at. Not only did I lose my initial investment of four hundred thousand pounds because of the railroad, I now owe that cheat a hundred thousand extra as a penalty to him. Which is entirely unfair, if you ask me, because his Australian railroad has turned a profit."

"That's the five hundred thousand pounds Archibald owed her," Samuel muttered to Cameron in an aside.

"I thought Archibald said the other hundred thousand was interest," Cameron replied in a barely audible voice.

"Sammy probably lied to him," Samuel said. "My sister is an accomplished liar."

"Do you think she's lying to us now, then?" Cameron asked.

Samuel slowed his steps slightly as Sammy turned the corner ahead of them, stepping into what, from a distance, looked like an office or a library. "Do you know, there's a fair chance she is. So let's just be on our guard, shall we?"

Cameron nodded.

Samuel headed on, following Sammy into what was, indeed, a large office lined with bookshelves. Much to his relief, the haggard and disheveled figure of Ian Archibald sat at a desk under a tall window at the far end of the room. His hair stuck up at odd angles, as if he'd shoved his fingers through it in consternation a few too many times. He had a large ledger open in front of him, and when he spotted Sammy, he shot to his feet.

"I cannot do it, Mrs. Thorne," Archibald barked the

moment Sammy stepped up to the desk. "I absolutely cannot manufacture money out of thin air. You have to let me go."

"Mr. Archibald," Sammy said in a perfectly pleasant voice, smiling as though she were hosting a garden party. "I'd like you to meet my brother, the world-famous composer and musician, Samuel Percy."

"How do you do?" Samuel said with a bow, sending a wry glance to his sister for her praise in his introduction.

"And this is his associate, Mr. Cameron Oberlin," Sammy introduced Cameron.

"How do you do?" Archibald nodded curtly to both Samuel and Cameron. Halfway through resuming his seat, he stopped and shot straight again with an awkward jerk. "Hold on one moment, I know you," he said, narrowing his eyes at Cameron.

Cameron cleared his throat. "We, er, met at Hyde Park. Right before she snatched you up."

Archibald's eyes lit with recognition, then narrowed in anger. "Where is my money? Have you come to bring me what that pervert, Lord Selby owes me?"

"I'll thank you not to speak to Mr. Oberlin or to refer to my friend in such a manner," Samuel said. He was more pleased than he should have been that he had an opportunity to defend Cameron so soon. And by the look of the young man as his shoulders hunched at Archibald's sharp tone, he needed defending. In fact, Cameron needed a great deal more than that. He needed comfort and pleasure and someone to make him feel good.

The thought couldn't have come at a more inconvenient time. Samuel shook his head and took a large step closer to the desk. "Why don't you make this entire visit smooth and easy by telling us now where Lady Selby and Lord Stanley are?"

"Oh, no," Archibald laughed humorlessly. He stepped around the edge of the desk, glancing between Samuel and Sammy. "I'm not telling anyone anything unless I'm allowed to leave this place and go back to London."

"You'll do nothing of the sort until you find five hundred thousand pounds for me," Sammy said, tilting her chin up and managing to appear both defiant and preening at once.

"As I have said at least a hundred times before, Mrs. Thorne," Archibald said through a clenched jaw, "you have more than enough items of interest and exotica to sell to make the money that you need. This place is crawling with items that any museum in Europe would fall all over themselves to possess."

Cameron walked around the edge of the desk to stare at the ledger and the rest of the papers on the desk's top as the conversation inched closer to the center of the room.

"How dare you?" Sammy gasped. "Those items to which you refer so cavalierly are my husband's legacy. They are my treasures, and I will not part with them."

Samuel laughed. "I always knew you were a dragon, Sammy. And dragons always protect their hoards."

Sammy snapped to him with a sharp look of offense that turned into a smile. "Do you know, I actually like that." She glanced down at her gown, then tilted her head to the side. "Perhaps I will have Gemma make me a dragon costume instead of attending the ball as a peacock. I look devilishly good in both red and green, and scales would be delightful on me."

"I'm convinced you already have scales underneath your clothes," Samuel said in a flat voice.

"If I do, then you do as well, brother of mine," Sammy said with a wink. "Should we ask Mr. Oberlin to confirm it for us?" She turned to the desk.

Cameron had just turned a page of the ledger Archibald had been working with, but at Sammy's question, he snapped his head up. "Um…er…I wouldn't…I don't…." His face went beet red, and for a moment, Samuel thought he might pass out.

Archibald narrowed his eyes. "I should have known," he said in a seething voice. "Lord Selby's and my brother's illness has infected you all. Well, I want no part of it." He headed toward the door.

"And just where do you think you're going, Mr. Archibald?" Sammy chased after him.

Samuel had no choice but to follow them out of the room. He glanced over his shoulder to Cameron, who had turned another page of the ledger and looked reluctant to leave it altogether. Samuel gestured for him, and Cameron tore himself away from what he was reading to follow.

"See anything interesting?" Samuel asked him as they followed the echoing sound of Sammy and Archibald bickering back to the main hall.

"The records aren't well-kept," Cameron said. "But I think Archibald is right. The value of a great many objects is recorded in that ledger. Your sister's collections are worth a fortune."

Samuel grunted. "And she isn't bluffing when she says she won't part with them. At least, she won't until a representative from some solicitor's office marches into the place with an order from the courts and an army of removers to take it all away."

"That's something Mr. Burberry would do," Cameron said with a wide-eyed look of dread.

"...holding me here against my will, even though you have me living in luxury," Archibald was in the middle of shouting as Samuel and Cameron caught up to him and Sammy in the front hall. Archibald was halfway up the stairs while Sammy stood like a queen in the middle of the circular hall.

"I have never been insulted with so much ingratitude in my life, Mr. Archibald," Sammy called up to him in a voice of false truthfulness. "Haven't I provided you with the largest guest room and the softest bed in the house? Aren't you allowed to leave to go out riding or to the pub whenever you'd like?"

"With an escort of those two brutes you employ," Archibald shouted down at her.

"You like Harry and Alfred," Sammy said in a coaxing voice.

"I would prefer to have my freedom, madam," Archibald growled back at her, continuing up a few stairs.

"Who needs freedom when you have a house as magnificent as this as your prison?" Sammy asked.

Samuel rubbed a hand over his face. He and Cameron had walked straight into a circus. He'd known all along his sister was eccentric and devious, and that she had enough money to support her mischief, but he'd had no idea she had the power to actually keep a man in her house against his will.

"This is ridiculous," he said in a voice only Cameron could hear at first, then raised his voice to go on with, "Sammy, you cannot keep Mr. Archibald here as a prisoner."

"And what do you suppose the man would do the moment I let him go?" Sammy demanded, whipping to face him. "He would fly off to London to be reunited with his married lover," she answered her own question. "And then he would purchase berths on the first ship leaving England. Is that truly what you want for your friend, Lord Selby?"

Samuel's brow shot up. "I'd no idea you were such a humanitarian or that you cared one whit about reuniting Lord Selby and his son."

"I'm sentimental that way," Sammy said with a simpering smile.

Samuel shook his head. "Only because you think you need Archibald to figure out how you can pay your debt to this Burberry chap."

"Oh, I see I'm the topic of conversation already," a deep voice sounded from behind Samuel.

He turned in time to see a middle-aged man with a large moustache, clothes that were just a bit too fine for Derbyshire, and a gold-tipped cane made of ebony striding through the front door and into the hall. The man's eyes sparkled with ill-intent as he glanced avariciously around at all of Sammy's trinkets and decorations.

"Burberry, my dear," Sammy said, abandoning her argument with Archibald to walk elegantly across the hall to greet her guest. The smile she wore was as false as the style of her gown, and yet, there was some sort of attraction between the two of them. "How lovely to see you. But you've arrived early, I'm afraid."

"Always arrive early," Burberry said with a toothy grin. "It leaves your enemies on the back foot and gives your friends more time to entertain you."

"And which are you?" Sammy laughed, though there was an edge to the sound.

"Both, of course," Burberry said.

He and Sammy shared a brittle laugh as Burberry took Sammy's hand and kissed it. Samuel was left without a single clue as to whether the two of them adored or hated each other. He had the feeling the answer might have been both in equal measure.

"Let me introduce you to my brother and his friend,"

Sammy said, stepping away from Burberry. "This is my brother, Samuel Percy, the world-famous composer and musician." She rested a hand on Samuel's arm and smiled up at him as though they had the closest and most affectionate of sibling relationships. "And this is his friend, Mr. Cameron Oberlin."

Burberry was in the middle of removing his coat and hat and handing them to Sammy's butler, but at the mention of Cameron's name, he jerked visibly. When he spun around and stared right at Cameron, his expression lit with surprise and delight—a particular kind of delight that had Samuel balling his hands into fists at his sides.

Worse still, Cameron had gone splotchy at the sight of Burberry. He took a shuffling step back, glancing around furtively, as though a magical exit that would take him out of a nightmare would suddenly appear to rescue him.

"Mr. Burberry," Samuel said in a deep voice, stepping forward to shake the man's hand. He squeezed it hard, letting the man know which of the two of them was stronger. He hoped that through that gesture, Burberry would know that he was not to be trifled with, and further, that Cameron wouldn't be trifled with either.

"I've heard so much about you, Mr. Percy." Burberry smiled widely, oblivious to the thoughts that Samuel was already forming about him. "And I believe Mr. Oberlin and I are already acquainted." He nodded to Cameron.

Cameron nodded tightly in return, then looked away.

"Excellent," Sammy said, clapping her hands

together. "Then why don't the three of you become reacquainted while I go upstairs and change for supper. Mr. Lee, would you tell Cook to have supper ready early?" Sammy asked her butler. "And Mr. Archibald, come back here at once and help entertain my guests."

"Ah, yes, Mr. Archibald," Burberry said. "How has your investigation into Mrs. Thorne's finances been going?"

"Not well, sir," Archibald huffed, coming down the stairs again. "Not well at all."

Mr. Lee gestured for them to enter the parlor off to one side as Sammy started up the stairs. Samuel took a step closer to Cameron, tempted to take his hand as they moved into the parlor.

"Are you well?" he asked the poor lad.

Cameron shook his head and said nothing, but proceeded with his head held high.

Samuel was certain beyond any shadow of a doubt that Cameron had had some sort of encounter with Burberry in the past. He'd reacted strongly in John's office when the man's name was mentioned. He'd said Burberry was his family's landlord and kept raising the rent. And the way the two of them looked at each other, Samuel wondered if Burberry were somehow involved in whatever scandal had driven Cameron out of Derbyshire a year ago. All of it added up to one conclusion—Samuel couldn't stand Burberry.

CHAPTER 7

"Your cook always did make the best roast mutton, Mrs. Thorne," Burberry told Sammy with a lascivious smile, winking at her down the length of the table, as they drew to the close of their supper an hour or so later. "I shall make it a point to either dine with you more often or to steal the woman away."

Sammy laughed, flirting right back with, "If you steal my cook, I shall just have to find another, better one. And you know I am fully capable of besting you in any competition you set forth."

Samuel fought not to roll his eyes as he sliced into his mutton and sent Burberry a frown. His dislike of the man hadn't lessened one hair since they'd sat down to supper. His opinion had only sunk when Sammy's cook had sent word that there was no possible way supper could be ready a full forty-five minutes early, thanks to Burberry's untimely arrival, but Burberry, and therefore Sammy, had sent word back to the woman, saying of course it would be ready.

Which was probably why the center of Samuel's cut of mutton was all but bleeding, it was so rare.

"I'd say this calls for a wager," Burberry fired back at Sammy, eyes ablaze with excitement. "You fire your cook tomorrow and I'll fire mine. Then, we'll race to see who can find the more accomplished chef to man our kitchens by the end of the week. In a fortnight, we will each host supper parties. The winner will be decided by our friends and neighbors."

"That is an intriguing wager," Sammy said, her eyes sparkling, as though she might consider it.

"You are gambling with people's livelihoods," Samuel scolded them. "The consequences of dismissing two chefs without reason and, if my impression of the situation is right, without references, would run the risk of ruining two lives."

Sammy sent Samuel a flat look. "You never were any fun," she said, biting into a particularly pink piece of meat. She cleared her throat, then assumed an imperious air and told Burberry, "I am sorry, Mr. Burberry, but I am not the gambling type."

Samuel rolled his eyes and sent a look across the table to Cameron.

Cameron had remained silent throughout supper. He'd eaten what was placed in front of him, but he didn't seem to relish it in any way, even though the food was, arguably, of a higher quality than Samuel assumed the young man was used to. When they'd been shown into the dining room, Cameron had taken the farthest seat from Burberry that he possibly could, and he hadn't looked at the man once during the meal. It seemed somehow fitting that Ian Archibald sat between Cameron and Burberry, providing a belligerent shield between the two.

"Why do you not propose to fire your men of business and wager to find a better one by the end of the week?" Archibald snapped. "That way I could finally be free of this macabre prison."

"I couldn't possibly do that, Mr. Archibald," Sammy said with exaggerated sweetness. "Not when I've hired you to perform a task for me which you have not yet completed." She snapped her last words, like a crocodile biting at his heels.

Samuel sighed and put his fork and knife down. He'd had enough of the rushed meal anyhow. "The answer to your financial problems is right before your nose, Sammy," he told his sister, near the end of his patience. "Why, I'm certain that Greek bust on the sideboard is worth a tidy sum, and that the British Museum would pay that sum."

"Is it authentic?" Burberry asked, his eyes gleaming.

"Of course," Sammy said. "Although it is Roman, not Greek. It is a depiction of the bust of one Antinous." Her smile grew downright wicked as she turned to Cameron, who had the misfortune of being seated at her left hand. "You know who that is, don't you, Mr. Oberlin?"

Cameron shook his head and mumbled, "No."

"Why, Antinous was the lover of Emperor Hadrian." She sent a devilish look to Samuel. "Hadrian was so devastated at Antinous's untimely death that he had the young man deified. Can you imagine that? Making your male lover into a god out of grief?"

Samuel wanted to strangle his sister. But she wasn't the only one.

"I'm certain there have been many a youth who is worthy of deification for his prowess in love," Burberry said with a growl in his voice, peeking down the table at Cameron.

So that was the story. Samuel picked up his knife and fork again just so that he could have something to squeeze his hands around. Otherwise, he would have been tempted to strangle Burberry. Cameron looked as though he wanted to be struck dead by a freak bolt of lightning, which told Samuel that whatever affair had happened between him and Burberry, it wasn't one Cameron remembered fondly.

"So, Burberry," Samuel said in too loud a voice. "What is this I hear about your political ambitions?" For Cameron's sake, he needed to steer the conversation in another direction.

"I plan to stand for the Conservative Party in the next general election," Burberry said with pride. "It is the natural progression for a man like me, you see. I've made my fortune, I've gathered my friends, and now I will progress into the public realm." He sent Sammy a cheeky wink as he did.

Samuel narrowed his eyes. Burberry might have had an affair with Cameron at some point, but he had his sights set on Sammy now. Which stood to reason somehow. A man as obviously ambitious and greedy as Burberry wouldn't be content to bed only one sex.

"Is there an election in the offing?" Samuel asked, fighting to appear nonplussed by what was turning into a bizarre supper party.

"There is always an election, even when there isn't. A man of your status must know that, Mr. Percy. I have begun to court my friends and exert my influence so that I am ready when the time officially comes," Burberry said, cutting into his raw mutton. The piece he held up, pausing on the way to his mouth, dripped bright red juice, turning Samuel's stomach. "I have a few ideas for ways I might win even more allies." He pointed his fork at Samuel, splattering red drops across the white tablecloth. "Ideas you might be able to play a part in."

"Me, sir?" Samuel asked, jaw clenched. He put his fork and knife down again, in no way able to even pretend he still had an appetite.

"Yes, yes," Burberry said thoughtfully, but ate his meat instead of continuing.

Samuel waited. He sent a look across the table. Cameron had put his cutlery down as well and stared as his plate as though the green beans would take on a life of their own and jump up to stab him. It didn't matter how long Samuel stared at him, Cameron would not look up and meet his eyes. Which only confirmed Samuel's assessment that Burberry had taken advantage of him.

Knowing that boiled Samuel's blood. Had poor Cameron gone his entire life with nothing but hardship and people abusing his kind nature? The man deserved so much better than that.

"This is what I propose," Burberry said suddenly, startling Samuel out of his thoughts. "You are a world-famous composer, are you not, sir?" he asked as though saying Samuel was a world-famous tightrope walker.

"I am," Samuel said in a dark voice.

"My darling brother just had a symphony premier at the Royal Albert Hall," Sammy said, reaching across the corner of the table to pat his hand. "Can you imagine? He invited me to attend as his special guest, of course, but I find the company here in Derby far more engaging." She batted her eyes at Burberry while also managing to appear as though she were staring daggers at him for stopping her from attending the premier.

"Indeed." Burberry brightened even more. The look in his eyes grew even more avaricious. "Well then, since we are dealing with such a renowned family, I'll up the stakes of my proposal."

A sinking feeling formed in the pit of Samuel's stomach. He should have known Burberry's idea would be another wager.

"How's this for a fair trade," Burberry went on,

glancing down the table to Sammy. "I will cancel the debt you owe me in full." Both Samuel and Sammy's brows shot up, and Cameron and Archibald both snapped their heads up from where they'd been wallowing in gloom and embarrassment. "If you, Mr. Percy, perform a concert at my estate in, say, a week's time."

Samuel's mouth dropped open to accept what seemed like a ridiculously uneven deal. The fact that it *was* so uneven stopped him from rushing to assent. "Is that all?" he asked.

"Of course not," Burberry sniffed. "You will perform a concert at my estate to which everyone who is anyone in Derby society will be invited, and you, Mrs. Thorne, will attend as my *very special friend* and hang on my arm all evening, showering me with praise and adoration."

Burberry sat back in his chair, spreading his arms as though he'd led a successful coup.

Samuel blinked. That was it. That was truly all the man wanted. There had to be more to the plot still, but one night of him and Sammy likely making arses of themselves for Burberry's benefit in exchange for the cancelation of a five hundred thousand pound debt was more than anyone could have asked for.

"Yes," Samuel said.

"No," Sammy said with ferocity at the same time.

Samuel whipped his head to the side to glare at his sister. "You would forego the chance to cancel a debt of this magnitude when all you have to do is attend a party?"

"I would and I will." Sammy reached for her wine glass, tilting her chin up and staring down her nose at Burberry. "That is my final statement on the issue." She took a long drink of her wine.

Samuel stared at his sister in utter consternation. "Then you will have to sell some of your treasures, my dear dragon," he growled.

"I will do no such thing," Sammy sniffed. "Mr. Archibald will come through for me and find the money in my late husband's estate, perhaps among his former business dealings." She sent Burberry yet another look that could be defined as either flirtatious or threatening.

Samuel was convinced he was on the verge of losing his mind. His sister had always been willful and eccentric, but everything had its limit. He rubbed a hand over his face and let out a breath that sounded like a growl. "You always have been the most vexing woman I've ever known."

"Why, thank you, dear brother," Sammy said, saluting him with her wine glass and a dazzling smile. "I aim to please."

Samuel remained stubbornly quiet throughout the rest of supper. Burberry and Sammy took care of the conversation themselves, discussing local matters, and leaving the rest of them out of things. When supper was finally finished and the five of them withdrew to the parlor for after-supper aperitifs, once Burberry was locked into a discussion with Archibald—one that appeared to be driving Archibald as mad as Samuel felt—

Samuel subtly slipped his hand under his sister's elbow and whisked her to the side of the room.

"Are you mad, woman?" he hissed at her once they were out of earshot of the others. "No," he said immediately, "don't answer that. I already know that you are."

"Samuel!" She pressed a hand to her décolletage—which Samuel noticed was particularly low that evening—and blinked innocently up at him. "How can you say that about your own sister?"

"Because it's true," Samuel growled. He let out an impatient breath and shifted his stance, turning his back on the others. "One party, Sammy. That's all it will take for you to clear an enormous debt. It's a better offer than you can ever hope to get otherwise."

"It is an offer that you do not understand," Sammy said with sudden seriousness in her eyes. "Burberry isn't merely offering to host a concert at which he can show the two of us off."

"Yes, I gathered as much," Samuel said, rubbing a hand over his temples.

"Then why are you pressuring me to give in to that criminal's demands?" Sammy took a step closer to him.

"Because this is an easy solution, and you are unwilling to consider the other solution," Samuel said.

"I won't do it." Sammy crossed her arms and turned up her nose.

"For God's sake, Sammy," Samuel growled. "Why not?"

"Because Burberry wishes to marry me," she said, lowering her chin a little.

Samuel blinked. "And what is the problem in that? The two of you obviously get along. You spent the entire supper flirting."

"Flirtation and marriage are two entirely separate things," Sammy insisted. "Flirtation is fun, enlivening. Marriage is the dullest thing I've ever done."

"Marrying Burberry would end all of your problems," Samuel said. "Yes, the man is awful, and I suspect he has offended my friend somehow—"

"The two of them had an affair," Sammy said, one eyebrow raised, as though she hoped to rile Samuel up with the information.

"I'd gathered as much," Samuel pretended to dismiss the matter, as though he didn't care. "But I also gather that Burberry enjoys female company as much as male."

"Yes, he does," Sammy said with an air that was far too suspicious for Samuel's liking.

Samuel stared flatly at her. "Sammy, you haven't," he said, his blood preparing to boil in his veins.

"The country is so boring," Sammy insisted. "Burberry made a wager, and I lost. What else was I supposed to do?"

"You were supposed to keep your legs together," Samuel growled. "That or marry the man, like any sensible, business-minded widow would do."

"Oh, it is not *truly* that I do not wish to marry him, I

just...I cannot let him *win*," Sammy said, turning away from him. "I would never be able to live it down."

Samuel gripped the sides of his head to keep it from exploding. "My God, woman. Are you really so stubborn, so vicious, that you would draw out everyone else's problems as well as your own simply because you don't want to let Burberry win some imagined competition between the two of you?"

Sammy pivoted back to him, her brow raised. "Yes."

Samuel made a sound of irritated agony, but Sammy went on with, "I have worked my whole life to hold my own. You know how difficult it is to navigate this society looking the way we look. If I show just one second of weakness, if I appear to be biddable in any way or able to be manipulated, then I will find myself on the wrong end of the whip at any moment."

"How do you know?" Samuel said, feeling a twist of reluctant admiration for her.

"How do you *not* know?" she fired back. "We are little more than performing monkeys to them, Samuel. The only way I can hope to hold my head up high in society is by behaving as an eccentric curiosity. I have the money to pull it off now, but the moment I succumb to the marriage vows once again, I become nothing more than a trinket on a man's arm."

"You will not have the money anymore unless you *do* succumb to those marriage vows," Samuel reminded her.

Sammy pressed her lips together and glanced away. Samuel could see that she was well aware of the truth, but she was fighting it tooth and nail. More than that, he had the itching feeling that something else was going on, something Sammy wasn't telling him. It didn't matter, though. His sister could be as stubborn and outlandish as she wanted, but the time was swiftly coming when she would have to put her silly games aside and face the harsh reality of the world she lived in.

"Agree to do this concert Burberry is proposing," he told her, hoping his voice sounded softer, even though he didn't feel soft toward her at all. "It will just be one night. Do what you'd like after that."

"It wouldn't just be one night," Sammy told him stubbornly. "You know that the moment I appear to show that much interest in Burberry, it will only be a matter of time before he is parading me around as another conquest."

"He's already conquered you," Samuel replied, one eyebrow raised. "And I haven't heard you complain about it yet."

Sammy flushed. "There is nothing to complain about there. But that doesn't mean I want to give up what freedom I have to become the laughingstock of Derby high society. It doesn't matter how one tries to hide those things, people always jump to conclusions and box one into a humiliating corner."

Her comment hit Samuel uncomfortably. It sounded a little too familiar. There was already a resemblance between him and Sammy, but it bothered him that it would extend beneath the skin and end with him mirroring her coldness and jaded view of the world. He glanced across the room to Cameron, prickles of guilt between his shoulder blades.

Those prickles turned to clenched muscles when he found Burberry speaking to Cameron and standing much too close as he did. The way Burberry looked at Cameron with a lascivious smile made Samuel want to throttle the man. Cameron looked as miserable as could be, but Burberry had backed him against a side table where he couldn't get away.

"Do you still think it's a grand idea to simply give in to Burberry's plans?" Sammy asked in a haughty voice. "How long do you suppose it will be before he asks to throw your friend Cameron into the terms of the agreement?"

"Over my dead body," Samuel grumbled.

Sammy hummed and smirked at him. "Then perhaps the two of us should think a bit harder about rushing to take Burberry up on his offer. Five hundred thousand is a large sum, but is it worth sacrificing the things we hold most dear?"

Sammy had a point. Samuel hated it, but there it was. He couldn't, in good conscience, do anything that might put Cameron in an uncomfortable position, not for a king's ransom, and not for the sake of what passed for family in his life. He told himself it was because he wanted to keep Cameron all for himself, but underneath that were warmer, tenderer feelings. Feelings that were the absolute last thing he wanted to consider when so much else was up in the air.

CHAPTER 8

*E*verything about The Black Widow's house made Cameron feel as though he'd stepped through the looking glass and into some sort of macabre, gothic novel. He'd seen the house from the outside so much that it had almost faded into the background of his imagination. Being inside of the place brought back every awed childhood emotion he'd ever entertained when staring at it from the other side of the gate. The art and artifacts it contained ranged from beautiful to frightening, the staff was exotic and attractive, and even the scent of the place hinted at spices and sensuality.

But sensuality was the last thing he wanted to feel with Burberry in the same room. It was bad enough that he'd had to sit through supper with Burberry carrying on a conversation with their hostess, as though nothing at all were out of the ordinary. Cameron couldn't tell if it was worse or better when Burberry flirted so shamelessly with

Samuel's sister. That meant the man wasn't flirting with him. But all that changed once they'd adjourned to the parlor for drinks.

"I seem to recall that you like a good bit of sherry after supper," Burberry said, pouring Cameron a glass as Samuel argued with his sister in the far corner of the room.

"I don't care for it," Cameron mumbled. He glanced desperately to Archibald, but Archibald was already on his way out of the room. The moment Mrs. Thorne took her eye off him, Archibald bolted.

That left Cameron very much alone with Burberry.

"That's not what I remember," Burberry said in a salacious purr. "I recall you being extraordinarily fond of sherry. Extraordinarily fond of quite a few things." He pressed the glass of amber liquid into Cameron's hand. His touch remained on Cameron's fingers far longer than it should.

Cameron cleared his throat and stepped away from Burberry, shaking on the inside. He went so far as to take a quick gulp from his glass to calm his nerves, even though he knew it was a terrible idea. A few sips of sherry or wine or beer or whatever it had been two years ago was what had started him down the dangerous path to begin with.

"You cannot imagine my surprise to see you back here," Burberry said, following Cameron across the room. "I didn't think we'd ever see each other again."

"It wasn't my idea," Cameron said. He reached a

table containing some sort of ancient, tarnished, bronze plate at the far end of one of the sofas and pretended to be interested in it.

"Your idea or not, I'm glad you're here," Burberry went on.

He was right up against Cameron before Cameron knew what was happening. So close, in fact that he pressed his hips against Cameron's backside. Cameron gulped hard at the sensation of the man's erection and spun around to push him away.

"I don't do that anymore," he said in a garbled rush, spilling some of his sherry on the carpet.

"Don't you?" Burberry arched one eyebrow invitingly, but took a step back. "As I recall, you were quite good. Why stop doing something you're good at?"

Cameron sent a desperate look across the room to Samuel and his sister, but the two of them were so deeply engaged in their argument that they wouldn't have been aware if a cow wandered into the parlor. Which, he supposed, was why Burberry had taken liberties.

"I've no wish to offend you, Mr. Burberry," Cameron blurted, "but I am not interested in continuing our former acquaintance."

"My, my," Burberry said with a hungry grin. "You have learned a few manners in London." He took a step closer, pinning Cameron against the table. "I wonder what else you've learned from the big, bad city."

"I've learned that I'm good for more than a suck and a fuck." Cameron winced. His statement would have been far more powerful if he hadn't mumbled it, and if he'd been able to look Burberry in the eyes as he said it.

"But you were very good at those things as well," Burberry said. He backed off, sending Cameron a lascivious look as he ran a finger around the rim of his sherry glass. "How long are you in Derby?"

"I don't know," Cameron answered quickly.

"Have you visited your dear mama and papa yet?" Burberry asked on.

"No, I have not. I'm not welcome there, thanks to you." Cameron only just managed to glance up to Burberry with a frown.

"And have you heard that I've raised their rent again?" Burberry asked with a mercenary look in his eyes.

"I have." Cameron nodded once.

Burberry smiled. "Would you like me to lower it?"

"I would," Cameron winced.

"I could always raise it even higher."

"Please don't do that," Cameron mumbled.

"No?" Burberry shrugged. "Then you know what you need to do." Burberry glanced down, as if issuing him a command to get on his knees.

Cameron's mouth dropped open. He couldn't possibly mean right there and then.

"Yes, like that," Burberry said, staring at Cameron's open mouth with a grin. "I miss it so."

Cameron snapped his mouth shut. He took a deep breath, trying to pull himself together. He wasn't the green and anxious boy that he'd been only a few years ago. Those things were no longer either a novelty for him or something he was willing to use to eke out a living. He was a grown man, and it was time he acted like one.

"It's not that I'm not appreciative of all you've done for me over the years, Mr. Burberry," he said, trying to stand tall. "And I will not pretend that we did not have some enjoyable times together. But that is all behind me now."

"Is it?" Burberry's mouth was tight in disappointment.

"I have good employment as a clerk in London," Cameron said. "I enjoy my work, and I have friends now."

"Very interesting friends, I might add," Burberry said with a wry grin, glancing to Samuel.

Samuel looked in Cameron's direction, which came as something of a relief. Samuel's expression was dark, and the way he stared at Burberry was enough to make Burberry back up farther.

"So, thank you for your kind offer," Cameron said, being polite, even though there had been nothing kind about Burberry's advance at all. "But I have to say no. If you will excuse me."

Samuel broke away from his sister and started to approach him and Burberry, but Cameron didn't think he was up to the confrontation. Even though it made him feel like a coward, he turned and marched out of the parlor. As soon as he reached the hall, he picked up his pace and ended up mounting the grand staircase two steps at a time until he reached the hall with his guest room.

As soon as he'd flown through the door, slamming and locking it behind him, Cameron let out an anxious breath. If he had known this trip would involve that sort of a reunion with Burberry, he would have put his foot firmly down and absolutely refused to go. The day was turning into one of the worst of his life. He couldn't go to bed fast enough.

He heaved a sigh and slumped his way across the room to the wardrobe, where he'd put away his things in the brief space of time between his and Samuel's arrival and supper. The wardrobe looked sadly bare, even with his extra shirts and a change of trousers. He undressed, shaking out his worn things in the hope that airing them would mean he could get another day's use out of them, then hung them in the wardrobe with his clean clothes. Even though it was February, he hadn't brought a nightshirt or robe with him for the simple reason that he didn't own any. He always slept in the nude. Although, considering he was a guest in someone's house, he opted to sleep in his drawers instead after he washed his face and brushed his teeth.

But sleep evaded him when he climbed into the huge, soft bed. It didn't matter how comfortable the bed was or how warm the room, thanks to the blazing fire set by the staff, his mind refused to turn off. Not to mention that it was barely eight o'clock. He tossed and turned, flipping from one side to the other, then finally settled on his back, staring up at the ceiling.

What would have happened if he'd never met Nathaniel Burberry? Burberry had been his family's landlord for as long as Cameron could remember, but what would have happened if Burberry had never taken a particular interest in him? It wasn't as though Burberry had been responsible for his attraction to men. He'd felt that in himself since he was a boy. Burberry had been the first man to actually call him out and invite him to do something about it, though. Cameron had known from the start that it was wicked of him to go up to Burberry's bedroom when he'd told his family he was running errands for the man. And lying had been the least of his sins. It was thanks to Burberry that he knew what he liked, thanks to Burberry's explicit instructions that he'd learned how to properly suck off a gentleman. Those skills had come in handy when he'd first arrived in London.

Just because he'd liked sex hadn't meant he'd liked Burberry. Not in the end. Not when Burberry had raised his family's rent after Cameron had told him he didn't want to do it anymore. And not when Tony had walked in on Burberry buggering him silly a year ago. Burberry had had the nerve to ask if Tony wanted to join in rather than showing any remorse. And, of course, Cameron had ended up banished, since Tony was utterly incapable of keeping his mouth shut.

Cameron tossed back to his side, furious with himself

that his bitter memories had caused the sweet reaction of making him go hard. He'd always hated the way his body reacted to stimulation, whether his heart wanted it to or not. He accepted it as a condition of humanity, but that didn't mean he had to lie there and wallow in it.

He threw the bedcovers aside and got up to pace around the room to walk himself back into a state of calm. It was a lovely room, though some of the artwork left much to be desired. The pink-faced cherubs carrying garlands of flowers to their voluptuous and naked ladies wasn't to Cameron's tastes at all, but the suggestive nature of the paintings on the walls did nothing to calm his agitation. The room contained a bookshelf, but he'd never been much of a reader, and the titles all seemed as dull as toast. He examined the clock on the mantelpiece for a moment, then went to look out the window, but the back garden was dark.

The only other curiosity in the room was a door near the head of the bed that he hadn't had a chance to go through yet. He marched over to it and tried the handle, and when he saw it was unlocked, he pulled the door open and stepped through.

Stepped right into what had to be Samuel's bedroom. Had to be, because Samuel was there, just pulling his shirt off over his head as his trousers hung low on his hips. Cameron was treated to the full, gorgeous sight of Samuel's naked torso, its muscles well-defined, a dusting of dark hair across Samuel's chest. The man had fine arms as well, which he saw all of as Samuel tossed his shirt aside. Perhaps most inviting of all was the trail of hair that pointed from Samuel's navel to the sagging waist of his trousers and the vee of muscle that was exposed as a result.

It wasn't until Cameron swallowed and squirmed as he went hard all over again that it dawned on him that Samuel wasn't remotely surprised to see him standing there.

"Cameron," Samuel greeted him with a nod, walking his shirt to a chair near his fireplace and draping it there. "Couldn't sleep?"

Cameron's mouth worked wordlessly for a moment, particularly when Samuel turned away from him for a moment, giving him a lovely view of the strong muscles of his back and a peek at the cleft at the top of his arse. The urge to see more, not to mention the need to touch what he saw, scrambled Cameron's mind.

When Samuel turned back to him, one eyebrow raised in question, Cameron managed to make a few garbled sounds before saying, "No."

"I'm sorry this has been such a trying day," Samuel said, moving to the edge of his bed and sitting so that he could remove his shoes. Cameron's heart squeezed in his chest as he speculated whether Samuel would strip off his trousers next. "I could see at every step of the way how difficult things were for you."

Cameron blinked and shook his head, forcing his mind to catch up to the moment. "I've had better days," he finally managed to say.

Samuel patted the bed next to him, inviting Cameron to join him. "Sammy tells me you and Burberry have a previous acquaintance."

Cameron took a few steps toward the bed, but changed his mind halfway there. Was he mad? He couldn't cozy up to Samuel, as though the air weren't crackling with sexual tension. Samuel's utter lack of shock at the way he walked right into his bedroom left Cameron feeling as though he'd walked into a trap.

"I've deduced that the two of you were lovers," Samuel said, his mouth pulling into a grin, but his eyes as cold as steel.

Cameron wanted to make a joke that, no, he and Samuel's sister were not lovers, but his mouth was too dry to form the words. It took a supreme effort of will for him to say, "I wouldn't call it that. I was young. We had sex. It felt good."

"On a regular basis?" Samuel asked with a combination of curiosity and jealousy in his expression.

Cameron nodded. "I kept meaning to stop. I wanted to. But I was young and...felt things. Burberry was the only one who I had to do them with. So I kept at it. Until Tony caught us together."

"And that's why you were chased out of Derby," Samuel said with sudden understanding.

Again, Cameron nodded. The situation was so unbearably awkward that he couldn't stand still. He paced the open space in Samuel's room, debating whether to simply go back to his room. He couldn't, though. Something was holding him to the spot. Samuel was the only ally he had at the moment, and he desperately wanted to feel as though he was not alone.

"I have to go visit my family," he said in a stilted voice, pushing a hand through his hair. "Tony will have told them I'm in town, and it would be worse if I didn't see them than if I do."

"Are you certain of that?" Samuel asked with a wry grin. "I must say, I'm not impressed with what I've seen of your family thus far."

"I wouldn't be able to live with myself if I didn't at least try. They're...they're my family," Cameron said without paying attention to his words. How could he pay attention when Samuel had finally cast aside his shoes and socks and stood to remove his trousers? He kept his drawers on, but they did nothing to hide the shape of Samuel's arse, or the fact that his cock was already half hard. And large.

"You've met my sister," Samuel went on with a grim laugh. "So you can see why family is not high on my list of things I treasure at the moment."

"Still, they're family," Cameron mumbled. He could barely pay attention to anything when Samuel turned to him, resting his hands boldly on his hips.

"Do you want me to come with you to see your family?" Samuel asked. "Perhaps tomorrow?"

Cameron dragged his eyes up from Samuel's drawers—embarrassed to have caught himself staring in the first place—and sighed. "You don't have to," he said in a rough voice, then cleared his throat. "I'm sure you have better things to do. Like sorting out your sister or convincing Mr. Archibald to tell us where Lady Selby is."

"I don't think either of those things are going to happen any time soon," Samuel said with a sigh, approaching Cameron slowly. "My sister is irredeemably stubborn, and I have a feeling Archibald just might be her match in that regard. On top of that, though my initial impulse was to take Burberry up on his offer to cancel Sammy's debt in return for a concert and what appears to be more of a promise of marriage on Sammy's part than just a bit of attention, now I'm not so certain."

Cameron gulped as Samuel grew closer. He told his feet to move, to back away, but they didn't seem to be listening. "Five hundred thousand pounds is a lot of money," he croaked.

"Something I've told my sister repeatedly now," Samuel said, still advancing on him. "But I don't like Burberry. I don't like him one bit. I think he was cruel to you."

"He wasn't, really," Cameron gasped as Samuel stepped all the way up to him, sliding a hand across Cameron's arm. "He didn't force me or anything."

"Still," Samuel said. "You deserve better."

He circled a hand around Cameron's neck, holding the base of his head as he slanted his mouth over Cameron's. Cameron sucked in a breath, then sighed aloud as Samuel parted his lips with his tongue, then slipped inside. The kiss was every bit as good as the one he remembered from the concert hall. It was better, because they both wore nothing but their drawers, and when Samuel leaned into him, caressing Cameron's arse with his free hand and pressing their bodies together, it felt like the gates of heaven had opened.

Cameron couldn't help himself. He closed his arms around Samuel's back, closing his eyes and giving everything he had to their kiss. It was fiery and wet, their tongues tasting and mouths sucking. The pleasure of it was exactly the sort of reward he felt as though he deserved after the miserable day he'd had. Best of all, for a few, blissful seconds, he felt as though it could be something more than just a kiss. Samuel had spoken so kindly to him, had felt sorry for the pain he'd endured that day. He was angry with Burberry on his behalf, as though he genuinely cared. Images of the two of them together and smiling, simple and companionable, rose up within Cameron that were almost as powerful as the pure heat and throb in his groin. Things could be so beautiful if—

"Let's fuck," Samuel said with a growl in his voice, his hand tightening on Cameron's arse.

It was as bad as a splash of cold water. He pulled away, shaking his head.

Samuel held him tight enough that he couldn't break away from their embrace entirely. "You're as hard as iron, Cameron. Don't try to tell me you're not aching for a fuck."

It took every ounce of strength Cameron had to

glance up and meet Samuel's eyes. "Yes, I enjoy fucking. But I'm not a toy to be used and tossed out of bed after."

"I never said—"

"Like Burberry did with me," Cameron added in a cold voice, staring hard into Samuel's eyes.

Samuel's mouth dropped open, and his eyes flashed with offense. For a moment. Then they softened with understanding. "What can I do to prove to you that you mean more to me than you meant to those others?"

Cameron frowned. "But do I? Do I really? Or am I just another conquest you've taken a particularly long time and gone through a lot of trouble to make?" He didn't think he could bear to feel that way again, like he was just a cock and an arsehole and not a man. Especially not with Samuel.

Samuel's expression pinched with pain, but Cameron couldn't tell if it was pain on his behalf or if Samuel was frustrated because he wasn't getting what he wanted. "Isn't this proof enough?" he asked, taking Cameron's hand and moving it to his erection.

Cameron sighed and lowered his head to watch his hand for a moment as he tested Samuel's length and girth through his drawers. "This is not affection," he said, lifting his eyes to meet Samuel's again. "This is not love."

"Then how about this?" Samuel leaned into him again, slanting his mouth over Cameron's. He treated Cameron to another searing kiss, then said, "This is friendship." Another kiss followed, and Samuel added, "This is deepest admiration and genuine affection." He reached for Cameron's prick as his kiss went on, deepening.

Everything within Cameron told him he should have stepped away. He shouldn't have sighed into Samuel's mouth or continued to stroke his cock. He should have done something when Samuel tugged at the drawstring of his drawers, causing them to sag so that he could stroke Cameron's cock skin on skin. Something other than mirroring the gesture so that he had his hand directly on Samuel as well. He should have stayed true to his scruples instead of fisting Samuel and being pleasured in return as they traded sighs and groans in each other's mouths.

The whole thing spiraled out of control within a minute, and with a gasp and a cry, Cameron came across Samuel's hand. It felt so good and lasted surprisingly long. Samuel came apart a few seconds after Cameron was done, spilling his cum across Cameron's hand, which hadn't stopped moving, even through his burst of pleasure. Cameron winced at himself internally, but, damn, it had been good. Simple and silly though it was.

He and Samuel sagged against each other for a moment, bodies hot and sweating enough to make the sensation of their skin touching beautiful and erotic. Samuel shifted to embrace Cameron lightly, nuzzling the side of his neck, which also felt uncommonly good.

But when Samuel whispered, "Come to bed with me," Cameron shook his head and stepped back.

"I shouldn't have done that, and I'm sorry," he said,

breaking away from Samuel entirely, eyes downcast. "I don't want to give you the wrong idea about what I'm willing to do. Because I can't treat myself so shabbily again. I'm sorry," he repeated before turning and striding back through the door into his own bedroom.

He shut the door behind him, wondering if there was a lock. Even if there was, he wouldn't have turned it. Too large a part of him didn't want to shut Samuel out entirely, even if that would have been best for both of them. Instead, he removed his drawers and wiped his hands before tossing them to the floor, then climbed into bed and pulled the covers over his head. He couldn't decide if what had happened was a beautiful end to a horrible day or if it had just made things worse. All he knew was that his body wanted Samuel more than ever, but his heart still wasn't sure.

CHAPTER 9

It was impossible for Samuel to decide which was worse, not being able to touch Cameron at all or touching him and having the young man flee. They'd gotten close enough to experience a moment of sublime release as they wanked each other off, then Cameron retreated, body and soul, because he believed staying the night with Samuel and doing more would be treating himself shabbily. Samuel was beginning to understand where Cameron's idea that indulging in sex would mean he was betraying himself had come from, but that only made him seethe hotter with indignation on the young man's behalf.

He was growing to care about Cameron Oberlin. He saw the heartache that the young man had been through. So why wouldn't Cameron give in and trust that Samuel only wanted what was best for him?

Because he was too bull-headed to actually say as

much to the lad, Samuel answered his own question. Because the part of him that despised the niceties of domestic life and wanted to defy the so-called norm must have shone from him like a beacon, and that wasn't what Cameron wanted.

"You don't have to do this, you know," Cameron mumbled to him late the next morning, as the two of them headed out through the gate of Sammy's Derby estate and started what was bound to be a long walk to the small hamlet just outside of town, where Cameron's family lived. "I need to warn my parents about Burberry's new scheme, and you don't have anything to do with that. Just because it's not going to be pleasant doesn't mean I can't face my mother and father on my own."

"I said I'd accompany you, so I'll accompany you," Samuel snapped.

He immediately felt ashamed of himself for the reaction. Cameron wasn't at fault for wanting to keep his private life to himself. Even if Samuel ached to be a part of it like he'd never ached for anything before.

Cameron seemed to sense the tension that had Samuel wrapped in knots, though he probably misunderstood it as sexual frustration—and it was absolutely that as well. Cameron peeked sideways at him as though Samuel were a tiger about to pounce as they skirted through the edge of town, making their way to one of the main roads leading north. The last thing Samuel wanted was for Cameron to feel even more ill at ease with him, so he scrambled for some neutral topic of conversation.

"I wasn't expecting to find Archibald so engaged in the work my sister has given him," he said, glancing sideways at Cameron. "I approached him after breakfast this morning to ask why he hadn't simply slipped away in the middle of the night."

"He has men guarding him," Cameron said.

"He does," Samuel agreed with a nod. "But it's not as though he couldn't bribe them to turn their backs while he packed his things and ran."

"Maybe he's afraid of them," Cameron suggested.

Samuel tilted his head to the side with a considering expression. "It's a possibility, but honestly, has Archibald behaved as though he's afraid of anything since we arrived at my sister's house?"

"No, not really," Cameron said, letting out a breath.

Samuel indulged in a quick half smile. Cameron was conversing with him, even if it wasn't on a topic that would advance their relationship, whatever that was. It meant there was a gateway open between the two of them. They could become friends after all.

Friends. Samuel nearly laughed out loud at the concept. He didn't want to be Cameron's *friend*, he wanted to be the one buried deep in the young man's arse while Cameron moaned his name in ecstasy. He wanted to be the one with his mouth around Cameron's beautiful cock when he came.

Except, behind those familiar, expected impulses, Samuel felt an itching for something more. He wondered what it sounded like when Cameron laughed from his belly, putting his whole heart into it. He wondered which of the paintings at the National Gallery would grab Cameron's attention the hardest and transport him into the world of the painter. Perhaps most intimately of all, he wondered what thoughts would fly through Cameron's head if Samuel played one of his original compositions for the young man. He wanted to take Cameron to the seaside and watch the sunlight glint in his blond hair. He wanted to curl up in front of a fire with him at Christmastime with mugs of chocolate and listen to carolers in the street. He wanted a lot of things that he'd only ever laughed at men for wanting before.

He must have let the silence between them run on too long. They turned off of the main road and started walking down a much longer, rougher one, and Samuel found Cameron staring at him covertly. Out of curiosity, Samuel waited to see whether Cameron would be the one to break the silence. That only lasted for a few, impatient minutes before Samuel had to break it himself or crawl out of his skin.

"I've just been thinking about whether Archibald's romance with Lady Selby is truly as devoted as we all assume it is," he lied, face heating.

"You doubt that they love each other?" Cameron asked, as though they hadn't just spent an awkward twenty minutes in silence.

"If Archibald is so unwilling to attempt an escape from my sister to fly back to London, then perhaps he's done with Lady Selby," Samuel suggested.

Cameron appeared to consider it for a moment, then shook his head. "It's more likely he's still poring over your sister's books because he's looking for a way to embezzle the money he needs to start a new life in America."

Samuel sent Cameron an impressed look. "What makes you say that?"

"The ledger," Cameron said as though it were obvious. "Whoever kept those books before did a terrible job of it. There are loads of inconsistencies and incorrect calculations that go back for years."

Samuel missed a step, pausing to stare at Cameron. "How do you know? You only looked at that ledger for thirty seconds."

Cameron shrugged, his face coloring. "I remember things the instant I see them."

That didn't lessen Samuel's awe in the least. "Remember them? At just one look?"

"Of course." Cameron blinked. "Don't you?"

"Not at all," Samuel said, starting forward again. He could see a cluster of cottages amidst fallow fields a mile or so in front of them along the frosty path they walked and assumed they were coming close to Cameron's old home.

"I mean, when you study something," Cameron went on, as though Samuel was the one who didn't understand. "As if your mind paints a picture of it that you can recall later and study."

"A picture?" Samuel shook his head. "No, lad, I think your mind is the only one that does that."

Cameron frowned and scratched the side of his head. "You mean, you don't see images in your head that way?"

"No," Samuel laughed. "But I do hear music. Lots of music. Before I write it down. It's as though my mind composes while I'm sleeping, then plays concerts for me that I only need to record on paper later."

"Huh." Cameron studied him for another moment, then made a face as though he was pleased to have learned something new, then glanced ahead down the road.

"So, you truly remember things, like pages from a ledger, as if that ledger were still clear in your mind after only one look?" Samuel asked after a few silent moments.

"I didn't think it was unusual," Cameron said.

"It's highly unusual," Samuel laughed, slapping a hand on Cameron's shoulder.

The moment of contact was sweet at first, particularly when Cameron smiled, but grew awkward as Cameron's smile vanished. At first, Samuel thought it was because of something he'd done. But when he realized that Cameron had glanced past him to the edge of one of the fields, where a group of children, who were old enough that they should have been in school, stood from some sort of game they were playing and stared at him, Samuel knew it wasn't him who had ruined Cameron's ease.

"I'm going to tell Ma," one of the boys—who must have been about twelve—shouted at Cameron, then turned and sprinted off down the lane. The other children ran after him. All of them sent Cameron mean and stubborn scowls, as if he'd come to steal their toys.

Cameron sighed, his shoulders sagging. "They'll know we're coming now," he said.

That was all he said as they walked the last half mile to Cameron's family home. Samuel buzzed with a protective energy, his nerves pulled taut as he looked for a way he could shelter Cameron from what was bound to be an unpleasant meeting. He didn't see what he could do, though, aside from grabbing Cameron's arm and tugging him back the way he'd come.

By the time they reached the hamlet, it felt to Samuel like every inhabitant of the dozen or so cottages that made up the group had spilled out into a common area with a well. Samuel could practically feel Cameron trembling with dread beside him. At first, he stepped closer, but when that earned him a shocked glare from a middle-aged woman wearing a thick shawl around her stooped shoulders, he backed away. Considering the reasons Cameron had been banished from his home, any proximity on Samuel's part would likely only make things worse.

"Hello, Ma," Cameron mumbled, approaching the woman with the shawl.

"Stay away from me, you spawn of Satan," his mother said, taking a step back.

Cameron stopped where he was, head hung so low that it both tugged at Samuel's heartstrings and made him want to growl with rage and tell every one of the villagers gathering to stare at Cameron just what he thought of them.

"Ma," Cameron went on, dragging his eyes up to meet his mother's, then glancing on to a man with a limp who stepped up behind her. "Pa. I came to warn you that Mr. Burberry is threatening to raise your rent again."

A few of the other villagers suddenly looked anxious and murmured to each other, as though they were the ones whose rent was about to be raised. Cameron's parents only seemed interested in glaring at him. Samuel was furious over that, but also struck by the realization that the properties Burberry owned weren't flats on city blocks, like he'd automatically assumed, but thatched cottages in the middle of the countryside which were clearly inhabited by the simplest sort of folk England had to offer. Somehow, that made Burberry's treachery even worse in Samuel's eyes.

"If Burberry is raising our rents, then you are to blame," Cameron's mother spat at him. "You and your wicked, sinful ways."

"It's nothing like that, Ma," Cameron insisted, shrinking under the derisive stares directed at him from all sides. "It's just Mr. Burberry being ambitious."

Samuel had the uncomfortable feeling Cameron was lying. He'd seen the way Burberry made advances on Cameron the night before. Burberry was as unscrupulous as they came, and Samuel wouldn't have put it past the bastard to threaten to raise rents if Cameron didn't lower his standards. Burberry was trying to do the same thing with his sister.

"You might not have caused it directly," Cameron's father spoke up, eyes narrowed at his son, "but it's your problem to solve."

"Right true it is," his mother added with a nod. "And where's that money you promised to send us?"

"Now see here," Samuel began, indignant that Cameron's parents expected him to pay for their lives when they were treating him like shite.

Cameron held up a hand as a plea for Samuel's patience, then reached into the inner pocket of his threadbare coat. He silently took out a small, crumpled handful of bills and handed them to his mother. Samuel noted that Cameron's mother took them without touching Cameron's hand, and that it was a deliberate slight.

"Now be off with you, filth," she said, backpedaling and making a shooing motion. "We don't want you or your negro friend soiling us good people.

Samuel hadn't expected to be slighted for his race at just that moment or by those particular people. It stung more than it should have, particularly given that they relied on their son to pay their rent while he'd just had a composition premiered at the Royal Albert Hall. He didn't see any point in staying to argue with the ungrateful wretches, though.

"I think we should leave," he murmured, stepping

closer to Cameron. "You're not going to get what you want from them."

Cameron flinched, sending Samuel a guilty look. It broke Samuel's heart to see that he'd guessed right and that Cameron was hoping for some sort of sign of reconciliation from his family. Samuel could have told him that where family was concerned, there was no hope.

"You listen to him," a younger woman standing close enough to have overheard Samuel said. "Your sort doesn't belong here among good folk."

Cameron glanced desperately at his parents for a long moment, then to the woman who had spoken, then to Samuel. At last, he nodded and turned to silently walk away.

Samuel fell in beside him, picking up his pace so that Cameron would match it, getting the two of them as far away from the hostile little village as possible.

"This is why I despise family and domesticity," Samuel grumbled once they were well away from the cottages. "It's all hypocrisy and arrogance." The grey and forbidding sky above them and the stubbly, fallow fields around them seemed to reflect everything Samuel thought about the people they'd just met.

Cameron glanced to him with surprise, and a bit of hurt. "They're not always bad like that," he said. "They care for each other, even if they don't care for me."

"That doesn't make them worth a fart in my book," Samuel huffed in return, striding fast to work off his indignant energy. "You can prattle on about the sweetness and joys of a domestic life, but that back there is the reality." He gestured over his shoulder with his thumb. "And I know you don't believe the things I do about what we're all entitled to in this world and what sort of pleasure we should take without caring so much as a hoot about what those supposedly good people think, but if that's what *they* are offering us, I'd just as soon have what *we* can give each other."

Samuel was rather pleased with his outburst, but somehow it only seemed to make Cameron sad. "I'm sorry you feel that way," Cameron said, squaring his shoulders a bit. "I'm sorry that's all you've experienced in your life."

"It's all you've experienced too, if you'd just open your eyes and see it," Samuel snapped back, then shook his head. "You could have so much more, my friend. So much more."

Cameron studied him for a long moment, slowing their pace once they reached the other side of the fields and could see the main road far in the distance. He didn't say anything, though.

That silence continued for so long that it began to make Samuel's back itch. He tried to think about other things as they finally reached the main road and headed back into Derby, tried to weigh what he should do about Sammy and her stubbornness, about Archibald and his reticence, and about Burberry's offer to let Sammy's debt go for a concert and a promise. But his thoughts kept shifting firmly back to Cameron and all the things Samuel wanted to do to make the poor man's life better. He needed loving up, that much was certain. Not in a sentimental or foolish way, but in a very practical one. The man deserved a warm bed, a good fuck, and a hearty meal after.

But somehow, even that lovely image didn't feel like enough. There was something Samuel was missing, something he felt compelled to discover, for Cameron's sake, to make up for everything he'd just witnessed.

When they reached the edge of Derby, Samuel strode on as if they would return to Sammy's house, but Cameron started down a different street.

"Where are you going?" Samuel asked him.

Cameron paused and let out a breath. "I have one other call to pay. You don't need to come with me."

Samuel's expression darkened. "Is it to Burberry?"

"No!" Cameron answered, as though offended Samuel would even ask. "It's to my eldest sister, Georgie."

Samuel instantly felt sheepish. "I'll come with you, then," he grumbled. "Though the last thing I want to see is you being set down by a family member who should be kissing your feet."

Of all things, Cameron smiled. It was brief, and small, but it was definitely a smile. He didn't say anything else as they walked on, though.

They headed through the collection of flats and townhomes near the edge of town and on to what appeared to Samuel like a miniature business district.

The buildings on the street they walked down had shingles for everything from solicitor's offices to physicians to a print shop. It was that print shop that Cameron entered, just as a fine drizzle began to fall.

"Cameron!" The joyful shout came from a plump, smiling woman with a toddler in one arm, who had been working a large, old fashioned printing press with her free hand. "What a blessed sight you are."

As the woman stepped around the printing press, Samuel noticed that the reason she was so plump was because she was heavy with child. More than that, an older toddler—a boy of perhaps three or four—clung to her skirts and moved with her as she approached Cameron to hug him tightly. The little boy clinging to his mother's skirts gazed up at Samuel with wide eyes.

"Georgie," Cameron said with more joy in his voice than Samuel had ever heard from him. "I'm sorry I didn't tell you I was coming. There wasn't time."

"Nonsense," Georgie said, her smile so bright it could have taught the heavens a thing or two. The more Samuel looked at her, the more he could see the clear resemblance between the siblings. When Cameron smiled, his eyes had the same brightness about them. "When did you arrive?" Georgie asked. "How long are you here for? Where are you staying? I'm certain James would be happy to have you stay with us, though you'd have to bunk with Avery here," she said in a rush, resting her free hand on the little boy's head. "And who is your friend?"

She turned to Samuel with the same wide-eyed look as her son, suddenly in awe.

Cameron laughed, and plucked the toddler, a girl, straight out of Georgie's arms to cuddle with her. "This is Mr. Samuel Percy, the world-famous composer and musician," he said, imitating the way Sammy had introduced him the night before. "We're working on a special assignment for my employer in London, John Dandie. And we're staying at his sister's house." He paused before adding with a mischievous wink, "His sister is Mrs. Thorne."

Georgie's mouth dropped open, and her eyes widened even more. "But of course. How could I mistake you for anyone else? You and Mrs. Thorne favor each other very much."

Samuel met the comment with a wry grin, wondering if the resemblance was the color of their skin or if Georgie could see past that.

But no, somehow Samuel could see that Cameron's sister deserved the benefit of the doubt. She had an air about her, something open and soft. It was the same sort of feeling he had from Cameron when the young man was in a peaceful place.

"I can't believe how much Victoria has grown since I last saw her," Cameron said, kissing the toddler in his arms over and over, as though she were made of sugar and marzipan.

"It's been a year," Georgie laughed. Then she sighed. "Good heavens, Cameron. It's been a year." Her brow knit in concern, and for a moment, Samuel thought she was going to cry.

"Don't you worry about that, Georgie." Cameron stepped toward her, hugging her sideways. "Yes, it was rough at first, but I'm well employed with Mr. Dandie and safe as you please. Oh, and this is for you."

He shuffled little Victoria in his arms, then reached into his jacket and pulled out a second wad of bills. That one was larger than the one he'd handed over to his parents. But rather than snatching at it, Georgie gasped and pushed Cameron's hand away.

"Oh, Cameron, I couldn't," she said, looking even more like she would cry. "You need to keep your money for yourself. Why, look at that poor suit you're wearing. Aren't you taking care of yourself? The print shop makes more than enough money for me and James and the children. You have to stop sending us money like this."

Samuel's brow flew up. Cameron's sister was as different from the rest of their family as could be. He instantly liked the woman, and even found the children charming. Particularly since the little boy, Avery, had moved away from his mother's skirts and now stood less than a foot away from his side, staring up at him as though he were a giant.

"I heartily agree with your assessment, Mrs.—" Samuel began, then realized Cameron's sister couldn't possibly be named Oberlin.

"Where are my manners," Cameron said, grinning from ear to ear. "I've introduced you, but Samuel, this is my sister, Mrs. Georgina Clifton. Her husband, James, runs this print shop."

"Did someone mention my name?" A handsome gentleman who must have been in his thirties stepped out of the back room, wiping his ink-stained hands on a clean cloth. Avery broke away from Samuel to run into his father's arms. James Clifton picked up his boy without so much as a second thought, stepping forward to shake Samuel's hand. "Cameron," he went on, shaking Cameron's hand, then thumping his shoulder. "It's good to see you again."

"You too, James."

Samuel couldn't believe the scene unfolding in front of him. Surely, Cameron's sister and her husband knew the truth about Cameron. And they could see the color of his own skin as clear as day. But instead of the wretchedness he and Cameron had received in the village, they were greeted warmly in the print shop.

"What are we all doing standing around here?" James asked, gesturing for all of them to move toward the back room. "We have some tea on, and Georgie made the most delicious lemon biscuits yesterday."

"James likes them," Georgie said with a wink for Cameron. "A little too much, if you ask me."

Samuel followed the cheery family into the back room of the shop. Past what looked like a workshop was a family living area. Samuel was offered a seat at the kitchen table, right along with the rest of the happy brood, and served tea and the most delicious biscuits he'd ever had. Cameron was offered the same, and both Georgie and James sat as well, as though there were nothing they wanted more than to take time out of their busy day to entertain a queer and a black man.

It was domestic. It was joyful. It was exactly what Cameron wanted. Samuel saw it in an instant. His heart felt lightened by the scene, and by the way Cameron smiled and sat at perfect ease, sipping his tea. And it squeezed Samuel's insides with regret. He was incapable of the sort of familiarity that surrounded him, which meant he'd never be capable of being what Cameron needed. And yet, for once, that sort of life didn't seem so foreign or so disagreeable after all. On the contrary....

They flew through topics of conversation—from Derby gossip to Cameron recounting the frosty welcome he'd received in their home hamlet to questions about Samuel's music—before getting around to what Samuel presumed was the reason Cameron had wanted to pay a call.

"I came to warn you that Burberry has threatened to raise rents again," he said, face going red, glancing down at his empty teacup.

"Have you seen him since returning to Derby?" James asked with a frown. Samuel sensed that the frown wasn't disapproval of Cameron, though.

Cameron nodded, then sighed. "He made me an offer last night, and when I refused, he hinted he would raise rents."

"That man is a devil," Georgie hissed. "It's bad enough that he took advantage of you—"

"I was as much to blame as he was," Cameron mumbled.

"I don't believe that for an instant." Georgie's back snapped straight, and when that wasn't enough, she powered herself out of her chair, one hand on her pregnant belly, and marched to the stove to set another kettle on to boil. "Burberry will lure any comely young person astray, male or female. He's been doing it for years, but no one is brave enough to stop him, because he's landlord to half of Derby." She slammed the kettle down on the stove.

"Is that true?" Samuel asked. He glanced to Cameron at first, but when Cameron merely nodded and lowered his head, he looked to James instead.

"It is," James said with a sigh, managing to look both furious and worried. "Both parts of it. Burberry isn't picky about who he seduces. Probably because it's all the same to him. It's all about lording it over those who are less fortunate than him, those who he thinks he can push around and control."

"Does he own this building as well?" Samuel asked.

"No, thank God," Georgie replied from the stove. "Not anymore."

"We managed to secure a loan from the bank to purchase the place from Burberry about two years ago," James said. "I'd rather have my home owned by a bank than by a thief."

"That's the worst part of it," Georgie said, returning to the table and taking Victoria out of Cameron's arms. The little thing had started to fuss, and when Georgie sat down, managing to hold the girl across her lap in spite of her belly, she opened her shirt and pulled out a plump breast to offer the girl.

Samuel's brow shot up, and he couldn't help but grin. Tits had never held much interest for him in that way, but he couldn't help but stare for a moment all the same. Cameron's sister was as free and mischievous as Sammy, which made him wonder which of them had the capacity to get into the most trouble.

"Finish your thought, love," James said, laughing at his wife.

"My thought?" Georgie blinked. "Oh! That's the worst part of it," she repeated. "Burberry doesn't even really own all of those properties. Not truly."

Samuel started, gaping at her. "I beg your pardon? Burberry doesn't actually own his properties?"

"No," James said with an irritated frown. "He was a member of a partnership that owned them all, Grasmere Ventures."

"Grasmere Ventures?" Cameron said, dropping the biscuit he'd just picked up from the plate in the center of the table.

Samuel frowned. "You've heard of it?"

"It was in the ledger," Cameron told him. "Quite a bit, actually. Your sister is owed quite a bit of money by Grasmere Ventures."

"Sister?" James asked, staring curiously at Samuel.

"Oh, I forgot to mention," Georgie said, her eyes going wide again as she glanced between Samuel and James. "Mr. Percy is Mrs. Thorne's brother."

"Is that so?" James looked impressed.

"For my sins, yes," Samuel said with a smile. "We're twins, actually."

"How extraordinary." James smiled. Samuel liked the man immensely. Even more when he pivoted to face him more fully and said, "Then perhaps there's something you could do about this mess. Burberry's partner in Grasmere Ventures, you see, was your sister's late husband, Mr. Thorne."

"That explains the ledgers," Cameron said, pushing a hand through his hair.

"I'm no legal expert," James continued, "but my brother works for the solicitor who formalized the contracts for Grasmere Ventures. The partnership was only to last during the two men's lifetimes. After that, when one of them died, the assets were to be divided, or else one party could buy out the estate of the other party."

"Perhaps that is what happened," Samuel said, frowning. He'd hoped they'd accidentally stumbled on an easy solution to more than a few problems.

"The only way to know would be to go through your late brother-in-law's things to find proof of a buy-out or dissolution of the partnership," James said with a shrug.

"Do you think that's what Archibald is actually doing

for your sister?" Cameron asked, blinking as though he'd had a sudden insight into the situation. "Do you think that's why your sister is so reluctant to simply sell her collections and why she believes Archibald can produce five hundred thousand pounds out of nothing?"

Both Georgie and James looked shocked at the amount. "Five hundred thousand?" Georgie said.

Samuel was just as gobsmacked as the others, because that seemed entirely possible.

He turned to Cameron. "We have to go back to my sister's house," he said. "We have to sit Archibald down and squeeze the truth out of him."

"Agreed," Cameron said, standing.

"And if it's true that my sister is entitled to half of what Grasmere Ventures owned jointly, then Burberry has a lot to answer for."

CHAPTER 10

Cameron would have stayed and visited with Georgie and her family all day if he could have. It was apparent to him at once, though, that Samuel was excited by the idea that his sister might be a partial owner, in some way, of all the property Burberry owned. Indeed, Cameron himself was arrested by the idea that someone other than Burberry might control the fate of his parents, and whichever of his siblings might end up living in a house Burberry owned someday. If there was a possibility that someone with a kinder disposition and less of a manipulative streak could be responsible for his family's welfare, then Cameron, too, was interested in discovering the truth. He'd worry about the fact that Mrs. Thorne might not be any more reliable than Burberry after they uncovered the truth.

They said their goodbyes—Cameron promised to visit Georgie again before he returned to London, if he could—and he and Samuel marched back across Derby to Thorne Hall. Cameron had the same, overwhelming sense of stepping through the looking glass once again as Mr. Lee let them in through the front door and he was faced with the wild and disturbing collections that lined the front hall, not to mention the rest of the rooms.

Archibald was back at work in the office when Cameron and Samuel strode in, full of energy and enthusiasm. They were, perhaps, a little too excited, as Archibald nearly jumped out of his chair and his skin as Samuel demanded, "What have you discovered about Grasmere Ventures in your work for my sister?" in a booming voice.

Archibald scrambled to hide some of the papers he'd been recording information from the ledger on—and a second ledger that hadn't been there the day before—on the desk in front of him. "How dare you barge in here, like avenging angels of some sort, and frighten me in such a way?" he demanded. "I deserve to be treated with far more deference than a single person has shown me since arriving in this house, and I will not stand for it anymore, do you hear me?"

Both Cameron and Samuel flinched back. Cameron was taken completely off-guard by the intensity of Archibald's reaction. Granted, he would have been startled by someone with Samuel's presence flying into a room and demanding answers, but Archibald was a little too startled, a little too guilty, as he covered up papers and shifted books around, turning pages. Cameron wished he were close enough to see what, exactly, Archibald was trying to hide.

"My question was not meant to offend," Samuel said, stepping forward again, hands raised in appeasement. "We've just come across some information that might help all of us to resolve the problems that face us."

Cameron let Samuel take command of the situation. He could see that Samuel was frustrated, and honestly, Cameron didn't blame him. Nothing was going the way Samuel must have expected it too, even when it came to him. Perhaps especially when it came to him. There they were, in the middle of confronting Archibald about what he might have found in Mrs. Thorne's financial records, and Cameron's face started to heat over his sudden and inconvenient memory of the night before. If Samuel was half as frustrated as Cameron had been when he went to bed—in spite of the blissful moment of release they'd shared—then he was likely half mad with confusion.

"You may not intend to be offensive," Archibald railed on, stepping out from behind the desk, "but you are. You and your mad sister."

"I will not dispute the fact that Samantha is as mad as a March hare," Samuel said in a growl. "Money combined with a willful nature will do that to a woman, to anyone. What I am asking is for you to calm yourself and assist us in getting to the bottom of a financial mystery that has suddenly presented itself."

"Don't you think that is what I've been trying to do all along?" Archibald snapped. "I have been held here against my will, more or less imprisoned in this room, forced to pore over the most poorly-kept book of records I have seen in my life, in some vain attempt to prove that your bloody sister has a small fortune lying around unaccounted for. I have better things to do," Archibald shouted. "I was near the top of my class at university. I was a successful investor and a partner at a financial office. I had the love of a beautiful woman. But everything was taken from me. Everything, dammit!"

"For God's sake, calm down!" Samuel boomed. He rubbed a hand over his temples, where Cameron could practically see his veins throbbing. "Yes, life has dealt you a challenging hand to play. But I haven't seen this much complaining since I was in short trousers, forced to listen to Sammy weep because she only received one treacle tart instead of two."

"I shouldn't have to endure these insults," Archibald went on, though in more of an understated, seething voice than a shout, as before.

Cameron inched subtly to the side, making his way around the far side of the desk, anxious to get a look at what Archibald was trying to hide. The ledgers were open to pages of incorrect calculations and entries made in a shorthand that didn't resemble anything he'd ever seen. Underneath the newer ledger, however, Cameron spotted the corner of what looked like a listing of dates and times for ships departing various points in England for New York City.

"No one is trying to insult you now." Samuel

continued his attempt to handle Archibald. "I merely wish to know what you have discovered about Grasmere Ventures." He extended a hand toward one of the sofas nearer to the fireplace. "Please, take a breath, perhaps have a drink," he started toward a small table containing several decanters, "and tell us what you have learned about Grasmere."

"It was a company that is now defunct," Archibald said, still seething with resentment. "But I refuse to say anything more about it or about your late brother-in-law's involvement with it until you promise me one thing."

Cameron glanced up from where he was trying to move ledgers aside without drawing notice. He was certain the one piece of paper was a timetable for ships, and from what he could see after lifting the cover of the other ledger, another was a letter from a solicitor in London, informing Archibald that several outstanding debts could no longer be put off.

"What do you want from us?" Samuel asked.

He made the mistake of nodding to Cameron. Archibald turned, noticed what Cameron was looking at, and marched back to the desk.

"Keep your hands off of my things," he snapped, scrambling to gather all of the papers that had more to do with his personal business than Samuel's sister's from the table. He hugged them all close to his chest with an almost feral look. "None of this is any of your concern. It is mine and mine alone."

Samuel sighed heavily. He muttered something

under his breath about circuses, then crossed to pour himself a drink.

Once he'd downed it, clacking the tumbler back onto the table, he pivoted to face Archibald and asked, "What do you want from us in return for your cooperation in helping to defeat Burberry?"

A small grin tugged at the corner of Cameron's mouth. That was a clever way to phrase the issue before them. After supper the night before, Cameron was certain Archibald didn't care for Burberry any more than the rest of them did.

"I want my freedom," Archibald said. "I want you to help me to escape this asylum and return to London. I want to be reunited with Annamarie so that we can continue on with our life together."

"The answer to that is simple, man," Samuel said, gesticulating in frustration. "It's been simple from the start. Tell us where Lady Selby and Lord Stanley are."

"If I tell you, you'll just leave me here to go after them," Archibald said with a humorless laugh. "Help me escape first."

"If we get you out of this house and help you on your way to London, you'll just give us the slip so that you can run away with Lady Selby and still have Lord Stanley to use to extort money from Lord Selby," Cameron said. The fact that Archibald was so badly in debt only proved that to him.

"There you have it, then." Archibald snapped his back straight. "You don't trust me and I don't trust you."

"So none of us gets what we want, Lord Selby remains parted from his son, and lives are in shambles," Samuel said, throwing up his arms and walking back to the liquor table.

"Whose lives are in shambles?" Sammy asked, striding into the room with a smile. She was dressed like anyone on their way to Paris would be, all in lace and pearls. Cameron thought she made a very pretty picture, but considering the trouble the rest of them were going through on her behalf, he didn't think much of her fashion choices or her cheer.

"Sammy." Samuel turned to her, abandoning the liquor to storm across the room to her. "This madness needs to stop, and stop it will."

"Oh? Have you found a way for me to pay off Burberry without having to sell any of my pretty things?" she asked, a genuine flash of hope in her eyes.

"We might have," Samuel said, calming just a bit as he came to a stop in front of her. "It has come to my attention that your late husband was a partner in an endeavor called Grasmere Ventures, which owned quite a bit of property. The property Burberry claims to own now. It seems as though Thorne might have had an equal share in the property, which means you, as heir to his estate, which I assume you are, since Thorne never had children, are entitled to."

"Really?" Sammy said with a scathing amount of sarcasm, her expression darkening. "I never would have thought of that." Her sarcasm deepened.

Samuel's shoulders dropped a bit. "So you knew about Grasmere and the possibility that you, via Thorne, are entitled to half of whatever Burberry earns through the partnership's holdings?"

"Why do you think I have gone to the trouble of striking up such an intimate friendship with the man," Sammy said in acid tones. "Of course, I'm entitled to half of everything Burberry and David owned through that blasted partnership of theirs."

Samuel blinked. "Then what is all this madness and fuss about? Why can you not simply arrange to take what is yours or use it as collateral to pay off what you owe Burberry?"

Cameron felt awkward on Samuel's behalf. He could tell there was a great deal to the matter that neither he nor Samuel knew, and that he'd rushed into what he hoped was a solution without truly knowing the lay of the land.

Sammy sighed and stepped away from him, heading for the liquor table herself. "Yes, David and Burberry were partners in Grasmere Ventures. Yes, the property held jointly through that partnership provides the bulk of Burberry's income. But the partnership agreement no longer exists."

"Because Thorne died," Samuel said, taking a tentative step toward her. "Because the terms of the agreement dissolved the partnership upon the death of one of the partners. But from what we were told by someone with connections to the office of the solicitor who managed the agreement, was at that point, the property was to be divided between the remaining partner and the deceased one's estate, or else the surviving partner could buy the estate out." Samuel paused, then asked, "Did Burberry already buy you out?"

"No, he did not," Sammy said, slamming the stopper of one of the glass decanters so hard into it that Cameron was surprised it didn't break. She took a long swig of the glass she'd just poured, then turned to face her brother. "Did your solicitor's friend also tell you that there was a fire at the office of said solicitor and that the original document of the agreement was lost?"

"No," Samuel said darkly, "he didn't."

"Did he also tell you that I have not yet been able to find any record of the agreement or any sort of copy among my late husband's things?" Sammy snapped.

"No." Samuel glanced to Archibald.

Cameron looked at Archibald as well. The man clearly knew everything they were talking about. It seemed obvious to Cameron now that Archibald was searching for any record of the Grasmere agreement. It was also clear to him that Archibald had his own aims beyond just that. He wondered just how much freedom Archibald actually had. He also wondered if the badly mismanaged records were Archibald's doing. It would be a simple thing for a man as financially-minded as Archibald to use the excuse of bad recordkeeping to squirrel away money for himself.

"And did your solicitor's friend tell you that the

whole reason I have spent any time at all at Burberry's home is on the chance that I might find a copy of the original agreement there?" Sammy went on.

Samuel blew out a breath and moved to lean against the back of the sofa. "Why did you not tell me all of this from the beginning? There has to be a way we can prove that you're entitled to half of what Burberry has."

"And to stop him from raising people's rents," Cameron added, though he wasn't comfortable getting involved in what felt more and more like a personal discussion between Samuel and his sister.

Samuel and Sammy both glanced to him.

"Yes, I suppose that would be the kind thing to do," Sammy said, walking slowly to her brother's side without quite looking Cameron in the eye.

Again, Cameron had the uneasy feeling that Sammy owning the deeds to so many people's homes would be rather like those people going out of the frying pan and into the fire. But if Samuel had any influence whatsoever over his sister, perhaps there would be a way to convince her to be fair.

If they could prove she was entitled to Burberry's properties, and if Burberry were willing to let it all go without a fight.

Cameron blinked as a thought occurred to him. Burberry was interested in Sammy. Perhaps his interest was because, if he were to convince Sammy to marry him, the entire, potential headache of Grasmere Ventures and who owned what would be eliminated. He would, indeed, be willing to forgive five hundred thousand pounds, because he would stand to gain much more than that, over time.

Cameron shot a look to Samuel. He didn't know what to say or how to say it, but he had to speak with Samuel alone.

Of course, being alone with Samuel brought with it an entirely different set of problems. Memories of the night before flashed back to Cameron. He'd been so determined to stand his ground and not give in to temptation yet again, but the moment he and Samuel had had their cocks out, the moment their mouths and tongues had met, all of his fine resolve had vanished. He was a fool to think he'd be able to hold his own in the face of temptation again.

Samuel sighed, rubbing his temples in a gesture that Cameron was coming to associate with him being frustrated. It was somehow sweet, even though it meant Samuel was in pain.

"All right," Samuel said in what sounded like a voice of forced calm. "I see the situation more clearly now. Archibald, you need to keep searching my late brother-in-law's records for anything pertaining to Grasmere Ventures that might have slipped through the cracks. Sammy, you need to continue to cozy up to Burberry in the hope that we might get a peek into the records he has."

"Which is what we've been doing all along before you arrived," Archibald grumbled.

Samuel ignored him. "Added to all that, of course, is that we will have to proceed with the concert Burberry wants us to orchestrate and attend."

"No," Sammy insisted, stomping her foot. "I won't do it. I won't let Burberry humiliate me by implying I've given myself to him on the cheap."

Samuel glared at her. "Then make an inventory of your collections and start contacting museums. It's one thing or the other, Sammy,"

Sammy crossed her arms and huffed through her nose. Cameron would have shaken his head in amazement at her stubbornness and immaturity. He would have done the same with Archibald too, who looked as pleased with the arrangement as little Victoria had looked when she started fussing earlier. But if there was one thing that Cameron had learned in the past, miserable year of his life, it was that age didn't bring maturity, and that grown men and women could act like imbeciles when they didn't get their way. And Samuel was right about money and willfulness being a dangerous combination. No wonder the upper classes of England were so daft.

"I will consider it," Sammy said at last in a stiff voice, standing.

"You would do well to," Samuel told her warningly.

Sammy tilted up her nose, as though she wouldn't be cowed by her brother. But instead of telling him off, as Cameron expected, she simply sniffed and said, "Supper will be at seven tonight. It will just be the four of us, no guests, so there is no need to dress." She sent Cameron a pitying look as she walked past him and left the room.

Samuel went back to the liquor table for his second drink.

Archibald took his armful of papers—which he was still clutching tight—back to the desk.

"Is there anything I can do to help?" Cameron asked, already knowing what the answer would be.

"You can get me out of here and take me back to London," Archibald said resentfully. "And if you will not do that, then you can leave me to work undisturbed."

Cameron nodded, then sighed. He sent Samuel a quick look, but Samuel seemed to be lost in his thoughts. That pretty much decided things for Cameron. Exhaustion pressed down on him, and since there were still a few hours until supper, he intended to take a nap. And God only knew what he would do from there.

CHAPTER 11

The singular positive thing to come out of the past two days of utter misery and frustration for Samuel was that the strains of a new composition began to play in his head. But it was a wild and discordant tune, and would have been more at home on a program with some of Franz Liszt's more recent, experimental pieces than a standard concert at the Royal Albert Hall. It was all a reflection of his intense frustration, of course, but knowing that didn't make Samuel feel better about things.

But as their sorry company suffered through a mostly silent supper and icy rain began to beat its prickly rhythm against the windows of the house, Samuel saw a tiny light at the end of the tunnel.

"Perhaps we should all consider the concert," Sammy said as she took a second and final bite of the apple charlotte her cook had sent up for pudding.

Samuel clenched his jaw around a bite of the sweet treat he'd just put in his mouth, closing his eyes in a bizarre combination of frustrated relief, then chewed and swallowed before answering, "I think that would be the most sensible option."

"But Burberry would have to agree to plan the event on my terms," Sammy went on. "I would want to choose the decorations, of course, and the guest list. We wouldn't want to have just anyone in attendance, not at such an important event."

Samuel stared down the table at her. Sammy had seated him at the foot of the table that night, opposite him, with Cameron and Archibald on either side. "And what about your concern that Burberry would humiliate you by making everyone believe you are his mistress? Everything you've just said would make it seem as though you were."

Sammy cleared her throat and dabbed at her mouth with her serviette. "It occurs to me that if we all worked together, if I were seen to be your sister over Burberry's guest, this proposed concert might give me the ability to be seen in society as a force to be reckoned with."

Samuel had the distinct feeling that his sister's mind was hard at work on how to play both sides of the muddle they all found themselves in. Hosting an event on Burberry's behalf, whether she liked Burberry or not, would allow her to stake a claim on a high place in Derby society, and with her famous brother there to support her, it wouldn't necessarily look like she'd succumbed to Burberry.

"And you will, of course, arrange things to give us time to slip away into whatever study Burberry keeps his important papers to find the Grasmere agreement," he reminded her, "instead of simply lording me over your Derby friends."

"I beg your pardon?" Sammy pulled herself out of her thoughts, blinking rapidly. "Oh, yes. That. Of course."

He honestly couldn't tell if Sammy were teasing him to get some of her own back or if she had chosen to focus more on the social aspect of the concert than the practical one.

By the end of supper, as everyone stood and headed out of the room to go about their own business for the night, Samuel wasn't certain he cared anymore. He was tired, his limbs felt heavy, and his mind was as frazzled as if he'd spent the day herding cats. All he wanted to do was peel off his clothes and the cares of the day with them, climb into the big, soft bed in his guest room, and fall asleep while listening to the freezing rain pelting his windows.

"Do you think we should send a letter or a telegram to John to tell him how things are progressing?" Cameron asked as Samuel headed up the grand staircase, surprising him.

Samuel paused, turning and waiting for Cameron to catch up. Once he had, the two of them proceeded up the stairs side by side.

"I don't know what we would say." Samuel shrugged, which turned into rolling his aching shoulders. "We've located Archibald, but the man is being a stubborn prat, as usual, and refusing to divulge Lady Selby and Lord Stanley's whereabouts. Beyond that, I doubt he cares about my sister."

"Mr. Edward Archibald might want to know that his brother is safe," Cameron pointed out as they reached the landing and headed down the hall toward their bedrooms.

Samuel huffed an unkind laugh. "I can't see how anyone would care a whit about their family at this point. Family is all just a bunch of troublemaking gits who were born to darken our lives."

Cameron seemed surprised by Samuel's outburst and fell behind by a half step. That immediately made Samuel feel self-conscious and guilty.

"Not your sister, of course," he said, gesturing for Cameron to walk on with him and step into his bedroom instead of continuing down the hall to his own. Cameron could use the door that connected their rooms to retire to his own bed for the night. At the moment, Samuel needed him to talk to and to go over the events of the day with. "Your sister and her family are lovely."

"Ma and Pa don't speak much to her or James," Cameron said, his shoulders dropping. He paused at the door of Samuel's room, peering in at the bed anxiously.

"Come on, man. I'm not going to bite," Samuel sighed. He would have added, "Unless you want me to," but under the circumstances, he didn't think it would have the effect he desired.

Cameron seemed to make up his mind when a door opened and shut somewhere at the far end of the hall. The sound startled him into leaping into Samuel's room, then shutting the door quickly behind him.

"If you're worried about being caught in a compromising position with another man," Samuel told him with a tired grin, shrugging out of the jacket he'd worn to supper and loosening his tie, "then you've no need. Even the servants in my sister's house are used to every manner of immorality and oddity possible. They wouldn't bat an eyelash."

"Oh." Cameron shifted awkwardly as he stood only a few feet into the room. "It's just that I haven't had the best experiences being found in a man's bedroom before."

Samuel chuckled at that, but his insides burned. Part of him wanted to know the full story behind Cameron being caught with Burberry and exposed, but the rest of him knew that the details would likely only enrage him, and he couldn't go into the next few days so angry with Burberry that he couldn't stand the sight of the man.

"So how do we convince Archibald to tell us where Lady Selby is so that we can call that part of our mission a success?" Samuel asked as he took his jacket to the wardrobe, hung it, then unbuttoned his waistcoat.

"Archibald is stubborn," Cameron said, taking a few, tentative steps deeper into the room. "And perhaps rightly so. Didn't Blake and Niall double-cross him once before about the medallion and the money he asked for?"

Samuel huffed a humorless laugh. "They did. Which doesn't make our task any easier." He turned back to Cameron after handing his waistcoat in the wardrobe and taking the cufflinks out of his shirtsleeves. "Did you see it, by the way? The medallion?"

"I saw the entire collection," Cameron said, inching just a bit more toward him. "She has the whole set displayed in that parlor, with all the other antiquities. It seems like such a small thing to have caused so much trouble."

"She should sell the lot of it to the British Museum, or some other museum," Samuel said, unbuttoning the top few buttons of his shirt and walking to stand near Cameron. "Personally, I'd be happy if she sold this whole estate and everything in it, took the money, and moved back to the Caribbean to live like a queen."

"But she's your only family," Cameron argued, gaping at Samuel. "Wouldn't you miss her?"

Samuel smirked. "You seem to have forgotten my view of family already."

"I haven't," Cameron insisted. "It's just that...." He hesitated, biting his lip in the way that put fire in Samuel's blood. "Don't you feel the need to care for anyone? To hold anyone at all so close to your heart that they feel like a part of it, even when they vex you?"

The question shot straight to Samuel's soul before he could muster his defenses to dismiss it. In fact, as he looked at Cameron's sweet, handsome face and the sad hope in his eyes, it dawned on him that he could care for someone that way. He could let someone occupy that empty spot in his heart marked "Family".

"I've never had any need for someone like that before," he said, turning away and walking to the corner of his room, where Sammy had seen fit to provide him with a handy little decanter of brandy. He poured himself a snifter, then turned to Cameron and asked, "Would you like one?"

"No," Cameron answered, moving toward Samuel. "What I would like is to figure out a way to protect my family from Burberry's machinations."

"Even though they vex you?" Samuel arched one eyebrow.

"Yes," Cameron said.

Samuel drank his brandy, then put the snifter down. "I would like that too," he admitted with a sigh. "Even though I think the majority of your family doesn't deserve it."

Cameron seemed to ignore him. An intense light burned in his eyes. "I've been thinking about it, and I believe I have an idea for how we might catch Burberry unawares, have time to search through his things for information about Grasmere Ventures, and spare both you and your sister the indignity of going along with his plans."

A burst of energy hit Samuel, though it was as much from the way Cameron had moved swiftly and deliberately closer to him than for whatever idea he had. "How?" he asked.

"I'll go to him," Cameron said in a nervous rush. He gulped, then continued with, "I'll meet his demands. I'll spend a night with him and let him do whatever he wants to me. Then, when he's asleep, I'll search his house for what we're looking for."

Samuel took an angry step toward him. "You will do no such thing," he snapped. "Don't even think of it."

Cameron looked as though Samuel had slapped him. "It's a perfect plan," he argued. "One that brings the least harm to the most people."

"It will bring harm to you," Samuel said. And that was something he wasn't willing to gamble with.

Cameron frowned, a different sort of stubbornness in his eyes than Samuel had ever seen before. "It's not as though I've never done anything like it before," he said. "Those two months I spent as a telegraph boy taught me that I'm capable of just about anything, if there's a higher purpose to it."

"Capable of making a whore of yourself?"

Samuel regretted the words the second they were past his lips. Cameron looked stung. Samuel grimaced and turned away from him, rubbing a hand over his face.

"I'm sorry, that was uncalled for," he apologized. "You were not a whore, you were a young man in an unfortunate position who did what he had to do to survive."

"I was a whore," Cameron said in a rough voice,

nodding once. "And I'd be one again if it meant helping you."

Something warm and affectionate slithered through Samuel's insides, in spite of the harshness of what Cameron was saying. There was so much care and admiration in Cameron's eyes, and Samuel knew he didn't deserve it. At the same time, a twist of resentment tainted every sweet feeling pulsing through him and made him reckless.

"You offer to fuck another man to help me, but you won't go to bed with me?" he asked, afraid he sounded too hurt. "Someone who cares about you?"

His fears were justified a moment later as Cameron's face softened and regret filled his eyes. "I've refused to go to bed with you because I don't think I could bear it if you were done with me once you had me," he said in a near whisper.

The air between them crackled with a rawness and vulnerability that frightened Samuel. He took a step closer to Cameron, close enough to touch him.

"What if I told you that I wouldn't be done with you," he said, disquieted by the emotion that made his voice tremble. He lifted a hand to caress Cameron's face. The things that spilled out of him were as new to him as they were to Cameron. "What if I told you that I didn't think I could possibly be done with you any time soon, because you're too deep under my skin."

Cameron sucked in a breath, his face coloring and his eyes turning glassy. "I...I wouldn't know what to think."

"Neither would I." Samuel stepped into him, resting his other hand on the other side of Cameron's face and slanting his mouth over his.

It was glorious to kiss Cameron. The man's mouth was made for sin, and in spite of Cameron's gentle ways and shy demeanor, he knew how to return a kiss in a way that fired Samuel's blood. Their lips parted, and with a sigh of need, Samuel explored Cameron's mouth with his tongue and nibbled on his lower lip.

Cameron didn't pull away. Instead, he moved into Samuel, tugging his shirt from his trousers so that he could smooth his hands along Samuel's sides and press his fingertips into his back. The simple gestures held so much more fire for Samuel than they had when any other man had done the same in the past. The way Cameron touched him went beyond an ordinary effort to stoke arousal and rush toward a conclusion. It was meaningful and precious, like something they'd both waited a long time for.

"Off," Samuel whispered the single word, rushing through the buttons of Cameron's pitiful jacket and threadbare waistcoat underneath to get to the parts of Cameron that weren't shabby at all.

Cameron nodded, mouth soft as they stepped briefly apart, shrugging out of his jacket and letting it fall carelessly to the floor. Samuel pulled his shirt off over his head and toed out of his shoes before reaching for the fastenings of his trousers.

"No, let me," Cameron stopped him once he had his shirt and shoes off as well.

Samuel moved his hands to the side and let Cameron approach to unfasten his trousers. He sucked in a sharp breath when Cameron finished with them and his drawers, pushing both down over his hips, then sinking to his knees before Samuel as he moved them down Samuel's legs. He helped Samuel step out of them, pushing them to the side, but didn't rise from his knees once Samuel was fully naked and desperately erect in front of him.

Cameron didn't hesitate or show any signs of reticence at all. He brushed his hands up Samuel's thighs, sending an erotic tremor through him, to cup his balls with one hand and grip the base of his cock with the other. Cameron stroked him a few times, causing Samuel to suck in a breath, and when he closed his mouth over Samuel's tip, licking and teasing it, Samuel let out that breath on a deep moan.

Samuel was certain within minutes that he was losing his mind. Cameron knew what he was doing with devastating skill. He teased and pleased Samuel's tip before drawing him into his mouth with progressively deeper swallows. The sensations that ripped through Samuel were so good that he had to grasp handfuls of Cameron's hair just to keep his soul from flying out of his body. Every time Cameron bore down on him, Samuel didn't think Cameron would be able to go any deeper, and each time he did.

"Fuck, Cameron, that's so good," he panted, quickly spiraling out to the very limit of his control.

That control nearly shattered when Cameron made a sound of such enjoyment that Samuel could only whimper in reply. It had never felt so good before, not with any of the nameless men he'd thought he wanted in the past, but that didn't mean Samuel was ready to rush to completion. He felt like they'd only just begun.

"Stop," he panted, nudging Cameron away. The sight of his hard cock sliding out of Cameron's mouth, wet with his saliva, and the way Cameron's mouth stayed open as he tried to catch his breath, were the most erotic things Samuel had ever seen. "I want this to last," he gasped. "But I'm not going to if you keep on like that. Stand up."

Cameron nodded and did what he was told, getting shakily to his feet. Samuel went straight for the fastenings of Cameron's trousers, undressing him as swiftly as Cameron had done for him. As soon as Cameron stepped out of his things, immediately ignoring them, Samuel took Cameron's cock in his hand. It was big and thick, with a perfectly flared tip that was slick with moisture. Samuel explored it fully and sensually, throbbing himself as he did. He reached for Cameron's balls, testing them out as well, before caressing his shaft and brushing a thumb over his leaking slit.

"I like that," Cameron gasped, tilting his head back with an impatient breath. "I knew I would."

That settled it, as far as Samuel was concerned. "I

need you in my bed," he said in a voice that was so earnest it was almost dire.

Cameron met his eyes and nodded. That was all Samuel needed to proceed. He took Cameron's hand and led him to the edge of the bed, then threw back the bedcovers with almost comic enthusiasm. He didn't care how eager he looked, though. He had wanted Cameron for what felt like ages, waited for him for what felt like a lifetime, and now they would finally consummate months of flirting.

He rolled into bed, pulling Cameron with him and tossing him to his back. It felt like heaven to spread himself over Cameron's lithe, muscular body and to nestle himself between Cameron's spread legs. The position brought everything important into immediate contact, and for a moment, Samuel rutted slowly against him, adoring the sensation of their hard pricks rubbing against each other and the friction caused by their closely-pressed bodies. It was simple, but sometimes the simplest things were the best.

He was even more convinced of that as he bent down to close his mouth over Cameron's in a searing kiss. The way their tongues mated, stroking and sucking, was perfection. The way Cameron circled his arms around Samuel's torso and kneaded his muscles—higher on his back at first before sweeping down to squeeze and caress his arse—was even better. Samuel thought he might lose himself entirely when Cameron spread his arse cheeks to finger his hole.

At the same time, that made him groan in frustration. "I didn't think to bring any lubricant," he told Cameron with painful regret.

"There are plenty of other things we can do," Cameron told him, surging up to capture Samuel's mouth again.

Samuel was so grateful for Cameron's acceptance and adaptability that he bore down on his mouth with a ferocious growl of need. He'd been with partners in the past who had scoffed at him and even judged him for not being prepared enough to give them what they wanted. He'd suspected some of those partners of wanting nothing more from him than the novelty of being fucked by a black man—possibly as a form of humiliation in their minds—but Cameron wasn't like that at all. Samuel wasn't even sure Cameron saw the difference in their skin tone—even though it made a beautiful contrast— only the similarity in their need to be touched and enjoyed.

"You're so lovely," Samuel said between kisses, meaning it far beyond the physical. "I want every part of you."

He followed up his words by shifting to kiss Cameron's neck as he arched his head back, deliberately leaving a mark that he only hoped wouldn't be visible above Cameron's collar on the morrow, before licking his way down to one of Cameron's nipples. At the same time, he fisted Cameron's cock, moving carefully, and paying special attention to Cameron's tip.

"I like this," Cameron panted, kneading the muscles of Samuel's shoulders. "I—oh!" He gasped as Samuel raked his teeth across his nipple. "Samuel, I'm not going to last," he went on, breathless and desperate.

"Then don't, love," Samuel said, pulling his body up Cameron's so that he could grasp both of their cocks together, and so that he could kiss Cameron again. "Come for me now. We've got all the time in the world to make love slowly in the future."

Cameron's eyes went wide for a moment before Samuel jerked his hips to rub his prick against Cameron's, fisting them as well. Cameron made a sound of pleasure, his mouth staying open in the most erotic shape Samuel had ever seen as he lifted out of their kiss so he could watch Cameron's face. And watching Cameron's face as he increased the intensity of sensation between them was a treat.

Cameron's eyes went hazy again as his breath grew shallow and his sighs needy. Samuel thrust against him, then Cameron's breath hitched for a moment as he burst, spilling across Samuel's hand and his own belly, then turned into a long moan of pleasure as Samuel pulled as much out of him as possible. The sight was so wonderful, and the feeling so intense, that Samuel came a moment later with a cry of his own, spending himself across Cameron's belly and blending their seed together.

It was delicious madness that something so simple could bring him so much satisfaction, but as Samuel relaxed and flopped to the bed beside Cameron, he couldn't remember enjoying himself so much with another man. He didn't even mind when Cameron rolled against his side, embracing him loosely—even though they were both too hot—as they caught their breaths. He didn't feel the instant need to get up and wash himself off or to thank Cameron with a cordial smile and send him on his way. He didn't want to do anything but lie there with Cameron as sleep pressed swiftly down on him.

His last thought before drifting off was that perhaps it wouldn't be so bad to have a long-term lover after all.

CHAPTER 12

Cameron was surprised to be awakened the next morning by the first rays of dawn filtering in through the frosty window. Not so much because he had slept solidly through the night—he'd been thoroughly exhausted, physically and emotionally, and he always had fallen hard to sleep after sex, when he could—but because he was still in Samuel's bed, nestled against his side. He would have thought for certain Samuel would have nudged him out of bed and sent him back to his own room after they'd finished with each other the night before. The dried evidence of how much they'd enjoyed themselves itching on Cameron's belly was definitely still there, so he hadn't imagined things. He just couldn't believe the entire night had passed and he was still in Samuel's bed.

It was a nice bed too, he thought, closing his eyes again and indulging in all of the sensations enveloping him for a moment. Even nicer than the one in his guest room. Cameron couldn't remember the last time he'd been treated to a thick, soft mattress, crisp, clean sheets, and layers of quilts that made him feel as though he were cocooned in luxury. And not once in his entire life, in spite of his variety of experience, had he ever woken up in the arms of the man he'd had sex with the night before.

He moved a hand slightly over Samuel's chest, letting Samuel's wiry chest hair tease his palm, trying to gauge whether Samuel was awake or not. He didn't think so, considering the steady rise and fall of Samuel's chest. Honestly, Cameron was glad he was still asleep. That meant that he could have just a few more moments to indulge in the wonder of what the two of them had done the night before.

It had never been like that for him. His encounters of the past had always been exciting, brought him off, and sent his pulse racing, but they'd also left him feeling used —not always in a bad way—and inferior. With Samuel, he had felt...not loved precisely, but as though he were a part of something, not the object of something. Samuel had seemed more concerned with bringing him off than getting off himself, which was new to Cameron. It made him smile in spite of himself.

That smile faded too quickly as reality thundered back in on him. He inched carefully away from Samuel. What was he thinking? It was madness to go to bed with a man who saw sex as nothing more than something fun and pleasurable when he himself wanted more than that.

Yes, it had absolutely been fun and pleasurable, and things had been said in the moment, but Cameron knew he'd be a fool if he believed any of those promises for the future. Samuel was who he was, Cameron knew himself, and neither of them were going to change anytime soon.

He pulled away more, slipping to the edge of the bed, eyes still trained on Samuel to make certain he didn't awake, then rolled out of bed. It was just his luck that the bed creaked as he did, then the floor groaned as he tried to tip-toe around it to gather his clothes.

"What are you doing?" Samuel asked in a groggy voice, propping himself up on his elbows in bed.

"Going back to my room," Cameron said, letting out a breath and the tension in his muscles, since he'd been caught. "You don't have to get up. I'll be fine."

"Nonsense." Samuel gestured to him, still bleary. "Come back to bed. It's too early to get up."

Cameron continued to gather his clothes, though he didn't bother putting them on. "What would be the point?" he asked.

Samuel blinked at him. "The point?" He shook his head. "What are you talking about, man? The point is to doze away the morning in each other's arms."

Cameron took his armful of clothes to the side of the bed, fixing Samuel with a wry smile. "What is this? Samuel Percy, world-famous composer, wants to spend the morning dozing in bed with a man?"

"Well, we don't have to doze," Samuel said with a cheeky grin.

Cameron's good humor evaporated. "I see." He nodded. "It's as I expected, then."

He turned to head to the door separating Samuel's room and his, but Samuel stopped him with a sharp, "What is that supposed to mean?" He sat up all the way, the bedcovers dropping down to his waist, exposing his fine, muscled chest.

Cameron was caught up in staring at Samuel for a moment before shaking himself and saying, "I should have known that what you really wanted was another go 'round with me."

Samuel's mouth dropped open, and he looked sharply offended. "Yes, of course I want another go with you. Because you're lovely and sensual and you respond so beautifully when I touch you. But can't we just lie here and snuggle for a while too?"

Conflicting extremes of emotion tangled themselves in Cameron's gut. He walked back to Samuel's bed, putting the pile of his clothes on one corner so he could cross his arms and narrow his eyes at Samuel. "I thought you didn't like domesticity. I thought you liked to thumb your nose at society and do things that would shock them to prove you're above them."

A sheepish flush painted Samuel's still sleep-blurry face. "What's more shocking and anti-society than two naked men snoozing together, all cozy and warm?" Before Cameron could come up with a reply, Samuel went on with a bit more snap in his voice. "And don't you tell me that you aren't aroused by the idea of living dangerously and fucking again, because you're already halfway there as is." He nodded to Cameron's genitals.

Cameron glanced down at himself. Of course, he was well on his way to being hard. It was morning, after all, and he was standing naked in front of a man whose cock he'd had in his mouth the night before. Though remembering that did nothing to prove his point about the sanctity of domestic bliss and everything to make Samuel grin fetchingly at him.

"What if one of the maids comes in to set a fire?" Cameron asked, trying to ignore what his body was screaming at him to do with increasing intensity. "What if they come into my room and see that the bed was never slept in? How are you going to explain me spending the entire night in your bed to whatever friends you have that encourage your rebellious and rakish ways?"

Samuel laughed gently. "Where did you learn big, fancy words like that, country boy?"

"From the Brotherhood and the big, bad city," Cameron answered. He didn't want to admit it, but he enjoyed the banter with Samuel. He enjoyed feeling as though he were Samuel's equal, even though he knew he wasn't. And, heaven help him, he wanted to crawl back into bed and let Samuel fuck him raw so badly that his entire body was flushing pink.

"Cameron," Samuel said in a scolding voice, the fire in his eyes starting to smolder, "are you contemplating ideas of being naughty and dangerous and taking what you want, regardless of what society thinks or what the rules of domestic bliss say you should want?"

"No," Cameron lied. "Not at all. I'm not like that."

Samuel huffed a laugh. "Love, you're like an oak holding up in a stiff breeze right now. Stop lying and come back to bed so I can suck you off."

Excitement swirled through Cameron like nothing he'd ever known before. It was all still a dream, he was certain. Samuel couldn't possibly be luring him into behaving badly. Not that he'd never been lured into behaving badly before. But there was a spark in Samuel's eyes that needled Cameron into loosening the death grip he had on his scruples and climbing back onto the bed with him.

He told himself he would just sit there with Samuel, passing the time and perhaps discussing ways they could solve all of their myriad problems and get back to London to finish their mission. That was what he told himself, but within seconds, he found himself propped against the pillows, his legs spread wide, with Samuel fondling his balls and kissing his way down his belly toward his prick.

"You're not the only one who can give head and make a man forget his name," Samuel teased him with a salacious look before gripping the base of Cameron's cock and bearing down on him.

Cameron let out a shaky moan, grabbing the headboard behind him and trying not to jerk up into Samuel's mouth. That was a losing battle, though, particularly since Samuel seemed to appreciate his enthusiasm. It was sheer madness. He should be in his own room, washing and dressing and putting his mind to all the ways they could convince Archibald to stop being such a toad and tell them where Lady Selby was. He should be steeling his resolve to offer himself up to Burberry for a night so he could find the proof they needed that Mrs. Thorne was partial owner of Burberry's properties.

But all he could think about was Samuel's warm, wet mouth swallowing him, and all he could do was moan with pleasure and writhe against him until he came with a gasp deep in Samuel's mouth.

"Sorry! I'm so sorry," he apologized, gasping for breath as the mind-blowing lightning of the moment dissolved into sated bliss. "I should have warned you I was coming."

"Not at all," Samuel said, excitement in his eyes, lips wet, as he muscled himself to kneel between Cameron's legs. His cock was stiff and beaded with pre-cum, and he sucked in a short breath as he started to fist himself. "It was my pleasure."

It took him only a few more, captivating strokes before he came across Cameron's belly with a strangled grunt. Cameron felt more than a little guilty watching him and getting so much enjoyment out of it. Particularly when Samuel panted, "What do you think of that, Mr. Domesticity?"

What Cameron thought was that he'd been a hypocrite to say he only wanted coziness and calm. What he felt was that he might be willing to sacrifice a sweet, little home and a quiet life if it meant he could explore the wicked desire he had for Samuel. Samuel would grow tired of him eventually—after all, he'd made no secret of who he was and what he stood for—but in the meantime, Cameron would be able to experience a kind of pleasure he'd never known before.

"What I think is that I wish you'd thought to bring some kind of lubricant," he answered breathlessly, meeting Samuel's eyes with an impishness he didn't know he had in him.

"By God, so do I," Samuel said in a deep, coarse voice. "I'll purchase some today."

He surged forward, slanting his mouth over Cameron's, kissing him senseless. Cameron realized that he'd never let go of the headboard, as if he were somehow chained to it, but that only excited him more. He kissed Samuel back, trying in vain to shut out the blossom of emotion he felt for the daring man. He would not fall in love with Samuel. It was merely an infatuation, merely sex. He would not fall into a pit of affection that he wouldn't be able to get out of. He would just enjoy the physical sensations Samuel made him feel.

A thump in the hall turned those thoughts into a moment of stark terror. Flashes of everything that had happened when Tony walked in on him and Burberry flared hot in Cameron's mind. He tensed, almost pushing Samuel off of him in his haste to protect himself.

"I need to go," he said, scrambling out from under

Samuel when the man leaned back. "We have things to do today."

"It's just a maid," Samuel told him, watching as Cameron scrambled for his clothes, then nearly fell off the bed in his haste to get up and retreat to his own room. "You don't have to worry about—"

Cameron didn't stay long enough to find out what Samuel didn't think he had to worry about. He dashed into his own room, then practically slammed the door behind him. Even then, he didn't feel entirely safe until he was washed, dressed, and groomed enough to head downstairs for breakfast. He did, however, catch himself laughing in wonder about everything that had happened more than a few times throughout the process of straightening himself out.

Sammy and Archibald were already seated at the table in the breakfast room by the time Cameron fumbled his way downstairs, but Samuel wasn't there yet. Cameron thanked God for small favors, as far as that went, because it meant he wouldn't have to blush and stammer his way through at least part of the meal. But it didn't mean he didn't find himself on the spot as soon as he'd served himself from the sideboard and sat at one of the empty places at the breakfast table.

"What do you think of this plan to stage a concert at Burberry's house?" Sammy asked him, as though they were in the middle of the conversation already, and as if Cameron's opinion on the matter meant anything.

"Er...." Cameron stammered, unsure what to say. He

was given a brief reprieve as one of Sammy's footmen—who looked as though he were from India, which fit right in with Sammy's unique collection of servants—poured his tea. "I suppose it's a lovely idea?" he finished once the tea was poured.

Sammy hummed as though she weren't convinced. "It's just that I thought there could be other ways to distract Burberry long enough to find what we might be looking for at his house," she said, raking him with a particular look. "Seeing as you and Burberry were once friends."

Cameron cleared his throat, squirming in his seat. "The thought had crossed my mind," he mumbled, staring at his ham and eggs.

"I believe he is still fond of you," Sammy said probingly. "Burberry has ravenous tastes." She popped a dried apricot into her mouth.

Archibald glanced up from the breakfast he was devouring to frown at Sammy. "Those two words do not go together. One has ravenous appetites or refined tastes."

"That just goes to show what you know about Burberry," Sammy said in a sly voice, sending Cameron a wicked look.

It occurred to Cameron with a devilishly uncomfortable feeling that both he and Samuel's sister had, at one point or another, been the object of those tastes. For some reason, that left him feeling far less keen about the idea of seducing Burberry so they could have a chance to search his home for the documents they needed.

Or perhaps he was fooling himself and that wasn't it at all. Perhaps the real reason he'd gone off the idea of sleeping with Burberry—or anyone else—again was because of what had happened between him and Samuel.

No sooner had that thought occurred to him, than Samuel strode through the breakfast room doorway, looking as though it were a sunny day in the middle of spring instead of a frosty one in February.

"Good morning, all," he said, sending Cameron an overt smile. That smile left Cameron feeling dangerously singled out and giddy with affection at the same time. "Sammy, have you made up your mind about the concert yet?" Samuel asked, moving to the sideboard and heaping a plate with food. Of course he would, considering the appetite he'd worked up.

Cameron shook his head at himself as Sammy answered, "I've just about decided to do it, whether I want to or not."

How was he supposed to conduct himself in a competent and businesslike manner and do the job John wanted him to do when he couldn't even look at Samuel anymore without blushing like a schoolboy? It was exactly the reason he'd held himself at a distance from Samuel for so long.

"I was hoping Mr. Oberlin here might have a better idea," Sammy went on, arching one eyebrow at Cameron.

"No, he does not," Samuel snapped, far too loud and too commanding for anyone's good.

Archibald scowled as he glanced between Cameron

and Samuel, and then Sammy. "This is a madhouse, it is," he mumbled to himself, tossing down his knife and fork.

"Do you have something you would like to add, Mr. Archibald?" Samuel asked, striding to the foot of the table and taking his seat as though he were a king sitting on a throne.

"No, no, not at all," Archibald said in an exaggerated, peevish voice. "I merely want the lot of you to do whatever you need to do to resolve this matter in the quickest possible way so that I can be released to live my life again." He paused, then added, "And then I wish that you would all go to hell, where you belong."

Cameron burst out laughing in spite of himself. He couldn't help it. Archibald was right; Thorne Hall was a madhouse. But he wasn't as certain that going mad was a bad thing as he'd been before. The feeling made him bold enough to ask Sammy, "Rather than making everything complicated and throwing me at Burberry's feet, why don't you just marry him and save us all the trouble?"

The room went silent. All three of the others at the table stared at him, and Cameron was convinced the footman was secretly staring at him as well.

Samuel broke into a grin himself. "There you have it." He sent his sister a wicked look. "The solution to everyone's problems."

Sammy stiffened, rolling her shoulders impatiently and staring at her breakfast plate. "I shall send word around to Burberry at once that we agree to his concert. I truly do think that is the best way for us to proceed."

"If you say so," Cameron mumbled.

He exchanged a look with Samuel. The flash in Samuel's eyes seemed to confirm the feeling he had that the rest of their trip would be spent attempting to convince Sammy to just marry the bastard—but not to raise rents—and put them all out of their misery. And trying to keep themselves from repeating exactly the same sort of scene that had ended with Cameron being banished from home in the first place.

CHAPTER 13

The only problem with using a Samuel Percy concert as a way to publicly declare Burberry and Sammy as paramours was that it took time to organize. Which meant Cameron was stuck as a guest in Thorne Hall—macabre decorations, mad conversations, and all—for days. He didn't mind the nights as much, considering he spent them in Samuel's bed, but even that carried with it an uneasy sense that he was betraying his scruples. It felt good, and while their bodies were entwined, Cameron felt close to Samuel. But it was the sort of thing he couldn't imagine lasting forever, or even very long.

"Why don't I bring all of my things into this room and spare the maids the necessity of keeping the other one up," he asked in the morning a few days after the initial plan to proceed with the concert was hatched.

He'd climbed out of bed early and stood by the washstand, scrubbing himself with a damp cloth while Samuel watched him admiringly from the bed. "I think it's been well-established that your sister knows and does not care what we've been up to."

"Share a room with me?" Samuel asked, sitting up, his expression uneasy. "As if we're some married couple visiting my sister for the Christmas holidays?"

At first, Cameron thought Samuel was teasing, and he laughed. "And what would be so wrong with that?" he asked, smiling.

When Samuel took a long time to answer, Cameron's smile faded. He turned to Samuel to find the man sitting in bed, staring at the bedclothes with a frown. "It would feel...defeating."

The uneasy feeling that hadn't truly left Cameron's gut since the night he'd first let his defenses down twisted into a tight knot. All of his worst fears seemed confirmed. "So I've defeated you, then?" he asked, trying and failing not to sound bitter or judgmental. "I've made you compromise your principles, as you've made me compromise mine?"

"No, I'm not saying that at all." Samuel frowned. "And I didn't make you compromise anything. You've been quite willing to compromise in any number of positions these last few nights."

Samuel was trying to tease him, trying to make light of the crack that had just yawned open in what had seemed like such bliss only a short time before. Perhaps it was his own fault for not insisting he get more sleep or take time to rest his overwhelmed mind. It just seemed to Cameron like his old problems were back in a new form.

"I'm not a joke, Samuel," he said, rushing through the rest of his morning ablutions. "I thought you knew that. I thought you'd changed your mind about how you see things."

"Don't be like that, love," Samuel sighed. He moved to the side of the bed, but still didn't get up. "You've shifted to see things a bit more my way and I've shifted to see them your way, but neither of us is going to flip over completely after just a few nights."

"Not even to make work easier for the maids in your sister's house?" Cameron asked.

"Sharing a bedroom while guests in someone else's house means something, Cameron," Samuel argued. "Something I'm not ready to commit to yet. I thought that asking to be given these rooms would be good enough."

Cameron's eyes went wide. "So this was all planned?" But of course it was. Samuel had intended to lure him into bed all along. Just like too many other men who saw him as a conquest and not an equal. Knowing that had Cameron writhing with discomfort and feeling far too similarly to how Burberry had made him feel years ago.

"I've upset you," Samuel said in a heavy voice. "That wasn't my intention at all. I was merely trying to view the situation realistically."

"And I was merely saying it would make things easier for the maid if we shared a room." He couldn't quite bring himself to look at Samuel out of fear of the sort of expression he'd see there.

As it turned out, he didn't need to actually look at the man to know what he thought. Samuel blew out a short breath and said, "Don't you feel more comfortable keeping a room of your own and going back to it in the morning? I know appearances matter to you."

Cameron finished with the washcloth and tossed it into the basin of water he'd been using, splashing some on the tabletop. "You mean that you would be more comfortable with me in your bed at night to fuck your way into a satisfied night's sleep, as long as I clear out in the morning so you don't have to keep pretending this is anything more than an extended telegraph delivery."

"Cameron, no. That's not what I mean," Samuel said, reaching toward him with a frustrated gesture.

Cameron snatched up his clothes from the night before from the chair they'd been draped over and marched back to his room without picking up the thread of whatever argument could have happened between him and Samuel.

"Cameron, wait," Samuel called after him as he threw open the door separating their rooms and walked through.

Cameron shut it behind him and waited, listening. He felt like a right fool for throwing a temper tantrum when he'd known full well what he was getting himself into. The last few days had been bittersweet to say the least, but he'd hoped the sweet would win out. When Samuel didn't pursue him—and judging by the lack of sound from the other room, didn't even get out of bed—Cameron was certain the bitter had won. He didn't know what he was doing, in spite of the myriad lessons he should have already learned in his life. He was no further along than he'd been when he'd been driven out of Derby.

There was even more bitterness to swallow later that morning, when he, Samuel, and Sammy walked out with Burberry to invite guests to the pending concert. At least, Burberry had insisted they were walking out through the center of Derby to invite guests to the concert. As soon as Burberry started accosting some of the finer gentlemen walking past them as they went about their business for the day, stopping them to discuss his political views as well as invite them to the concert, Cameron began to think that they'd all been had. Burberry just wanted to use Samuel's renown as a campaign endorsement, just as he likely wanted Sammy for her money.

He would have been content to stay out of things, but Burberry had other plans.

"You. See if you can find a barrel or something for me to stand on so I can make a speech to these good people, boy," Burberry ordered him, snapping his fingers.

"I beg your pardon, sir, but I am not your dogsbody," Cameron said in a sullen and offended voice.

Burberry glared at him, eyes wide. "You weren't this

hesitant to do what I said a short while ago," he snapped. "You rather liked being ordered around, if I recall."

Cameron's back went stiff. Particularly as several of the men who had gathered around seemed to know what Burberry was referring to. The only satisfaction in that was that they glanced to Burberry with equal shock, then rushed away.

"Now look what you've done, you nasty little invert," Burberry muttered, stepping closer to Cameron and narrowing his eyes. "If I lose votes because of you, you'll pay for them. Or, at least, your loved ones will."

Cameron's gaze skittered past Burberry to Samuel at the comment. Samuel had been quiet all morning, since their earlier confrontation. Cameron had considered it a relief not to have to deal with the consequences of that confrontation, but now he wasn't as certain. Particularly as Samuel didn't rush to his defense. Whatever the two of them had enjoyed could only evaporate that swiftly if it hadn't been anything at all to begin with. That knowledge filled Cameron with a strange sort of anger and indignation.

"If you lose votes, it is because of your own actions," he told Burberry.

He tried to stand tall and show a little pride in himself, but one frown from Samuel and he was back to feeling like a green country rube who would never be able to navigate the sophisticated world of men like him. It rankled him that Samuel was so willing to go along with Burberry's crazy scheme as well, even though they had all agreed it would be best. They'd all agreed before stepping out that morning that they'd let Burberry rule the day so that they could ingratiate themselves to him. Now, however, it seemed like a terrible idea. It seemed like an excuse for Samuel to back away from a fire he'd stepped too close to for his comfort. And yet, perhaps it was necessary for their grander scheme? Logic told Cameron one thing, and his wounded pride and his heart insisted on another.

"We are all responsible for our own actions," Burberry sneered and huffed a short laugh at Cameron's show of defiance. "And if your family ends up turned out of their cottage, boy, it will be because of your own actions. Or the lack thereof." He raked Cameron with a quick glance, then turned away. "Mr. Applegren," he addressed a gentleman who strode past, as if on his way to something important, "I was just coming to see you. You must meet my friend, the world-famous composer and musician, Samuel Percy."

Cameron glared at Burberry's back, then stepped away, putting as much distance as he could between himself and the vile man. Samuel was forced to keep up with Burberry, which only irritated Cameron more.

He was surprised when Sammy drifted over to his side as he leaned against one of the shops on the street where Burberry was making his spectacle.

"Now you know the frustration I endure on a daily basis," she said, striking a feminine pose by his side. "Burberry is a pill."

"I've no idea how he can get away with half the things he does without being arrested and put in the stocks at every turn," Cameron grumbled.

"He's a wealthy and powerful pill," Sammy said, blinking as though she were surprised Cameron hadn't made the connection. "My dear boy," she went on, "surely you have lived enough to see that money cancels out nearly every sin. Have you not observed the absurdities that the aristocracy is capable of?"

Cameron crossed his arms and sent her a sullen look. "I have."

"Are you not aware of the scandalous behavior of certain members of the House of Lords, or the antics of the royal family itself?" she said, blinking at him. "Laws, be they civil or social, are made for the lower classes and those without financial means. They do not apply to men like our friend Burberry."

"He's not my friend," Cameron said, his mood darkening. "He never was."

"But my brother is your friend," Sammy went on, sympathy in her eyes. "And if his fortunes continue on the way they are now, he will have fame and wealth for the rest of his life, which means he will be surrounded by Burberrys and their like. And so will you, if you stay with him." She paused, then added, "Which you want to, I can tell."

Cameron rolled his shoulders uncomfortably against the wall behind him. "He doesn't want that."

Sammy arched one eyebrow. "Are you so certain?"

"Yes," Cameron said. He wished he were lying, but it was the truth. He was a diversion for Samuel, nothing more.

Sammy hummed in consideration, and they both turned to watch Samuel and Burberry for a moment. Burberry had gathered another small crowd of gentlemen and was addressing them as though he were at a political meeting instead of a street in Derby. He gestured and glanced to Samuel repeatedly, and whatever he was saying, the surrounding gentlemen looked impressed. Cameron supposed it was a good sign. The more people Burberry convinced to come to his concert, the more likely he was to be distracted while Cameron and the others rifled through his things in search of information about Grasmere Ventures.

Cameron sighed. In truth, he just wanted to get it over with so he could go back to London and his work with John Dandie and forget this odd interlude had ever happened. He felt that even more acutely when Samuel glanced his way in the middle of whatever conversation Burberry was leading him through.

The swell of emotion that hit Cameron as his eyes met Samuel's was like a sour stomach after consuming a sweet treat. He still admired Samuel with everything he had, still thought the man was beautiful and intelligent and clever. He was an accomplished lover too, which shouldn't have surprised Cameron at all, given Samuel's preferences for numerous short-term conquests instead of one lasting one. But it was all going to end, and then what would Cameron do?

"Heaven's sake, Cameron. What are you doing loitering in the streets on a cold day like this?" Cameron was cheered by the sound of his sister's voice as she waddled down the street toward him, Victoria in her arms and Avery holding her hand.

Cameron stood, smiling. "Georgie." His heart was suddenly ten times lighter, particularly as he lifted his nephew into his arms once they grew close enough. "Mrs. Thorne, I'd like you to meet my sister, Georgina, and my nephew, Avery, and niece, Victoria."

"How do you do?" Georgie asked with wide eyes, trying to work out how to curtsy while holding a toddler and heavily pregnant, then settling for extending her free hand to Sammy.

"Oh." Sammy said with a forced smile, taking Georgie's hand. "I am quite well. It is a pleasure to meet you." She let go of Georgie's hand, then turned her brittle smile to Cameron. "If you will excuse me, I believe my brother needs my help. And I have an aversion to children of any kind."

She stepped away so quickly that she tripped on the hem of her skirt. She recovered masterfully, though, rushing on to stand between Burberry and Samuel as Burberry continued addressing his audience.

"She's ever bit as grand and strange as I always thought her to be," Georgie laughed.

"You cannot even begin to imagine," Cameron agreed with a humorless laugh.

Even with Avery in his arms, he couldn't keep his smile in place. He watched the scene with Samuel continue to unfold, knowing he didn't belong in it.

After only a few moments of that, Georgie hummed as though she'd figured out a riddle. "I see," she said.

"What do you see?" Cameron asked with a sigh. Georgie was one of the few people from whom Cameron had never felt the need—or the ability—to hide anything.

She inched closer to him and lowered her voice. "I suspected the other day as I watched the two of you interact," she said.

There was no point in Cameron asking what she suspected. "It's bloody inconvenient," he grumbled.

"Bad word," Avery gasped, slapping a plump hand over his mouth.

Georgie laughed. "We've been teaching him not to repeat the things his father says. I see that extends to his uncle too."

Cameron laughed, adjusting Avery in his arms. "Quite right, young man. Bad word. We shouldn't use bad words at all."

"No," Avery said with a firm nod.

Cameron's smile grew wider for a moment, then faded. "I would have liked to have had children."

The look that came to Georgie's eyes came close to breaking Cameron's heart. "It's not impossible," she said. "I'm certain there are plenty of poor, dear, unfortunate souls floundering away in orphanages around London or, God forbid, in the streets that could use a father."

Avery began to squirm, so Cameron put the boy down. He stayed in a crouch once he did, since Avery apparently wanted to continue to play with the brim of his hat, even though he didn't want to be held.

"Perhaps," Cameron said, glancing up at his sister. "But it also makes me wonder if I shouldn't have summoned all of my courage, grit my teeth, pushed aside my natural inclinations, and found an agreeable young woman to marry and have a real family with."

"Don't say that," Georgie said, her eyes going round. "You would have been positively miserable."

"Would I have been?" Cameron asked, standing. He faced Georgie, his back to Burberry, Samuel, and the others, as he was beginning to think it should have been all along. "I'm not certain I would have been any more miserable than I am now."

"Poor boy." Georgie stepped closer to him, resting a hand on the side of his face. "Life hasn't been easy for you."

"Life has no obligation toward me whatsoever," he said with a shrug. "And I'm happy enough in London. I enjoy my work. I have a few friends now. I belong to an organization, called The Brotherhood, that I like, even though the club is so grand I feel like I'll be cast out of it at every moment. What right have I to ask for more?"

"We all have a right to ask for love," Georgie said, patting the side of his face before stepping back. She glanced past his shoulder, presumably at whatever spectacle Burberry was making of himself.

Cameron shook his head. "I don't think I do have a right to ask for love. From what I've observed of my sort so far, that's not what most of them want. I know a few exceptions, but not many." He sighed. "The longer I live, the more it's been made clear to me that I have a choice between loving who I want to without fulfillment or going against myself to have the sort of family that would make me feel like I have a place in this world. I can't have both."

He shrugged, scuffing his toe into the pavement in front of him while looking down. He could feel Georgie watching him, feel her pity.

"I would say you could come back to Derby and live with me and James," she said in a low voice, "but I know that after what happened last year, that probably isn't an option."

"No," he said, still looking down, hands thrust in his pockets. He took a breath and blinked up at the sky. "I have to stay in London now. I have a responsibility to John Dandie." He bit his lip, trying to blink away the impossible muddle in his soul. "Maybe I will just find myself a girl who doesn't mind if I'm a bit shy around her. I could probably do what I need to do to get a family." He winced. "It can't be that hard, can it? Men like me have been living that lie forever."

"It's not the right lie for you."

Cameron jerked straight at the sound of Samuel's

voice directly behind him. His body went hot and cold as he turned and found Samuel only a few feet away, staring at him with a look of sadness and consternation. He didn't know how much of what he'd just said to Georgie Samuel had overheard, but by the look of things, it was too much.

CHAPTER 14

Samuel couldn't believe what he heard from Cameron. Worse still, he knew it was his fault. He'd let Cameron down that morning. He'd known the young man fancied himself the domestic sort. He'd even been drawn into the fantasy that he might be able to enjoy a long-term relationship with Cameron. Maybe he could, but what he'd said to Cameron that morning was God's honest truth. He couldn't change who he was overnight, and neither could Cameron. In any way.

He knew that men like them had pretended away their lives in what passed for normalcy in the socially acceptable world from time immemorial, marrying, fathering children, and only ever diving into their true natures in the darkness and in secret. But to think of someone as beautiful and vibrant as Cameron giving up his true nature for what could only be a pale imitation of happiness was too much for Samuel. But rather than meeting Samuel's eyes with a look of agreement, or perhaps even an appeal to rescue him from his shackling imagination, Cameron looked embarrassed and indignant at being overheard.

"I don't see that it is any business of yours," Cameron said in a low voice, glancing around to see if anyone was paying attention to them.

In fact, Samuel had walked away from his conversation with Burberry and the odious men Burberry had gathered around him to show off his new toy—which was precisely how every conversation Burberry had dragged him into that morning had made Samuel feel—in such a way that the group he'd left stared after him. They could think him rude or wonder why he'd broken away from them to speak to a scruffy lad and a pregnant woman with children when Burberry was in the middle of inventing a list of accomplishments ascribed to Samuel that bore no resemblance to the truth, or they could go to hell, for all Samuel cared. Cameron was far more important to him than any concert, no matter the reason he was proceeding with it.

"You know full well that it is very much my business now," Samuel said in a low voice, stepping closer to Cameron.

Cameron took a step back to stand by his sister's side. "Is it?" Cameron's full lips pinched into a tight line as he continued to glance around anxiously.

Samuel wanted to tell him that no one passing would care about their conversation if Cameron didn't react to it as though they were saying or doing anything wrong. He had to remind himself that they weren't in London, though. They were in Derby, a town that wasn't so big that any passing man or woman might not know Cameron's face and know the story of why he had been banished along with it. The fact that his sister seemed to accept him still was an aberration, not the norm. The rest of Cameron's family's reaction to him was far more ordinary. Samuel was cruel to press the issue at a time and place when it could quite literally hurt Cameron, not to mention himself.

He cleared his throat and stood back, attempting to assume a formal manner when his feelings were anything but formal. "I am aware that I have disappointed you with my opinion on things," he said, hating how banal he was forced to seem, "but I can assure you that I have come to value you in a way that tests my preconceived notions of things."

Cameron narrowed his eyes. For a moment, Samuel worried that the young man was too unsophisticated to understand the words he'd used to express his sentiments. But Cameron said, "If you've changed your mind once because you got your way, who's to say you won't change it back again because you're bored?"

"I didn't mean—"

"You may have changed your mind," Cameron spoke over him, "but I haven't." He took a small step toward Samuel and lowered his voice to say, "You don't know what I've been through. Is it too much to ask that I have a little contentment in my life, a family of my own to share it with?"

Samuel blew out an exasperated breath through his nose. "That's not what I was driving at."

Impatience made his back itch and his feet unable to stand still. Why couldn't he simply say the things he wanted to say to Cameron, and why couldn't Cameron just accept him as he was?

He glanced over his shoulder to Burberry. Sammy had taken up the place he'd vacated by Burberry's side and seemed to have the gentlemen Burberry was trying to woo—to his political cause as well as to the concert— captivated by whatever she was saying. She also had a hand on Burberry's arm. Any outsider would think that the two of them were fond of each other and perhaps on their way to the altar. But that only frustrated Samuel more. How could Cameron long so blindly for something that was used and abused by so many, for everything from financial gain to social status?

"Do you really want to simply imitate that lot?" he asked Cameron in a hiss, nodding to Burberry's group. "Treating marriage and family as though it is nothing more than a game or a trinket to be worn to communicate status?"

"I want to create something of my own that combines the best of both worlds," Cameron said, scowling. Underneath the anger of his scowl was a sort of disappointment that Samuel found withering.

"You want to create that by abandoning who you are

and playing a role that doesn't suit you for the rest of your life?" Samuel asked.

Cameron let out an exhausted breath and rubbed a hand over his face. "I just want peace. I just want to live a life where no one hates me and casts me out. Is that too much to ask?"

Samuel opened his mouth to reply, but he wasn't sure what to say. Could he promise Cameron that sort of a life? He couldn't. Not even if their sort were accepted, or if either he or Cameron were a woman. The color of his skin precluded him from ever finding true peace in the world where his talents had planted him. The best he could offer Cameron was pleasure.

He took too long searching for a way to answer. Cameron shook his head, turned to kiss his sister's cheek and pat his niece and nephew on their heads, then turned to walk off.

"Where are you going?" Samuel called after him.

"For a walk," Cameron called without turning around.

Samuel pulled off his hat and rubbed a hand across his head in frustration. He had never wanted anyone or anything in his life as desperately as he wanted Cameron Oberlin, and he had never been as much at a loss for how to have him. Truly have him. Not just for a few nights of passion in what was turning out to be the strangest interlude of his life.

"If you hurt him, I will kill you."

The threatening comment was delivered in such a

soft voice, and by such a diminutive woman—a heavily pregnant one with a toddler in her arms and a tiny child clinging to her skirts—that Samuel's brow shot up and he turned to Georgie in shock when he heard it.

"I beg your pardon?" he said, blinking rapidly, not sure if he should grin and laugh or be horrified.

"You heard me," Georgie said, adjusting Victoria in her arms. "My Cameron has been through more than enough in the past few years. If you hurt him further, I'll creep into your fancy London flat in the middle of the night and cut your balls off with a rusty knife."

Samuel's jaw dropped open, still flabbergasted.

Georgie took a step toward him. "Cameron is the purest, sweetest soul I have ever known," she went on. "He was the apple of our mother's eye until she found out what he was. It hurt him, you know. To be rejected that way, by everyone he'd every cared about, by his family. Cameron has always been devoted to his family. We were the most important thing to him. He did twice as many chores as the rest of us, cared for Grandpapa when he was ill, missed school to help Pa in the fields. That boy did everything for us. Who gives a single shite who he'd rather go to bed with? Even David and Jonathan loved each other in the Bible, so why can't Cameron love that way as well? But everyone turned their back on him the moment that devil, Burberry, led him astray. Everyone. And you don't know what it did to him."

"I wouldn't ever—"

"You heard him," Georgie interrupted him again. "All he wants is peace and a family of his own again. If you truly care about him, you'll give that to him. If you think he's merely a sweet diversion to whet your appetite, then you're no better than Burberry. If that's who you are, then leave him alone and let him find the happiness he deserves."

Samuel was so bowled over by Georgie's impassioned speech—not to mention the tears of zeal she'd broken into halfway through, or the way she loved Cameron so completely that it put him to shame—that he could only stand there and gape. Georgie let out a tense breath and shook her head, then grabbed Avery's hand and walked away. It was a surprisingly powerful and commanding gesture for a woman as pregnant as she was.

"Dear, dear," Burberry's voice spoke behind him a few moments later. "It appears you've just been told off in spectacular fashion."

Samuel whipped around to glare at Burberry. His expression must have been fierce, because Burberry took a step back, holding up his hands as if he would have to physically defend himself.

"I will concede that it is none of my concern," Burberry stammered. "Only, it looked as though you could have used some help to keep the harpy at bay."

"How much of what she said did you overhear?" Samuel asked point blank. For Cameron's sake, he had to know how much trouble he might have just landed himself in.

"None of it," Burberry said. Samuel couldn't tell if he was lying or not. "I tend not to listen to the ravings of women when they are in that state," he added with a sniff.

Samuel's revulsion for Burberry deepened. "She was defending her family," he said, walking away from the spot of the conversation and toward his sister, who was still entertaining the cluster of men who had stopped to listen to Burberry.

Burberry chuckled. "That's what they always say." He fell into step by Samuel's side. "If you ask me, it's merely proof that women should be kept indoors, away from polite society."

Samuel stared at the man incredulously. "You think that, and you wish to marry my sister?"

"I never said—I don't—what makes you think—" Burberry flushed and stammered for a moment. Samuel sent him a flat look, as if to say anyone who thought his motives were anything other than trapping Sammy into a marriage that would be convenient and profitable for him was fooling themselves, and that Burberry himself was the biggest fool of all.

"All is well?" Sammy asked Samuel once they were side by side. She slipped her hand into the crook of Samuel's elbow and smiled vapidly up at him, but her eyes were serious.

"Not really," Samuel muttered.

"Mr. Percy, I would like you to meet another very important friend of mine." Burberry shifted back into political mode, gesturing to a middle-aged man who had joined the conversation after Samuel had walked away to check on Cameron. "This is Mr. Dalziel, one of Derby's most prominent solicitors."

"I've just been hearing a great many interesting things about you," Mr. Dalziel said, holding out his hand to Samuel.

Samuel shook it, then found himself trapped in yet another round of false flattery and political jargon as Burberry used the imagined connection between them to make himself sound like a man of influence. Samuel suffered through the conversation with as much of a smile as he could manage, nodding when it was appropriate and making light conversation when Mr. Dalziel asked about both his recent concert in London and about what it had been like to grow up in the Caribbean. The only bit of consolation Samuel had about being shown around like a trophy was that the men Burberry was trying to convince to vote for him, once the election rolled around, were as thick-headed and uninteresting as he was, so impressing them didn't take much effort on his part.

"I think that went surprisingly well," Burberry said with a proud smile as he, Samuel, and Sammy walked on to a sleepy café just off of the town's central thoroughfare. "The concert will be fabulously well-attended, and with any luck, the ballot boxes will be favorably stuffed come the election."

"Do you even know when there is going to be an election?" Sammy asked with a teasing smirk as they helped themselves to seats in a private corner of the shop, near a window.

"There is always an election right around the corner," Burberry said. "And one must always be prepared for it."

After what he'd witnessed that morning, Samuel was confident that Burberry had no more of a chance to win an election for street cleaner, let alone Parliament. But it didn't mean the man couldn't court a dangerous number of friends. Burberry was just influential enough to cause a great deal of trouble in Derby and within the surrounding area, particularly for the people whose rents he controlled.

Those thoughts were quickly forgotten, though. Once their tea was brought, he found himself staring out into the street, wondering where Cameron had gone and if he would come back. And once Cameron did come back, Samuel wondered what he would say to him, how he could act around him now.

He didn't need the emotional knots Cameron had tied him in. He didn't have time for his thoughts to be completely distracted by the young man's sweet and tragic presence. His life had been perfectly full without Cameron in it. He was celebrated publicly, as much as a man like him could be, he had friends in all walks of life, and he had lovers whenever he wanted them. His life hadn't truly lacked for anything.

Except that the more he thought about it, the more it felt as though he had nothing at all. He had diversions, not a life.

"But if you ask me," Burberry said in a laughing voice, as though he and Sammy had been talking all along without caring that Samuel's attention had drifted, "what I find quaintest of all is how the master has become the servant and the servant the master."

Sammy managed a brittle laugh, then sipped her tea to hide her irritation. Samuel glanced from her to Burberry.

"You and that Oberlin boy," Burberry told Samuel, as if explaining a joke. "What with you being...." He waved a hand at Samuel. "And him being a sturdy, English lad. And yet, he follows you around as though he would run your errands and shine your shoes, if you asked him."

Samuel caught Burberry's implication, and for a moment, he was so offended he couldn't breathe. "I will not hear Cameron spoken of in such a way," he said, eyes flaring with indignation. "Cameron is a bright, good young man, and your implication is obscene."

Burberry flinched, his expression filling with shock, at first, then a new kind of startled understanding. "I was merely implying that it's amusing to see an English boy defer to a black man, but if you're saying...." An uneasy awkwardness passed down Samuel's spine as Burberry's smile turned salacious. "I had no idea."

Samuel had the horrible feeling he'd exposed far more of himself than he'd intended to. He cleared his throat. "I am merely looking out for the young man. He is a valued employee of a good friend of mine."

Burberry chuckled, a whole new expression of camaraderie in his eyes. "You forget," he said, leaning forward and lowering his voice. "I'm *acquainted* with the young man in question." He winked lasciviously.

Samuel cleared his throat again, squirmed in his seat, and sent his sister a look. Sammy had a sweetly vacant look in her eyes as she sipped from her teacup, glancing out the window. The woman had a decided knack for pretending not to be present when she was sitting with her knees bumped up against Samuel's. And probably Burberry's too, considering how small the table was.

"A bit of advice, if I might," Burberry said, leaning closer still to Samuel. "Young men, like Mr. Oberlin, can be just as sweet a distraction as young women, or so I've found. Particularly as they are so eager over the discoveries they've just made about themselves that they're not picky about whose sausage they sample. I find them to be far better at it than the young ladies their age, though the ladies are more accommodating in other ways. I've had several young friends like Mr. Oberlin and enjoyed them immensely."

Samuel was so revolted by everything Burberry said and implied that he was certain the cream on the table would curdle in solidarity.

"But as lovely as those boys are, they're terrible for one's reputation," he said in a tight whisper. He leaned back a bit and picked up his teacup. "Certainly, men like us are far better equipped to weather the storm of scandal that inevitably comes with indulgence. There was some fuss last year when my acquaintance with Mr. Oberlin was made public." He shrugged, then sipped his tea. "But that's largely in the past now. And the more I am seen with the right sort of people—the more I am seen to *be* the right sort of people—the more those people forget the indiscretions of the past."

Samuel was appalled. But at the same time, a whisper of an idea took hold in the back of his mind. "You've found yourself in this sort of...situation with more than just Mr. Oberlin?" he asked.

"Several times." Burberry shrugged again and sipped his tea.

Samuel glanced to his sister. Sammy still wore that vacant look that would have convinced anyone passing by that she was away with the fairies. He wasn't entirely certain how, but he had the notion that she already knew about Burberry's past conquests, and that Burberry knew she knew. Otherwise, even he wouldn't have been so much of a dolt as to speak about these things while she was there at the table. And yet, Sammy still seemed taken with Burberry, at least in some regard. Their friendship must have been colossally beneficial to her in some way.

What struck Samuel the most, though, as Burberry ordered another pot of tea from the tired-looking young woman tending the café, was that, through his casual admission of sin, Burberry might just have handed them another weapon to use against him. If Burberry truly thought he stood a chance of winning any sort of election at all, he would need to keep his past and his proclivities a secret. There was no telling what the man might do, or what he might give up, to keep men like Cameron, and the others Burberry purported to have had liaisons with, quiet.

And yet, for Samuel to use the threat of exposure in that way against Burberry was the very height of hypocrisy. His career—and potentially his life—would have been over if he'd let the same sort of information about him leak out into the public sphere. It didn't matter whether he hated Burberry or not, there was a code of honor in place amongst men like him that he was loath to break.

Which meant they were all right back where they'd started—desperate to prove Sammy had a share in Burberry's money instead of owing him a small fortune. The only way they were going to be able to find that proof was by dancing—quite literally—to Burberry's tune at the concert.

CHAPTER 15

Samuel's feeling of disquiet stayed with him, not just for the rest of that day, but for the next few days. It helped nothing at all that Cameron didn't come to his bed that night…or any other night leading up to the concert. He could have simply knocked on the door that separated his and Cameron's rooms and gone to him, but that seemed like crossing a line—one Cameron wouldn't want him to cross. Samuel didn't think the door between them had a lock, but entering Cameron's room uninvited felt as though it would be crossing a boundary.

What Samuel couldn't figure out was whether it was his boundary or Cameron's that he would have been crossing. Luring Cameron into his bed with kisses and promises of ecstasy was one thing. Actively going to Cameron's bed and hoping he would be accepted for the night—or longer—felt as taboo as seeking out a partner for the night in St. James's Park. No, it felt even more taboo than that. It would be admitting to something, claiming something within himself that he didn't want to think about.

He avoided thinking about it during the two days leading up to the concert by rehearsing the small orchestra Burberry had arranged for and organizing the arrangement of the surprisingly large conservatory in Burberry's house. It occurred to him that Cameron or Sammy could have simply searched the house while Samuel was practicing with the orchestra, but Sammy seemed more interested in flirting with Burberry—Samuel was utterly gob-smacked by his sister's ability to toy with the man when he was fairly certain she hated him—and Cameron had refused to go to Burberry's house at all. In fact, he'd taken to rising early in the morning and leaving Sammy's house before the rest of them were up, only to return well after supper. He and Samuel exchanged enough words for Samuel to know that Cameron was spending all of his time either with Georgie and his niece and nephew, or else at his parents' hamlet, trying in vain to get them to accept him.

The whole thing had Samuel buzzing with annoyance late in the afternoon on the day of the concert, as they all gathered in Sammy's front hall so that they could ride to Burberry's estate together.

"I do hope Burberry's cook is up to scratch tonight," Sammy said, checking her reflection in one of the hall's many mirrors. "Burberry didn't say it was a supper party, but he cannot expect us to go through all the trouble of arriving early and helping the orchestra to set up, and for me to help him greet his guests, without feeding us first."

"I'm certain he'll provide us with something," Samuel mumbled. He had no patience for his sister anymore, particularly when the sight of Cameron coming down the stairs dressed in a new and stylish suit knocked the wind out of him.

Cameron was beautiful. The suit was expertly tailored to fit him and accentuate the breadth of his shoulders and his trim waist. He'd had his hair cut as some point since that morning as well, and it was styled rakishly to one side, even though center parts were currently in fashion. The troubled look on his face made him seem far older than he ever had to Samuel, and twice as serious. Cameron wasn't a green country boy at all, but rather a strong, slightly tragic man. A man Samuel would have given just about anything to peel out of his suit and make love to until they were both panting and exhausted. And God only knew what sort of promises he would make to the man after that.

He was well aware of staring for too long and with too many stars in his eyes by the time Cameron reached the hall and glanced awkwardly back at him. "Georgie took me shopping," he explained in a mumble. "She picked this out, made me purchase it with the money I tried to give to her, and cut my hair after. Is it all right?" He sent his reflection in one of the hall mirrors an anxious look.

"It's more than all right," Samuel said, his voice hoarse and his breath catching.

Cameron's cheeks went bright pink as he whipped his head back to Samuel. For a moment, hope and longing shone in his eyes. But only for a moment.

"I'm not late, am I?" Archibald charged down the stairs Cameron had just descended so gracefully. "I had a devil of a time finding anything that might be suitable for this sort of evening."

Samuel dragged his eyes away from Cameron to frown at Archibald. He was dressed well enough, but everything about the man annoyed Samuel in the extreme. Almost a week had passed, and the man was still stubbornly tight-lipped about Lady Selby's whereabouts and whatever devilry he was up to with Sammy's finances. Samuel was more convinced than ever that Archibald was prevaricating about Lady Selby as a way of figuring out how to embezzle from Sammy.

Sammy seemed to harbor the same distrust for the man. "Why, Mr. Archibald, what are you doing dressed like that?"

Archibald stopped fussing with his suit jacket and glanced across the hall to Sammy. His mouth hung open in surprise for a moment before he asked, "Is this not the appropriate attire for a musical evening?"

"It is," Sammy said, striding closer to him in her midnight blue gown, "but you will not be attending the concert."

Archibald gaped at her. "I thought we were all going."

Sammy shook her head. "Not you. Not when you have persistently failed to come up with a means for me to repay my debts."

Archibald gaped harder. "I thought the entire purpose of this evening was to sneak through Burberry's house to find the information you need to prove your late husband, and therefore you, are entitled to half of Burberry's earnings through Grasmere Ventures."

"That is precisely the point," Sammy said with a smile. "But the three of us have that well in hand."

Archibald was beside himself. "I have been trapped as a virtual prisoner in this house for weeks."

"I've let you go to the pub a few times," Sammy argued.

Archibald ignored her. "I am the only one among you who has any idea what a business contract looks like."

Cameron shifted restlessly, as though he knew what one looked like too, thanks to his work with John Dandie. But he didn't say anything.

"I am the greatest asset you have in this search, and you are saying I am not allowed to come?" Archibald finished indignantly.

"If I let you out of the house, you'll only bolt when you have the first opportunity," Sammy sighed. "And your work for me is not yet done. If our efforts tonight fail, I will still need you to scour my estate to come up with the money I need."

"You cannot expect me...there is nothing...how can you expect...." Archibald practically vibrated with fury. "This is intolerable, madam," he snapped at last. "I have half a mind to call in the police and accuse you of kidnapping and false imprisonment."

"Yes, please do that," Sammy said, accepting her coat when her maid brought it out from one of the side halls. "And while they're here, perhaps we could all ask them about Lord Stanley's whereabouts. I'm sure the Duke of Selby would like to know."

Archibald practically turned purple with rage before turning sharply and storming off. When he was several yards down a side hall, he roared with fury. The sound was so comical that Samuel turned to Cameron, ready to share his amusement.

Cameron might not have heard the conversation at all, for all the seriousness in his expression. His shoulders were hunched, his brow furrowed, and if Samuel hadn't known any better, he would have thought Cameron were on his way to the gallows.

"Your carriage is ready, Mrs. Thorne," Mr. Lee announced from the doorway.

Samuel stepped closer to Cameron as Sammy's maid helped her on with her coat. "Cameron, we've been avoiding each other long enough. We need to talk."

Cameron glanced up and met Samuel's eyes in surprise. "You choose now to say we need to talk?" he asked with a startled blink. "*Now?* When we're moments away from leaving the house for this damnable concert?"

Samuel let out a breath and rubbed a hand over his face. Cameron had a point. His timing was terrible. "After the concert, then," he said. "Or perhaps in a quiet moment before the performance begins."

"I'm not sure," Cameron mumbled, stepping away from him.

Samuel caught his arm, then moved in close enough to smell Cameron's shaving soap. "We need to talk about what you said to your sister. Even if you weren't serious about forcing yourself into that sort of life, we need to talk about the implications of what made you think that."

Cameron carefully extracted himself from Samuel's grip. "Haven't you already made your thoughts on the matter clear?"

"Stop dawdling, you two," Sammy called to them from the doorway. "We've a concert to mastermind and important financial documents to purloin."

Samuel gritted his teeth and rolled his eyes at his sister, but followed her to the door and out to the waiting carriage all the same. Cameron was right about the two of them not having time to discuss everything that they so desperately needed to discuss. But Samuel was right about the necessity of finally talking about it.

The drive to Burberry's estate was short. Samuel had been surprised by the size and relatively good taste of the place when he'd seen it for the first time. The property was in a fashionable area, and the house was stately and attractive. Burberry couldn't possibly have decorated it himself, as the furnishings were far too tasteful and elegant. It was the sort of house that Samuel could have found himself living comfortably in. The gardens—or what he'd been able to see of them through the windows while rehearsing with the orchestra—must have been lovely in spring and summer.

Cameron had nearly the exact opposite reaction to the place. He shrank in on himself from the moment he stepped out of the carriage, and he seemed to avoid looking at anything but his feet as the three of them were shown through the front hall and into the conservatory, where Burberry and most of the members of the local orchestra had already gathered.

"Ah, there you are at last," Burberry said, coming over to greet them. Which meant sliding across the room and taking Sammy's hands, then kissing her knuckles, and shaking Samuel's hand with an overly-chummy wink. Burberry barely acknowledged Cameron. It was probably for the best, but Samuel found himself paradoxically annoyed all the same.

"Mr. Percy, you simply must tell the first violinist that he should allow me to introduce you and the orchestra rather than doing it himself," Burberry said, tugging on Samuel's sleeve to lead him over to the orchestra.

Samuel should have known that simple comment would be the herald of trouble. As it turned out, the concert master, a Mr. Sims, had been bullied and badgered by Burberry over not only the introductions, but changes to the program that Burberry wanted to make so that he could give a speech to his cronies. There was also a matter of feeding and paying the orchestra members, which hadn't been discussed at all. Within moments, Samuel found himself up to his neck in complaints and tiny fires he needed to put out—literally, in the case of a bassoonist who stepped back into one of Burberry's fireplaces and ignited the hem of his trousers. Samuel's hope was that Cameron could use the distractions to sneak off immediately to search for documents related to Grasmere, but that plan was thwarted when he was, instead, drafted into helping Burberry's staff serve *hors d'oeuvres* to not only the orchestra, but a few guests who arrived early.

On top of that, it was discovered that the reason some of Burberry's concert guests arrived early was because half had been told the event was a full supper that would begin at six, and the other half were told it was simply a concert that would begin at seven. The confusion meant that, once again, Samuel felt as though he were the ringleader at a circus.

"It baffles me that Burberry could organize so much as a drinking contest in a pub, let alone think he could run for public office and win," Samuel told Cameron with a huff as soon as he had a spare moment to stand next to the man at the edge of the room. The guests had more or less all arrived, the orchestra was tuned and ready to go, and his part in things was now only to stand back and watch, then accept praise once the concert was done.

Cameron didn't seem to share his humor, though it

was clear that the young man was equally baffled by the topsy-turvy event. "I'm not entirely convinced Burberry actually does want to hold public office," he said, arms crossed tightly, as though the place made him uncomfortable. "I think he just likes to listen to himself make speeches."

"You're probably right," Samuel said with a laugh.

He rested a hand absentmindedly on Cameron's shoulder. Both of them stared at it for a moment before Samuel cleared his throat and drew his hand away. There was something about the touch that felt both right and wrong simultaneously. Touching Cameron made him happy in the simplest of ways, even if the touch didn't truly mean anything. But that sort of happiness was at odds with so many other things within Samuel that it felt awkward when he thought it should feel good. He tried to cover his uneasiness in the only way he knew how.

"You've been to this house before, haven't you?" he said with a cheeky, sideways grin that was on its way to being more.

Cameron swallowed and nodded.

"So you likely know all of the nooks and crannies, the quiet rooms and the hiding places," Samuel went on.

Cameron glanced warily at him. "I am familiar with the house. I have a few ideas about where Burberry might be hiding important financial documents."

A strange, stifled feeling worked its way through Samuel, particularly when the concert master stood to help the rest of the orchestra tune. Samuel, too, felt as though something in him were warming up and getting ready for excitement. It was the same thrill of the chase and sense of going against the grain of polite society that he felt before whisking a likely fellow away for a night of debauchery, and yet, it was more.

"That's not what I meant," he whispered, leaning closer to Cameron, unable to hide his smile. "I was referring to secret places in this house for an entirely different reason. That conversation we need to have," he added. "Or perhaps more."

Cameron sucked in a breath and straightened. Samuel could feel the tension that rippled from him, and it wasn't entirely negative. "I thought we were here for a specific reason," he muttered, barely moving his mouth.

Samuel shrugged and nudged his shoulder against Cameron's as the orchestra continued tuning. "Standing here, looking at all of these fine ladies and gentlemen taking their seats for the evening, demanding to be amused and diverted, reminds me of all the reasons I detest society." Even more than that, the way his sister flirted with Burberry at the front of the room, in full view of all those fine ladies and gentlemen—which was as much a part of their arrangement with Burberry as the concert itself—only fueled that dislike. Samuel leaned even closer to Cameron. "Doesn't it make you want to do something to prove that you're not like them? Doesn't it make you want to thumb your nose at their rules and show them that you revile their pretensions?"

Cameron looked at him as though he'd grown another

head. "What does it matter how this lot lives? You don't have to join in if you don't want to. There are other ways to live."

"That is precisely what I'm saying," Samuel insisted.

The orchestra descended into the flutter of musical chaos that always happened after tuning. Samuel loved the sound. It was a reflection of all the ways life could spin out in different directions, if given half a chance. Burberry helped Sammy to a seat, then made his way to the front of the room.

"Once Burberry introduces me," Samuel whispered to Cameron. "Why don't the two of us slip away."

"I'm already planning to slip away to search for information," Cameron whispered in return, turning to Samuel with wide eyes.

"Let's slip away for another reason." Samuel winked at him, brushing his hand against Cameron's. "Wouldn't it make you feel alive to have a tryst right under all of their noses? Wouldn't it be the perfect revenge for the way you've been treated, to show them they don't own you?"

Cameron pushed away from the wall and Samuel as Burberry's guests applauded lightly as Burberry took the stage. "Ladies and gentlemen, I have a very special treat for you this evening," Burberry began.

Cameron's face twisted into a mask of distaste. "You complain about this lot with every breath you take," he whispered. "But at heart, you're no different than they are. You say you don't care what they think, but you do.

You want them to notice you, but for all the wrong reasons. You aren't who I thought you were."

Cameron marched away, slipping out the door into the hall. Samuel was left to gape after him, feeling as though Cameron had reached in, grabbed his heart, and taken it away with him.

"Tonight, I have the extreme pleasure of presenting you with this fine orchestra to play an original work by our guest of honor, my dear, personal friend, the world-famous composer and musician, Mr. Samuel Percy," Burberry said at the front of the room.

He gestured to Samuel, and the assembly of Derby's high society turned to him in all their splendor, applauding and smiling at him with dazzling smiles and wide-eyed acceptance. And as much as he loved applause, Samuel felt as though he might die on the spot. Because Cameron was right; he was one of them, just as he'd always wanted and feared.

CHAPTER 16

Cameron's stomach twisted and his heart felt heavy as he marched away from the conservatory and Samuel. The audience of sycophants and boobs that Burberry had gathered to watch the entire spectacle burst into applause before Cameron made it even halfway down the hall, and somehow that seemed fitting. Someone was finally congratulating him for what he had a horrible suspicion he should have done in the first place —walk away.

He fought off a miserable and morose impulse to burst into tears as he turned the corner at the end of the hall, heading in the direction in which he thought Burberry's office was located. It wasn't fair. He was a grown man now, not a green boy who'd had his head turned by the promise of physical satisfaction by a powerful man. He should be in better control of himself on every level. But as he passed a servants' staircase, unsure of where he was going—both in Burberry's house and in his life—he collapsed to sit on it, hiding his face in his hands.

He wanted Samuel. He couldn't deny it. It didn't do him a lick of good, but he still wanted the man. Even knowing that he was nothing more than a diversion for Samuel. It was a blow to his pride and a bitter pill to swallow to feel in his gut that he would be willing to continue to go to Samuel's bed just for the pleasure of being with the man, and with the hope that maybe, somehow, he might be more than just a warm body for right now.

That hope had just proven itself to be in vain, though. The way Samuel had propositioned him only minutes before had felt like every cheap offer Burberry had ever made to him. Cameron rubbed his hands over his face as he hunched on the stairs, wishing he could wipe the memory of Samuel's suggestion away. For a man who composed such beautiful music, Samuel seemed to be completely incapable of hearing the song Cameron was trying to sing to him. Love—even if it was just sex—shouldn't be a means to get back at society or something to smirk and boast about. It should be something to cherish, something to bring two people closer together. Everything Samuel had suggested to him just now had crushed the dream that perhaps Samuel had changed to become more domestic and less like Burberry after all.

"Are you all right?" a small, female voice asked, shaking Cameron out of his misery.

Cameron sucked in a breath and stood at the sight of the young maid coming down the stairs. He sniffled and wiped his eyes with the back of his hand, ashamed that he'd been crying in the first place, let alone that he'd been caught. "I'm fine," he mumbled.

The maid didn't look convinced. "Burberry after you too?" she asked cryptically.

Hot and cold prickles raced down Cameron's spine. "How did you...." He was too ashamed to finish the sentence.

"Charlie heard him say something about nabbing a prize tonight," the maid went on with a sympathetic look. "And we all know what that means."

Cameron shuffled on the spot, running a hand through his otherwise perfectly-coifed hair and glancing down.

The maid rested a hand on his arm. "Besides, I know who you are," she went on. "Charlie tells me the rest of the staff felt badly over the way Master Burberry used you last year. He feels you were treated poorly after."

Cameron snapped his eyes up to stare in horror at the maid. He never should have returned to Derby. He never should have poked his head out in public after Burberry had destroyed his reputation. He should go back to London—where there were too many people, including men like him, for anyone to give a fig—and never speak to another living soul outside of work again.

At the same time, a more sinister voice in the back of his head wondered if he might be able to use the situation in front of him to his advantage.

"Do you know where Burberry keeps his business papers?" he asked the maid. "Contracts and agreements and such?"

The maid blinked at him in surprise, then tilted her head and looked at him suspiciously. "Are you thinking of undermining the man in some way?"

Cameron hesitated, bit his lip, then admitted, "Yes."

The maid smiled. "Then I know precisely where you need to go. Follow me."

She headed down the hall with a skip in her step, not toward the side of the house where Cameron thought the office might be located, but through the dining room and the butler's pantry, then down another set of servants' stairs and across the servants' hall to a locked room near what looked like a wine cellar. She went up on her tiptoes, reaching above the doorway of the room across the hall from the locked room, then came down with a small, shiny key.

"Mr. Burberry is devious," she said as she fit the key into the door and turned the handle, "but the bastard isn't particularly smart."

Cameron nearly choked on his tongue when the maid opened the door to what appeared to be a closet filled with ledgers and files and papers. It looked like the sort of thing he was tasked with maintaining in John's office, only far less organized.

"Burberry is a dolt," he said, stepping into the closet and turning in a circle to take in the full extent of it.

"Well, then. I'll leave you to it," the maid said, handing Cameron the key.

She skipped away, leaving Cameron with a mountain of papers and no idea where to start. He did the only thing he could—took down ledgers and glanced through the papers piled on the deep windowsill at the back of the room to gauge what he was dealing with.

The process went more slowly than he would have liked, since the closet had no light source, other than the window. He had to turn toward the hall with every new bit of paper or dusty ledger he looked at so that he could read them. The majority of the bits and pieces he found himself faced with were leases on the properties Burberry owned and statements from banks. The picture of Burberry's finances did come together, albeit slowly. The bastard had every bit as much money as everyone said he did and more, but from what Cameron could tell, most of it was ill-gotten gains. Burberry had ruined more than a few businessmen and farmers, and he was in the process of ruining more. Paradoxically, Cameron changed his mind about Burberry's ability to run for political office and win. So many prominent men owed Burberry that they would be easy to blackmail into voting for him.

None of that held more than a passing interest for Cameron, though. He needed to find anything related to Grasmere Ventures that he could. Logic said that those documents wouldn't be on the surface of what he was looking at, since the deal was made years ago, so he searched on the dustier shelves, reaching up for a small box on the top of one shelf.

"Isn't this an interesting predicament." Burberry's voice behind Cameron just as he closed his hand around the box shocked him into clumsiness.

Cameron knocked the box off the shelf entirely as he spun around to find Burberry wedging his way into the closet with him. The contents of the box spilled to the floor, but as Cameron glanced down to see if the way the papers inside scattered was enough for him to gauge what had been in the box, he noticed something far more disturbing—the state of Burberry's trousers.

"Any reason you're messing about with my personal things, boy?" Burberry asked, taking a step closer to Cameron. "Or is it that you'd rather be messing about with my *personal things*?" he said in a husky voice.

"I don't do those things anymore, Mr. Burberry," Cameron said, forcing himself to keep his back straight and to stare at Burberry as the man he was now and not the boy he'd been back then. It was more of a challenge than he wanted it to be in the confines of the closet. The air suddenly felt stuffy and filled with the scent of old paper and panic.

"You wouldn't have to do those things," Burberry said, raising a hand to run his fingers down the front of Cameron's suit jacket. "We could find other things for you to do. You look so fetching in this suit tonight, so much like a man and not a boy, that I'm sure we can find a great many more manly ways for you to keep us both occupied until my concert is over."

Cameron flushed, but not with shame. It was Samuel's concert, not Burberry's. The man was a first-rate bastard to try to take that from Samuel. But that was what Burberry did. He took things from people, like their homes, their money, and their pride.

"No, we won't be doing any of that," Cameron said, pushing Burberry back so he could step out of the closet.

Burberry's face twisted into seething disappointment as he backpedaled into the hall, Cameron stepping after him. "You forget, boy. I hold the deed to your family's home. I could make their lives very difficult."

A pinch of the panic Cameron had been carrying around with him on his family's behalf for years gnawed at him, but it felt old and toothless. "You could," he said with a nod. "But they could go somewhere else. They could pick up and move, start a new life, start over. As I have."

Burberry narrowed his eyes even more, but for once, Cameron felt like it was because he'd lost control of the situation, lost the one thing he'd always used to lord over other people, and he didn't know how else to get his way. "I'm warning you, boy," he said. "You don't want to cross me."

Cameron almost laughed. Burberry's argument was nothing at all. "Tell me about Grasmere Ventures," he said instead. "Is it true that Mrs. Thorne is entitled to half of the income you make off of everything that was a part of the deal you had with her late husband?"

Burberry blanched and took another step back. "You can't prove anything," he said.

Cameron glanced over his shoulder at the room full of documents. "Can't I?"

"There they are."

The moment was interrupted by Sammy, who had just turned the corner at the bottom of the servants' stairs and spotted them. Samuel was right behind her. The two of them picked up their pace as Burberry glanced from his room full of documents to the wine cellar to the rest of the hallway, as if looking for a way to escape.

"You cannot prove anything," he said at last, leaping forward to shove Cameron out of the way, then slamming the door to his closet.

"If we can't prove anything, then why stop us from getting into that closet?" Cameron asked.

"There's nothing in there for you to see," Burberry said, spreading his arms across the doorway once the door was closed, as if that would prevent them from seeing what was inside all the more.

Cameron held up the key he still held in his right hand. "I've got this," he said simply.

"Give that back to me." Burberry leapt at him, but Cameron dodged out of his way.

Burberry rocked back, baring his teeth at Cameron for a moment, then lunging forward with his hands stretched toward Cameron's throat. Before he could get anywhere near, though, Samuel stepped between Burberry and Cameron, using his body as a shield.

"If you so much as think of harming a hair on this young man's head, I will kill you with my bare hands," Samuel growled.

Cameron felt a quick surge of gratitude and lust, which was immediately followed by shame and heartache. As beautiful as it was to have someone as grand and wonderful as Samuel defend him so intensely, it was just a moment of passion and not a lifetime of mutual admiration.

Even those thoughts didn't have long to settle in Cameron's mind before the scene shifted yet again.

"Will you all please stop behaving like quarreling boys in a schoolyard," Sammy said with more exasperation than upset in her voice. She stepped between Samuel and Burberry, placing a hand on each man's chest to keep them apart. "I'm certain there is a way we can resolve all of our differences in a gentlemanly and civilized manner." She seemed to be enjoying the intensity of the conflict more than any reasonable person should, as though she thrived on madness.

Cameron relaxed out of the defensive pose he'd taken up when Burberry lunged at him. He tugged at the bottom of his jacket, eyeing Sammy nervously. The woman had a gleam in her eyes that Cameron didn't like at all—as if she had finally maneuvered all of the pieces on a chessboard into exactly the right configuration and she was about to call "Checkmate!"

"Sammy, now is not the time to interfere," Samuel told her, sending his sister the same sort of look that Cameron would have, if he'd felt he was allowed to. It was scolding and impatient, but also deeply wary. "Burberry has made a serious threat against a young man whose life he has already made a misery. And there is no telling what else might have been said or done, or what might have happened, if we hadn't arrived on the scene."

Cameron's brow inched up fractionally. Was Samuel actually concerned over what Burberry might have done to him?

Of course he was. Anyone who knew his history with Burberry would have been. That didn't mean that Samuel's feelings for him—if they even qualified as such —had changed from what they'd been earlier in the trip.

"Burberry wouldn't have hurt your young beau, Samuel," Sammy said, stepping to Burberry's side and slipping her hand into the crook of his elbow. "Because that would have been very gauche of him, wouldn't it?"

Cameron's face heated, not only at the way Sammy referred to him as Samuel's beau, but because of the deeply uncomfortable way she fawned over Burberry. Was the woman mad? She knew Burberry was a lecherous old devil, and she likely knew how many lives he'd made miserable with his machinations. But perhaps she didn't care.

"Sammy, what in God's name are you doing?" Samuel asked his sister in a deep and tight voice.

"Getting my way at last, I should think," Sammy said, blinking innocently. She glanced over her shoulder at the door to the closet, then looked to Cameron, holding out her hand. "The key, if you please."

Cameron gulped. It went against his better judgement in so many ways, but he handed the key to her.

Sammy's smile was glittering—the same way that the body of a deadly spider glittered. It suddenly made perfect sense to him that Sammy was known as The Black Widow. She was just as venomous and lethal. "I've been looking for the tidy bundle of your financial dealings for ages, Nathaniel, dear," she said, fawning over Burberry. "How very clever of you to keep everything downstairs. I'm sure it is the one place I never would have lowered myself to search."

"I'm cleverer than I look," Burberry said, shifting anxiously, sweat beading on his forehead. The way he held Sammy's arm reminded Cameron of how a man might look if he were holding a hungry tiger on a defective leash, no idea when it might break.

"Would I be safe in assuming the contract you and my late husband signed is contained in that closet?" Sammy asked.

Burberry gulped, but didn't answer.

"I see." Sammy smiled. "Well then, I win the bet."

Burberry blew out a breath. His shoulders slumped and his head dropped. "Very well. You win."

Cameron frowned, glancing between the two, then at Samuel.

Samuel looked as confused as Cameron was, but also furious. "What bet?" he asked, snapping out each word. "Explain yourself."

Sammy smiled and batted her eyelashes at her brother. "After David died, I knew very well that I was entitled to half of Grasmere Ventures. But as I told you, the late Mr. Thorne lost his copy of the contract and the original was destroyed in a fire. Burberry here still had his copy, though, which he lorded over me." She sent Burberry a mock angry look.

"I told you that I had no issue with giving you what was yours, as long as you gave me what I wanted." For a moment, Burberry looked seductive, or at least attempted to. The result would have been laughable, if the situation weren't so insane.

"In the course of discussing the matter," Sammy went on, mostly for her brother's benefit, "I was pleased to discover the extent of Burberry's fortune. I offered to marry him on the spot."

"I beg your pardon?" Samuel said, his eyes going wide and his mouth hanging open in disbelief, once the question was out.

"Burberry callously refused, however," Sammy went on. "Even after I skillfully seduced him. He wanted me to be his mistress, mind you, but not his wife. I refused to give him the honey unless he was willing to take the bees with it."

"I almost gave in at that point," Burberry admitted sheepishly. "But I had a fortune to protect."

"And I had a collection to complete," Sammy said, smiling at Burberry. "After all, I had lost one wealthy husband, so of course I needed another. That was when Burberry and I made our wager."

"What wager?" Samuel asked, emphasizing each syllable, his voice shaking with fury. He raised a hand to his temples as though he had a splitting headache. Cameron wouldn't have been surprised if he did. His own head was done in by everything Sammy and Burberry were saying.

"Burberry hid the Grasmere Ventures contract, along with a few of the other contracts and deeds he showed me. He told me that if I could locate them, he would consent to marrying me, and if not, I would yield to him and become his mistress in the most public and humiliating way." Sammy smiled at him. "But now I have found them and get the plum with the pudding, thanks to the two of you."

Samuel drew in a long, tight breath, closing his eyes,. "Are you telling me that the only reason Cameron and I are here is so that you could manipulate us into searching Burberry's house in order that you might win a bet?" He only opened his eyes at the end of the question.

"No, darling," Sammy said, smiling at her brother. "I didn't know you were going to visit, remember? And even then, I wasn't certain how I would be able to employ your help. I was hoping Archibald would come up with the idea of seeking out the Grasmere Ventures contract sooner. I also intended for him to come up with a secondary financial plan, if the unthinkable happened and I lost the bet. But that man has proven to be a dismal disappointment. Young Cameron's sister—or was it your brother-in-law—ended up being far more useful in that regard. You cannot imagine how thrilled I was when Cameron came up with the scheme of searching Burberry's house without me having to suggest the idea at all. That's what makes this victory unexpectedly sweet."

"This entire endeavor...." Samuel began, but had to stop and gather his patience. Cameron was certain the man was about to explode. "Everything we have endured since arriving here was all a part of some ridiculous wager you and Burberry had?"

"I will remind you once again, brother," Sammy said, still smiling, though her eyes were cold, "that you showed up on my doorstep of your own volition. I did not invite you, and I am not keeping you here." Her words were clearly meant to tell Samuel to go away.

Cameron didn't need to be told twice. "You are all mad," he said, taking half a step down the hall and away from them. "All of you. I don't know if it's wealth that has corrupted you or a warped sense of power because of it, but you're all barmy. You're playing with people's lives, not toys. And you're destroying those lives as though they are matchsticks. I am no matchstick." He took a few steps down the hall before turning back to say. "I'm done with you. I'm done with the lot of you, and this place, and with being seen as nothing but a toy."

He sent his last look straight at Samuel, though it broke his heart to do so, then picked up his pace and ran toward what he assumed was a kitchen—a kitchen that would have a door that could get him out of Burberry's madhouse as quickly as possible.

CHAPTER 17

"Cameron, wait!"

Cameron got no farther than the kitchen itself before Samuel's voice stopped him. He was painfully aware of Burberry's kitchen staff pausing in the middle of cleaning up after supper—not to mention much of the rest of Burberry's staff peeking out of the doorway to the servants' dining hall to see what the commotion was all about—as Samuel jogged into the heated, steamy kitchen after him.

"If you're leaving this madhouse, I'm coming with you," Samuel said once he'd caught up.

Cameron frowned at him. "You can't. You're in the middle of a concert. I presume it's still going on."

Samuel glanced up at the ceiling, as if the orchestra were performing directly above them, which they weren't. "I don't think I care what a group of Burberry's friends might think of me for disappearing in the middle of the evening."

"Of course you care," Cameron told him. Just because Samuel's sister had proven herself to be the worse of the pair didn't mean that Samuel was suddenly an angel who wanted to fly into his arms, kiss him soundly, and spend the rest of his life together with Cameron in domestic bliss. The confrontation in the hallway hadn't changed the lewd suggestion Samuel had made earlier, or the truth of the man that had caused the suggestion in the first place. "Go back to your adoring public," Cameron went on, taking a few more steps to the door.

"I know I've said something to offend you." Samuel grabbed Cameron's arm to stop him.

It was the beginning of an argument—possibly an apology—but it was cut short as both Samuel and Cameron glanced at Burberry's cook, kitchen maid, scullery maid, and a pair of footmen who were loitering for no reason other than to see a show.

Samuel let go of Cameron, straightened, and cleared his throat. "It was not my intention to insult you with what I said before," he said with too much formality. "In fact, my intention was exactly the opposite."

"Was it?" Cameron felt as though the eyes of the entire world were on him, not just a few servants he would never see again. It made him bold and careless. "I don't think it was at all. I think it was merely the truth coming out."

"The truth that—" Samuel stopped, pressing his lips together and tugging at his sleeves. Cameron could see frustration bubbling off of him, like the steam coming off the pots sitting on Burberry's stove. "The truth is that I admire you deeply," he went on, putting emphasis on his words while flickering anxious looks to Burberry's servants.

It didn't matter that Samuel was no more able to make any sort of declaration of true feeling while they were being watched, his hollow words of admiration weren't enough for Cameron. "Admire me all you want, Samuel," he said, shaking his head. "I was hoping for more, but I see, once again, just how impossible that is. Even if you made me believe for a moment that things could be different, all you want is to be just like those people upstairs."

Cameron headed on toward the door, certain that it led directly outside, when it opened suddenly and a man who looked like a carriage driver stepped through. The man opened his mouth to say something, but stopped when he realized he'd walked in on something.

"What if things could be different?" Samuel asked, chasing after Cameron. "What if...what if *I* could be different?"

Cameron stopped within a few paces of the driver and the door. He turned back to Samuel, daring himself to be honest and say what he truly felt—that he wanted so desperately to love him and be with him, but that he could only do that if Samuel treated him like a lover and not a telegraph boy. The rapt attention of Burberry's servants—the ones who were already watching and a few more who had piled into the kitchen to see what all the fuss was—made that impossible.

"None of us can be who we are not," Cameron said, meeting Samuel's eyes for a moment before turning away.

"I don't even know who I am anymore," Samuel called out in frustration.

"Of course you do, darling," Sammy said as she swept into the room. The servants all scattered. Cameron paused before stepping out into the courtyard, curious to hear what she would say. "You're Samuel Percy, world-famous composer and musician. And you have an adoring public waiting upstairs for you to make the announcement of your sister's engagement to Mr. Burberry."

A few of the servants gasped in surprise, though to Cameron's eyes, they seemed a little horrified at the prospect of getting a new mistress. Cameron glanced to Samuel once more, as if asking him why he was hesitating. His audience awaited.

Samuel's mouth worked wordlessly for a moment as he glanced between Cameron and his sister. At last, he huffed out a breath, rubbed a hand over his face, and told Cameron, "We'll talk about this when I return home."

That was all the answer Cameron needed, though he doubted it was the one Samuel thought he was giving. The choice had been made, and it was not Cameron.

Samuel was who he was. He was a glittering curiosity, as odd as anything Sammy had in his house, but one that belonged with the sort of people Burberry was friends with. He would never be the man Cameron needed to stand by him for the rest of his life.

With a sad nod, Cameron turned and continued out into the cold, February night. Without his coat—or rather, the one Sammy had pulled out of her late husband's things, since she'd deemed his own coat not good enough—the walk home to Thorne Hall was almost painfully cold. Or perhaps that was merely the disappointment over Samuel that wouldn't leave Cameron alone. He'd had so much hope. Samuel had showed so much promise when the two of them were together. He'd been reluctant to let Cameron leave his bed in the morning, almost as if he wanted merely the feeling of the two of them together, without the imminence of sex to distract them. It had almost been as though Cameron could finally close his eyes and rest in a lover's arms, knowing that he would be safe and cared for.

He would never truly be safe or cared for, though. Which meant all he had to look forward to was a life spent looking out for himself. It could be a good life. Working for John provided him with an income. He would still send money home to his family, but perhaps he could keep enough to find a suitable flat instead of just a room in a boarding house. He didn't need sex. He'd had enough of it as a means of survival to last a lifetime. He could have his safety in keeping himself to himself.

By the time he reached Thorne Hall, he knew that would never work, but neither did he have a solution. He would just have to muddle on until he came up with one. That started with returning to London. Tonight.

"Where are the rest of them?" Archibald asked before he had made it across the front hall to the stairs. Archibald glanced toward the door, as if Samuel and Sammy would walk through.

"They're still at Burberry's," Cameron said. He hesitated with one foot on the bottom stair, then said, "Did you know this whole thing was some sort of bet that Mrs. Thorne and Burberry made so Mrs. Thorne could get Burberry to marry her?"

"What?" Archibald's reaction was so violent that Cameron had his answer without having to hear a specific "No."

Cameron nodded. "Mrs. Thorne was hoping you'd come up with the idea of looking for the Grasmere contract on your own. The bet was whether she could find it in Burberry's house." He paused before saying, "She won because I found it, and now she and Burberry are getting married."

"So the whole thing has been for nothing," Archibald said, pale and splotchy with fury, gripping the sides of his head. "All these weeks I've spent trapped here, all of my efforts to turn sows' ears into silk purses for her. She was using me as a piece of a prank, and all for nothing?"

The madness of the evening and the heartbreak that still had Cameron off-balance made him reckless. "Did you find a way to embezzle the money you want from Mrs. Thorne?" he asked bluntly.

Archibald turned a whole different shade of puce as he stared at Cameron. Then he closed his mouth and swallowed. "Yes."

Cameron nodded. "Do you have any of that money now?"

Archibald's eyes grew rounder. "Yes."

"I'm going to pack my things and head for London immediately," Cameron said. "I wasn't sure where I was going to find the money to pay for my train fare. I probably would have done something desperate. But if you're willing to pay our way, I'll figure out how to get you out of the house without any of Mrs. Thorne's staff stopping us."

Archibald dashed forward and was halfway up the stairs before Cameron made it to the second step. "I'll be ready in ten minutes."

Ten minutes was all it took. Cameron had brought so little with him that it was the work of seconds to stuff it all into his traveling bag. He didn't bother changing out of his fine suit, figuring his more refined appearance could only help him once they reached the train station. He tried not to think about what he was doing as he closed his case and marched back through the house, meeting a flushed and harried Archibald at the top of the stairs. Archibald, too, only had a small valise with him.

"Is that all you have?" Cameron asked, steering Archibald away from the main stairs and off toward a side hall. Mr. Lee was lingering in the hall below, waiting for Sammy and the others to come home, and he would surely try to stop them if he knew what the two were up to.

"You forget," Archibald growled, a light of determination in his eyes. "I was kidnapped out of Hyde Park without anything at all. Everything I have here was purchased for me by that harpy."

Cameron nodded. He didn't need to know more. He found a quiet servants' staircase and gestured for Archibald to follow him down. But when they made it to the downstairs hall, one of the burly guards who Sammy had hired to watch over Archibald was there, chatting up one of the maids. As silently as he could, Cameron gestured for Archibald to follow him back upstairs.

"I should have warned you that the harpy has all of the doors in her house guarded by those men for my sake," Archibald grumbled.

"How about the windows?" Cameron asked in a whisper, heading to the unused parlor across from the servants' stairs.

"We won't know unless we try," Archibald said.

They did try, and they were successful. The parlor window stuck a bit, but between the two of them, they managed to get it open. There was a small, uncomfortable drop into darkness, but when Archibald—who was so eager to escape that he went first—didn't injure himself, Cameron jumped out after him.

"Why didn't you climb out a window before?"

Cameron whispered as they scurried across the frosty garden, keeping to the shadows.

Archibald took a moment to answer, and when they stepped into a patch of light cast by a streetlight on the other side of the garden wall, Cameron could see he wore a sheepish look. "I didn't think of it," Archibald mumbled. "And I thought perhaps I could find a bit more cash to…to compensate myself with."

Cameron would have frowned in disapproval if that money wasn't exactly what would get them back to London. As far as he was concerned, money truly was the root of all evil. He wouldn't complain for the rest of his life if he never had more of it than he needed to put food on his plate and a roof over his head.

Once they were away from Thorne Hall, their flight became easier. It was a bit of a walk to the train station, but no one seemed to question two men with suitcases making their way there. It wasn't so late at night that the trains had stopped running, and by the time they reached the station, Archibald had recovered enough to walk banally up to the ticket window to purchase two first-class tickets back to London.

"Why did you bother with first-class?" Cameron asked, once they were ensconced in their compartment and the train rolled out of the station. "Third would have been fine."

Archibald laughed. "With the money I have in my possession now, why not go first-class?" He sent Cameron a smug look. "Besides, I'd rather not be disturbed by porters and pesky fellow travelers."

Cameron had the feeling Archibald would rather not have been disturbed by him on the journey as well. Archibald didn't say another word, and once they were away from Derby with the train rocking gently and making a steady *cluh-clack cluh-clack cluh-clack* sound as it wound through the countryside, Archibald tucked himself into a corner, lowered his hat over his eyes, and fell asleep.

Cameron couldn't sleep. The anxiety of everything he'd done was almost as overpowering as the angst of why he'd done it. Samuel might be angry when he returned to Thorne Hall and found him gone. He might be hurt. Either way, the farther they got from Derby, the guiltier Cameron felt.

At least, where Samuel was concerned. As far as getting away from the insanity of Burberry and Sammy and their gambles and plots and schemes, Cameron couldn't get far enough fast enough. He never wanted to see either of the mad couple again. He would have written Derby off entirely, if Georgie and her family didn't live there. Perhaps there was a way he could convince them to move to London and set up a printing business there.

He drifted off into a light sleep on those thoughts. When he awoke, it was still dark, and he had no idea how much time had passed. Archibald had slumped in his seat, proving that he was very much asleep. That gave

Cameron an idea. He wasn't entirely comfortable with the idea, but at the same time, he didn't want the entire journey to be a bust.

As carefully as he could, he reached for Archibald's traveling bag as it sat on the seat beside him. Archibald didn't stir as Cameron picked it up and transferred it to his lap, so he went ahead, undoing the buckles and fastenings and prying it open. There was no telling how long it might take to find what he was looking for. He shifted through a few items of clothing and some toiletries, finally finding papers at the bottom of the bag. Cameron's eyes went wide at the stack of bills he found tucked into an envelope—apparently, Archibald's efforts to steal from Sammy had been extraordinarily fruitful—then narrowed as he found exactly what he was looking for.

It was simply a piece of paper with an address scrawled on it. An address in London. There was no way to be entirely certain it was the address where Lady Selby was staying, but Cameron could see the entire map of London in his mind, and the street listed on the slip of paper in his hand was a refined neighborhood north of Oxford Street. He searched deeper in Archibald's bag, looking for anything else that might indicate Archibald's plans regarding Lady Selby and Lord Stanley, but found nothing. Archibald hadn't brought the shipping timetable Cameron had seen him with a week before. But the address was good enough. It was a place to start.

He put everything back in the traveling case the way

it should be, then returned the case to Archibald's side. He then spent the rest of the journey debating how he should confront Archibald about Lady Selby.

As it happened, Cameron counted himself extraordinarily lucky that he'd searched Archibald's things and found the address. As soon as the train came to a stop in St. Pancras Station just as dawn peeked through the wide windows above, Archibald was out of his seat, opening their compartment door.

"I would be grateful if you could tell me where Lady Selby and Lord Stanley are, and if you'd be willing to return Lord Stanley to his father," Cameron said, following Archibald down to the platform.

Archibald glanced over his shoulder at Cameron as they made their way from the platform to the heart of the station. "Are you mad? If I tell you, then Selby and that deviant, Cristofori, will be pounding down my door, threatening to have me arrested within the hour."

"They just want Lord Stanley back," Cameron insisted. "I think Lord Selby is even eager to give Lady Selby a divorce, so—"

Archibald didn't give Cameron a chance to finish making the case. He clapped a hand to his hat and broke into a run as soon as they passed the partition and were in the station proper. Cameron was too stunned at first to do anything but gape. Archibald darted through the nearest door and into the street.

Cameron followed him, but he knew in an instant that Archibald had done what they'd all said he would do the moment he had his freedom. He'd bolted, and he'd disappeared. Cameron couldn't find him in the crush and swirl of early-morning commuters making their way to and from St. Pancras Station, or just passing by in their hurry to get where they were going. It was too dark still to get a clear view of the street in front of the station. As predicted, Archibald had slipped out of their grasp once again. But at least this time Cameron had the address of where they could begin to search for him.

CHAPTER 18

It didn't mean anything. All of the glittering diamonds around the necks of the ladies who approached Samuel to congratulate him at the end of Burberry's concert, all of the approving smiles from gentlemen in tailored suits, all of the silk and lace swirling around him, the offers of society and acceptance —none of it meant a damn thing.

"Smile, Samuel," Sammy whispered in his ear as the two of them and Burberry made the rounds through the conservatory once the final applause died down and the orchestra packed up their things to go. Simple musicians weren't worthy of the time or attention of the wealthy and titled classes, after all. "You would think you were on your way to the gallows instead of being embraced by the very best Derbyshire has to offer."

Sammy primped and preened for those people whom she saw as the best. The announcement of her sudden engagement to Burberry had gone over well with Burberry's guests, as did the novelty of having a black composer of such renown in their midst. Sammy lapped it all up, smiling with false modesty and alternating between hanging off of Burberry's arm, simpering at him as though she were in love, and clinging to Samuel while gazing up at him with sisterly pride. It was all an act, of course. The only thing Sammy cared about was the victory of convincing a man she despised to marry her and the prospect of being mistress of all his money.

Samuel used the excuse of shaking the hand of some old man, who winked and laughed, as though he understood the great joke that had been played on them all by introducing a black man into society, to pull away from his sister. He was exactly where he'd always thought he wanted to be, celebrated and praised by the top tier of the English country gentry, but all he could think about was Cameron. He would have taken an afternoon of sitting with Cameron's sister and her family in their cozy kitchen, sipping tea and eating biscuits, to the glittering fool's gold he found himself surrounded by now.

He'd hurt Cameron. Everything he'd done, even the way he'd wrapped Cameron in pleasure when he'd taken the brilliant young man to bed, had been an injury. The false gleam of the world Samuel was trapped in the middle of was an affront to everything that made Cameron the unique and wonderful man he was. Cameron had been implying—or saying outright—all along that he deserved better. Cameron deserved better than an offer to fuck out of spite for the rest of the world. He deserved a man who would see how perfect he was in his quiet imperfections, who could make him feel safe and appreciated, not lusted after like a prize. Like Sammy saw Burberry.

That final comparison struck him as he was attempting to accept the praise of a fresh-faced, innocent young woman who had apparently attended with her mother. The poor girl gazed up at Samuel in awe, glanced around her as though the false opulence of Burberry's conservatory were a palace. All Samuel wanted to do was lean in to whisper in the poor girl's ear, "Run. Run as far and as fast to get away from this life as you can."

What he said instead as soon as the woman and her mother moved on was, "I want to go home."

He turned to address the remark to his sister, but deep in his soul, it felt as though he were making the complaint to the universe. He wanted to go home, to have a home to go to. He wanted to walk through his own front door and find Cameron waiting for him, just home from an honest day's work at Dandie's office, shirtsleeves rolled up, handsome smile painting his relaxed face as he cooked supper for the two of them in their own kitchen. He didn't even know if Cameron could cook, but he would have been willing to wager that he could. The two of them would sit across from each other at the kitchen table, talking about the cares of their days, as if such small things truly mattered. Perhaps they would stay up for a bit reading—individually or to each other—before climbing a simple, narrow staircase to their bedroom. They would make love with all of the knowledge of how each of them liked to be touched instead of just fucking until they were satisfied. Then they would fall asleep in each other's arms, confident that the next day would bring them just as much contentment and light as the one before.

"By God, I want to go home," Samuel repeated, breaking away from his sister and marching toward the conservatory door.

"Samuel, you cannot just walk out before we're done with you," Sammy said with an annoyed snap in her voice. She picked up her skirts and followed after him, sending apologetic looks to those of Burberry's guests who wondered why a black man was charging through their midst.

"Artists," Burberry laughed as Samuel turned to leave the room, clearly thrilled that he could command everyone's attention on his own now. "They are terribly eccentric, aren't they?"

Burberry's guests laughed. Samuel laughed as well, but without humor. Burberry—and Samuel's sister—took eccentricity to an entirely higher plane with their antics.

"Samuel, you are embarrassing me," Sammy hissed once they reached the front hall.

One of Burberry's footmen ducked away to fetch Samuel's coat when he asked, then Samuel turned to his sister. "Samantha, you have been an embarrassment to me since the moment we set foot on English soil."

"I beg your pardon?" Sammy clapped an offended hand to her breast.

"You are selfish, fickle, willful, and shallow. And after this evening, I'm beginning to think you are genuinely mad as well." It felt uncommonly good to finally say those things aloud.

Sammy snapped her back straight and attempted to look down her nose at Samuel, even though he was taller. "And what is wrong with wanting to live a comfortable, interesting life, surrounded by pretty, expensive things, highlighted by unique amusements?" she demanded.

"The fact that you have no qualms about hurting people to win that life for yourself," Samuel said, accepting his coat from the footman and putting it and his hat on. "The fact that you love wealth and status and collecting things so much that you are willing to marry a vile man who you don't even like in order to have it all."

"And what is so horrible about that?" Sammy went on, still defiant. "Women have been marrying horrible men to secure their comfort since the dawn of time. They have been forced to marry them as well. And considering the plight of our grandparents and ancestors, everything they went through, why shouldn't I be the one to take advantage of these people?"

"Because it makes you just as horrible a person as they are," Samuel said.

He was finished with the conversation, finished with a lot of things. He turned sharply and marched out of Burberry's door as the footman held it for him, hoping he never had to see Burberry again. He walked back to Thorne Hall in the dark, already making plans in his mind to gather up Cameron and their things, head to the train station, and catch whatever train would take them back to London, or as far away from Derby as possible. But first, he would beg Cameron's forgiveness. He'd get down on his knees if he had to. He had a great deal to learn when it came to matters of the heart, but finally, after what felt like his entire lifetime of listening to the orchestra inside of him tune, he was ready to compose his magnum opus, his love song.

Thorne Hall seemed exceptionally quiet, compared to the fuss and chaos of Burberry's house. Samuel took it as a good sign. He didn't bother shrugging out of his coat or taking off his hat as Mr. Lee met him at the door. He headed straight up the stairs, taking them two at a time, and down the hall to his bedroom. When he reached his room he did remove his coat, but only then to ease his movements as he threw open the wardrobe to take out his things. His suitcase rested at the bottom of the wardrobe, and he took that out first, throwing it open with a feeling of satisfaction that reached deep inside him.

"Cameron," he called toward the door separating their rooms, "pack your things. We're going back to London."

A smile touched Samuel's lips as he raced around the room, gathering his things to throw into the suitcase. He didn't even care if they were folded or crumpled as long as he could pack them away quickly. The more he worked, the more desperately he wanted to get away from his sister's house and the madness of Derby.

"Cameron, come on," he called to the door again. "I know you're eager to get out of this asylum. Get out of bed and pack your things. We're going home." It felt so good to say that Samuel's smile widened.

That same smile faltered a few moments later when there wasn't so much as a single thump from the other room. He knew Cameron was angry with him, but he didn't think the man was *that* angry. He finished his packing, closed his suitcase, then marched to the door.

"Cameron?" he asked as he pulled the door open.

His heart nearly stopped as he glanced into the adjacent guest room. It was empty. A fire was still lit, but there were no lanterns. The fire alone was enough to see that the bed was not only unoccupied, it was perfectly made. Samuel stepped deeper into the room, glancing around as though Cameron might be hiding in a corner. The room was completely empty, though. Worse still, when Samuel checked the wardrobe, he found that empty as well.

"Cameron?" he murmured, fear lacing his voice.

His plaintive question wasn't going to be answered. Cameron was gone. Samuel shouldn't have been surprised. He'd known the young man was miserable in Derby. He'd known it was only a matter of time before Cameron stopped putting up with the shite that people kept throwing at him and marched off to claim his own life. But the fact that he'd done it without him was enough to bring Samuel to his knees.

He raced back into his room, throwing on his coat and hat again and grabbing his suitcase. He ran out of his room, charging down the hall and the stairs, even though a voice of reason at the back of his head told him rushing wouldn't do anyone any good. He had to find Cameron, had to explain everything that had happened and everything he'd realized about himself. He wouldn't be able to live with himself if he let Cameron walk out of his life without so much as an explanation.

"Where is he?" Sammy's voice demanded from the top of the grand staircase just as Samuel reached the bottom.

Samuel whipped around, nearly tripping down the last few stairs. He hadn't realized Sammy had left Burberry's house right behind him. She'd likely had the advantage of her carriage and might have arrived moments after he had.

"Where is that lying, cheating bastard?" Sammy repeated, marching down the stairs to meet him.

Fury like nothing Samuel had ever known raced through him. "I will not have you speaking about Cameron in such language," he boomed. He dropped his suitcase and stormed up the stairs to face her. "Cameron is the sweetest, most lovely, most tragic man I've ever known. Your Burberry has made his life a living hell, and I will not have you turning around and calling Cameron names because of it."

He grabbed Sammy's arms and shook her. "He deserves so much better than this," Samuel insisted. "He deserves comfort and peace, a life of ease and friendship and love. He deserves to be treated with all the respect that people claim they are giving me when they bow and simper while secretly laughing behind their hands. Cameron deserves more than your derision."

Sammy gaped and blinked and shrank away from Samuel, not out of any pain or discomfort Samuel was inflicting—he was being far more careful with his sister than he should have been—but out of pure shock. "I meant Archibald," she said at last, her voice high and offended.

Samuel let go of her and stepped down a stair. "Oh."

Sammy rolled her shoulders, peering down at him. Clearly, she was done with him, but her expression held a certain amount of emotion, perhaps even compassion. She stepped down one step, then another. "You love that young man, don't you?" she asked.

Every one of Samuel's instincts screamed at him to deny it. He hadn't gotten to where he was—in society or the musical world—by admitting to unpopular truths. But he owed it to Cameron. "Yes," he said with a nod. "I do."

Sammy let out a sharp, "Hmm." She stared hard at Samuel. "I don't think I've ever seen you in love before."

"That's because I've never been in love before," Samuel replied snappishly.

Sammy narrowed her eyes at him. "What's different about this man, then?" she asked. "Why him and not any other lover you've had." A slight falter in her glance seemed to be asking Samuel, "Why not me?"

Samuel swallowed, holding Sammy's gaze, and said, "Because he has the kindest heart of anyone I've ever known. Because life has handed him nothing but misfortune, and he has risen above it all, keeping his integrity intact, even when he's been forced to do unfortunate things to survive. Because he is all heart, and because he doesn't want anything other than peace."

"Unlike the two of us," Sammy said, her mouth pulling into an odd shape—as if she were trying to sneer, but was too genuinely touched by what Samuel had said to manage the reaction. She took a breath and shifted her stance. "You and I have had terrible lives," she went on.

Samuel frowned. "How so?"

Sammy shrugged sadly. "Look at how we were raised. We were never a part of anything, not even our own family, really. We've never looked right, never sounded right. You sought your redemption in your talent. I sought mine in catching the eye of wealthy men who could secure my comfort. Neither of us has the first clue what we're doing, though."

"No, we don't," Samuel admitted on a sigh.

"Because we were never taught how to love," she went on.

She was right. Even now, as Samuel looked at her in all her finery, hearing the wisest words she'd ever spoken, but still feeling as distant from her as though he'd stayed in Barbados, he knew she was right. It almost hurt that, while he knew she was his sister and had shared their mother's womb with him, she didn't feel like family. Not at all.

Sammy rested a hand on his arm. "Go chase after your young man," she said. "Catch him and get him to teach you what love is. Because you're not going to learn it any other way. You certainly won't learn it from me." She drew her hand away and fixed him with a sly grin.

It was the strangest feeling Samuel had ever had. Something connected him and Sammy, but it wasn't the bonds of family or love, or even friendship. The list of things about his sister that revolted him was far longer than the list of things he cared for in her. And in his gut, he had the feeling that once he walked out the door of Thorne Hall, he would never see her again. But in that moment, he was grateful to her in ways he couldn't quite put his finger on. As mad as the entire interlude under her roof had been, it had changed his life in ways he hoped were good.

"Thank you, Sammy," he said. He hesitated. It felt wrong to hug her, but just as wrong to stand there staring at her. In the end, he settled for resting a hand on her shoulder. "Have a good life," he told her, then winked and added, "Or, at least, have the life you want to live."

"Oh, I will," she said with a mischievous grin.

Samuel turned and headed back down the stairs. He picked up his suitcase at the bottom, then continued on to where Mr. Lee was standing ready at the door.

"Samuel," Sammy called after him. When Samuel

turned back to her, she said, "If you find Archibald, tell that impertinent little devil that I know he stole a small fortune from me, and if I ever catch him, I'll do far worse than keep him locked in the comfort of my house for the rest of his wretched life."

Samuel actually smiled at her threat. "I'll tell him. Though if I do catch him, you might have to wait in a queue of people who want to give him what for."

Sammy returned his promise with a lopsided smile, then headed up the stairs.

Samuel swept out the front door and into the cold, February night, turning his steps toward the train station. He hoped it wasn't too late to catch the last train back to London. He would have manned the boiler himself—if one still did that sort of thing with trains—to get them to the city faster. His whole life and his heart waited for him in London. He only hoped it wasn't too late for him to make amends with Cameron and beg the man to show him how to live the life he truly wanted.

CHAPTER 19

Mrs. Fielding locked the boarding house at eleven every night, and not even a storm or a flood could convince her to unlock it until six in the morning. That meant that Cameron spent the better part of an hour sitting on the cold step, dressed in a fine but rumpled suit, waiting for the door to be unlocked before he could drag himself into the marginal warmth of the drafty front hall.

"And just what do you think you're doing, sitting out on my front stoop like a vagabond?" Mrs. Fielding barked at him once she had him inside. "You've been sitting out there all night, I'd wager, letting all the other vagrants think they can get away with darkening my door."

"I'm terribly sorry, Mrs. Fielding," Cameron mumbled, exhausted from getting so little sleep and sore from the time he'd spent sitting in the cold. "I've just returned from a work trip up north. I wasn't expecting the train to reach London at the hour it did."

It wasn't precisely a lie. He hadn't expected the train to reach London so early because he hadn't planned the journey at all. Just thinking about everything that had happened the night before and the aches it had caused in his soul made Cameron even wearier than he was. Nothing seemed to want to go right in his life.

"I won't have it, do you hear me?" Mrs. Fielding harangued him as he plodded up the stairs to his room. Cameron noted a few of her other boarders poking their heads out of the dining room to see what was going on, much the same way that Burberry's servants had watched his confrontation with Samuel in Burberry's kitchen. "I won't have you lounging about, lazy as you please, in a suit you likely stole, making other wretches think I run a home for the indigent."

Cameron objected to being called lazy, and to the assumption that he was a thief and loitering for his own enjoyment, but he was too exhausted to argue.

Except that Mrs. Fielding seemed intent on picking a fight. "I'm not here to cater to your sort," she continued, following Cameron all the way to the door of his room. "I run a respectable establishment, I do. I won't go having men like you taking up space that other, more decent fellows might have."

"And what sort am I exactly, Mrs. Fielding?" Cameron asked as he reached his door and opened it. He felt so brittle and so raw that it was all he could do not to shout at the woman the way he wanted to shout at the entire, cruel world for being so unfair to him.

Mrs. Fielding seemed surprised by his question. She rocked back, blinking at him for a moment. "Why, you're a good for nothing lay about," she said, as though it were obvious. "All young men like you are."

"Like me?" Cameron pressed her, close to hyperventilating with indignity and impatience.

Mrs. Fielding blinked again. "You know. Young men from the country. Duffers and tosspots and the like."

Cameron clenched his jaw to marshal his patience. He was tired of being treated as somehow lesser because he was a country lad. He was tired of being looked down on because of whom he wanted to go to bed with, even if Mrs. Fielding didn't have the first clue about that part of his life. And he was completely done-in by the way people like Mrs. Fielding thought anyone who wasn't as rich as the queen was worthless. He'd seen how wealthy people deported themselves, and even though it might have made him vain, he was a damned sight better than the lot of them.

He took a breath to stop himself from exploding with all the resentment he'd kept bottled for so long, then said, "Mrs. Fielding, have I ever paid my rent past due?"

"Er, no," Mrs. Fielding said.

"Have I ever had guests when I wasn't supposed to, or had alcohol on the premises or come home drunk and slovenly?"

"N-no, you haven't." Mrs. Fielding hunched her shoulders, looking sheepish.

"Have I made a mess of my room or left unmentionable laundry where I shouldn't?"

Mrs. Fielding let out a breath, her face softening. "No, lad. You've been just fine." She bit her lip. "Forgive this old woman for being set in her ways and her prejudices."

Cameron relented with a sigh. "We're all set in our ways and our prejudices, ma'am," he said. "But I'll be moving out by the end of the week."

Mrs. Fielding looked shocked, and indeed, Cameron felt shocked. He hadn't known he would take that sort of action until he'd opened his mouth. But the truth was that if he truly thought he deserved better, like he'd been telling himself all along, he would need to be the one to start treating himself better first. And that began with finding himself a tidy little flat, like his heart truly wanted, instead of living at someone else's mercy in a rented room. There had to be something in Darlington Gardens that would suit him.

As soon as he shut the door to his room behind him and tossed his suitcase on the chair, Cameron dragged himself to his bed and flopped on it, not caring that he was still dressed. He fell straight to sleep without even climbing under the bedcovers. It was the most glorious and hard-won nap he'd had in his life.

That life felt as though it were pressing in around him again as he rose an hour later, washed, dressed in clean clothes, then left for the city and work. All he wanted was for his life to settle into the quiet pattern it had fallen into after he'd started working for John, but before Samuel had come along. He would be content to muddle his way through John's paperwork for the rest of his life and to confuse himself over the various legal briefings John asked him to sort through.

At least, that was what he told himself. The moment he stepped into John's office, his heart wasn't so certain. The office was filled with subtle reminders of Samuel, and in the most paradoxical of places. His eyes were immediately drawn to the hat rack where Samuel had hung his coat when he'd come to discuss the matter of his sister, the edge of the sofa where he'd sat, the small stove where Cameron had broken a teacup at the mention of Burberry's name. And chances were that the next time Cameron went to The Chameleon Club, he'd be reminded of the way he and Samuel had flirted—back when he was too shy to do more than smile at Samuel. Worse still, he might even come face to face with Samuel in the club, and then what would he do?

John strode out of his office—presumably because he heard the door open and shut—and his mildly expectant look turned to pure surprise at the sight of Cameron. "You're back," he said with a welcoming smile.

Cameron nodded, and John's smile dropped to a look of concern.

"What happened?" John asked.

"Everything," Cameron sighed. "Nothing." He began

to shuffle toward the stove to fix himself tea—seeing as he hadn't had breakfast, or anything else since the bits of supper he'd managed to eat at Burberry's the night before.

John waved him away from the stove. "Sit. I'll fix your tea. And tell me what happened in more detail. You look like you've been run through a wringer."

"I feel like I have as well." Cameron did as John ordered him, but he couldn't bring himself to sit on the sofa. That was where clients sat. Instead, he perched on the edge of the desk. He glanced over at the piles of paperwork waiting there for him and gave it all a vague smile. Thank God he would have something to do, even if most of the work John gave him was a complicated bundle of words he didn't know the meanings for and legal things that baffled him.

John approached him with a warm cup of milky tea and a worried frown. "Were you able to locate Ian Archibald?"

"Oh, yes," Cameron said with a wary look. He took a long drink of tea, feeling as though it might just be enough to heal his soul, before going on. "Archibald was staying at Mrs. Thorne's house."

"So you found Samuel's sister without a problem?" John asked, his concerned look deepening.

Cameron hid his bitter, heartbroken reaction by taking another sip of tea.

"Oh, dear." It was all John had to say to convey that he had a suspicion of how things had gone.

"I will be polite to my former hostess and simply say the woman is as barmy as a bag of toads," Cameron said.

John's brow shot up. "That's being polite?"

"I wouldn't know where to begin to explain the rest of it," Cameron said, finishing his tea.

John took the cup from him. "Do you want another one?" he asked in a careful voice.

Cameron started to shake his head no—two cups of tea was decadent, and he was just a lowly clerk who didn't understand his job half the time—but he changed his mind and nodded. "Yes, please."

John stepped away from him to fetch more tea, but asked, "So what makes Samuel's sister so much like barmy toads?"

John was likely trying to put Cameron at ease, but ease was the furthest thing from Cameron's mind. "Not that the details are particularly important, but she ended up leading me and Samuel on a merry chase over a debt that turned out not to be a debt, but a wager."

John brought the fresh cup of tea to Cameron, and as he handed it over, he asked, "What did that wager have to do with Ian Archibald and our search for Lady Selby and Lord Stanley?"

"Absolutely fuck all," Cameron said bitterly. He hid his embarrassment for cursing in front of John by starting in on his second tea.

"I'm not sure I understand." John tucked his hands under his arms and stood back, studying Cameron with a frown.

"I don't understand any of it either," Cameron admitted. "It was a mistake to go up there. The whole thing ended up being a right royal cock-up."

John continued to stare at him, though his expression changed to a different sort of curiosity. "Did something happen between you and Samuel?"

A sizzle of self-consciousness shot down Cameron's spine. "Did you send us up there together just so that something would happen?"

It was John's turn to look self-conscious. He covered it with a hopeful grin. "Did it work?"

"Depends on what you were hoping to see happen," Cameron said. Now that he had tea in him and had warmed up, all he wanted to do was slump into a blob on the desk. "Did we end up in bed? Yes. Yes, we did."

John's brow lifted hopefully. "And?"

Cameron didn't want to be angry with the man. He owed his life and his livelihood to John. Without John, he'd still be whoring himself out as a telegraph boy, or worse. But the man was an unforgivable bastard if he'd deliberately set him up for something to happen with Samuel.

"Was it your intention that Samuel make it clear to me that he just wanted a bit of a tumble and that he would rather rub shoulders with toffs and nutters—or thumb his nose at them by breaking all the rules of society in a handy water closet somewhere—instead of just being with someone he might love in a peaceful life?" Cameron asked on.

"Oh, dear," John said again, with more feeling. He dropped his arms and lowered his shoulders. "I'm sorry, Cameron. I thought Samuel only enjoyed that sort of nonsense for show. I didn't think he was genuinely committed to it."

"I'm not."

Cameron nearly jumped out of his skin at the realization that Samuel was standing in the doorway. More than that. He'd entered the office at some point during the conversation and stepped close enough to hear.

John recovered long before Cameron could, turning to Samuel with an uneasy smile and saying, "Samuel. You're back as well."

"I am." Samuel nodded, though is eyes were fixed firmly on Cameron.

Cameron stood straight, fumbling his teacup and splashing tea on his trousers as he did. His hand was shaking, so he sat the cup on the desk before saying, "I don't think I have anything left to say to you."

Samuel took another step toward him, shrugging out of his coat and throwing that and his hat over the sofa. "Well, I have a great deal left to say to you."

Uneasiness and hope twisted up Cameron's insides. At the same time, he wasn't willing to indulge that hope. He felt as though he'd been through everything with Samuel already, heard his promises and been disappointed with his unwillingness to change. But he was drawn to the man all the same, stepping away from the desk and forcing himself to have the courage to look Samuel in the eye.

"I was wrong to ask for what I did at Burberry's house last night," Samuel said. "I knew I was wrong the moment the suggestion came out of my mouth. I only said it because I was so enraged by the hypocrisy of the people gathering around Burberry, like flies around offal."

Cameron swallowed, then found himself breathing shallowly. It felt very much like Samuel was about to say all the things he wanted to hear. But was it just that? Just pretty words that Samuel knew he wanted to hear?

Samuel took another step closer to him. "I should have caught on to my sister's games and Burberry's wickedness far sooner than I did," he went on. "I should have taken you out of that mess the moment I knew how much of a mess it was."

Cameron opened his mouth to argue, though he wasn't certain what he might actually say. Should he argue against the way Samuel let himself get caught up in other people's schemes because they gave him a chance to perform, which was what Samuel did for a living, or should he argue that Samuel failed to protect him from Burberry when that wasn't his responsibility in the first place?

He didn't get a chance to say anything. Samuel took another step closer, a step that brought him so close that Cameron imagined he could feel the heat pouring off of him. "I know you think that all I want is the acclaim of a public life and the pleasures that wealth and influence bring with it. I would have said that was what I wanted as well, until I met you."

He reached out, resting a hand on the side of Cameron's face. Every bit of the sensual joy that he'd felt with Samuel, whether it had fit into his picture of morality or not, floated back through Cameron. The tenderness and the guilt in Samuel's eyes showered sparks through him, but sparks had a way of hurting when there were too many of them.

"For so long, I have been so intent on proving to everyone around me that I am worthy of their praise, regardless of the color of my skin, that I have lost sight of what truly matters," Samuel went on in a softer voice.

"And what does matter?" Cameron asked, feeling strangely stronger. For once, he felt as though he knew something Samuel didn't, the answer to his own question. Because *he* mattered. To himself, at least. And for far too long, he'd pretended he didn't.

"You," Samuel said with a simple shrug, a smile coming to his eyes. "You and your clever mind and your simple wishes. You matter, Cameron. You matter to me."

His words were lovely, but Cameron couldn't put all of his trust in just words. "Thank you for saying that," he managed to mumble through the awkwardness that twisted his insides.

Samuel surprised him with a wry grin. "But you don't believe me, do you."

"How can I?" Cameron asked. "We've been down this path before."

"How about this path?" Samuel stepped fully into him, clasping his hands on either side of Cameron's face. "Will this convince you of my sincerity and of how much you've come to mean to me?"

He slanted his mouth over Cameron's, kissing him with tenderness at first, then with passion when Cameron didn't pull away. Cameron couldn't have pulled away if he'd wanted to. It felt so good to be cared for, to be loved, even if it was just an illusion. Perhaps most startling of all, Samuel wasn't kissing him in some hidden back corner of another man's house or in the privacy of a bedroom, they were kissing in the middle of John's office, with John standing right there, watching, in full daylight. There was a sort of declaration in the kiss that hadn't been there in Derby, and more than anything, Cameron wanted to give himself over to it. He wanted to believe that Samuel was sincere.

But mostly, he wanted to be kissed. If he were honest with himself, he wanted more than that. Because he could still remember what it felt like to be skin to skin with Samuel and to feel encompassed in the man's ardor. Perhaps his newfound self-respect could extend to respecting himself enough to lay claim to what he wanted when he wanted it.

He didn't have a chance to make a decision on the subject. Just as Samuel made a sound of relief and anticipation and shifted to close his arms around Cameron, John's office door flew open. Cameron felt the old, frighteningly-familiar terror of being found with a man all over again. He pushed away from Samuel so fast and hard that he stumbled backward, knocking painfully into the desk. Samuel had to catch him to keep him from falling over, which only meant they found themselves back in each other's arms in an even more ridiculous way.

"Oh. Terribly sorry. I didn't realize this was the witching hour," Arthur Gleason said as he stepped the rest of the way into the office with a smarmy look.

"What do you want, Gleason?" John asked, his voice sharp and his eyes suddenly filled with fire. He marched past Gleason to shut the office door, giving them all privacy. Though Cameron suspected it was just as likely that crossing the room was John's way of getting closer to Gleason.

"I've come to tell you that I've found Annamarie Williamson," Gleason said. "Or rather, I've discovered that she will not be found."

In an instant, nothing else mattered. Cameron scrambled out of Samuel's arms and stood straight, brushing a hand over his suit.

"What is that supposed to mean?" John asked, rounding on Gleason with wide eyes. "Where is she?"

"I can tell you where she's not," Gleason said, his expression growing more serious. "She's not in London anymore. She's already slipped away."

CHAPTER 20

Samuel was still shaken and brittle from everything that declaring himself to Cameron had taken out of him. And he hadn't really had a chance to do it properly yet. He had so much more to say, so many more kisses to bestow, and mountains of forgiveness for being a callous boor to beg for. But all of that was rendered unimportant by Gleason's interruption and John and Cameron's reaction to it.

"What do you mean she's slipped away?" John took another step closer to Gleason, red splashing his face.

John was several inches taller than Gleason and broader as well, but Gleason radiated a certain amount of power and cunning that made him seem to loom larger than John. "I mean just that," he said. "I tracked down the nursemaid Lady Selby hired to care for Lord Stanley at last and extracted a confession from her."

An uneasy feeling slithered down Samuel's back.

"How did you manage that?" he asked, eyeing Gleason warily. Gleason had stooped low enough to work for Sammy just a few months before to locate the Egyptian medallion Blake had once owned, therefore, Samuel figured he was capable of committing numerous other atrocities, such as harming a woman to find out what he wanted to know.

Gleason seemed to see right through Samuel. He sent him a sour look, then said, "I bribed her with sweets and flowers." His gaze traveled past Samuel to Cameron and seemed to relent a bit at the horrified look Cameron wore. "And enough money so that she can set up the bake shop she's been wanting to start with her sister for years now." He turned toward John. "It's all about uncovering the background of your mark and learning what will cause them to betray their employer's secrets."

"But what good does that do if all you discover is that the woman has already left London?" Samuel asked, unimpressed with Gleason's air for the dramatic. He crossed his arms and waited for an answer.

"She hasn't been gone for long," Gleason answered with narrowed eyes, looking irritated that Samuel was unimpressed. He glanced to John. "In fact, she may not have left entirely yet."

"So you burst into my office in the middle of an extremely private moment between my friends," John said, his voice shaking with fury, "making a dramatic declaration about the very case we have all twisted ourselves in knots over, and your declaration might not be true after all?"

"It's true," Gleason insisted, shoulders pulling back in offense. "The maid wouldn't lie. Not after what I offered her."

"So where has Lady Selby been staying in London then?" Samuel asked. He didn't have a dog in the fight where the rift between Blake and his wife was concerned. At least, he hadn't originally. Now he felt as though it were his duty—to Cameron, if to no one else—to help bring the case to a close and to reunite Lord Stanley with his father. "Did the nursemaid tell you that?"

Gleason's mouth tightened to a thin line. "There was no need," he insisted. "She was adamant that Lady Selby has left for New York already."

"She can't have," Cameron said with a strange, thoughtful look. "No ships have left for New York at any point in the last fortnight. There is one departing later today, though, at three this afternoon."

"I beg your pardon?" Gleason blinked at Cameron.

"When was the last time you checked the timetables for departures?" John asked Cameron, sending Gleason a triumphant smirk.

"Back around the first of the month," Cameron said. "Right around the time Mrs. Thorne whisked Archibald out of Hyde Park."

Gleason laughed. "And you remember timetables for that long?"

"Yes, in fact, he does," John said, stepping toward Cameron. "Cameron's memory is like nothing I've ever seen before. He can recall things after seeing them once to a degree that would astound you."

Gleason's brow shot up, but he wasn't entirely convinced.

"I've seen him do it," Samuel said. He grinned at Cameron. "It's just one of the many extraordinary things about this young man."

Cameron blushed, but underneath the smile he sent Samuel was a world of unresolved tension.

"That's all well and good," Gleason said before Samuel could do anything to sort his situation with Cameron, "but if that's when the ship is leaving, we should go straight to the dock and intercept Lady Selby."

John rubbed a hand over his face, as though he grudgingly agreed, but didn't want to say anything.

"Or we could go to her house to see if she's left yet," Cameron suggested.

"We don't know where she's been staying," John reminded him.

"Number fourteen, Manchester Square," Cameron said. All three of the other men in the room gaped at him. "I found the address on a bit of correspondence in Archibald's bag while he was asleep on the train back from Derby."

Samuel blinked. "So you helped Archibald escape from my sister after all?"

"And I take it the man got away from you," John added.

Cameron glanced anxiously to John. "I didn't think it would matter whether he got away from me or not, since I found the address."

"You should have told me as soon as you came in," John said, striding to the stand to fetch his coat.

"Stop haranguing the young lad," Gleason marched after him, seemingly glad to have a reason to chastise John. "He was busy snogging his sweetheart."

John sent Gleason a bitter glare over his shoulder but didn't say anything. Samuel nudged Cameron to follow after him and Gleason. The four of them made their way out of the office, carefully locking it behind them, then hailed the first cab that they could to take them to Marylebone and Manchester Square.

"It seems that nursemaid committed one final act of loyalty by telling you she'd already left," John said to Gleason as the carriage jostled along, clearly trying to get under the man's skin. Samuel had the distinct feeling John wanted to get under Gleason's skin in other ways too. "Not as clever as you thought you were?" John needled Gleason more.

"I accomplished a damn sight more than you did," he flung at John, then turned to Cameron, who sat opposite him in the rear-facing seat. "Memory skills like yours could come in handy in my line of work, Mr. Oberlin. Are you certain you wouldn't like to come work for me instead of this one?"

The way he said it, with a flirtatious glint in his eyes, tapping his foot against Cameron's, annoyed Samuel to no end.

"He's happy where he is," Samuel answered before John could, shoving Gleason's foot away from Cameron's.

Gleason laughed, as though he enjoyed nothing more than antagonizing people. The man was a bit of a shite, as far as Samuel was concerned, though John seemed utterly taken by him. The air in the carriage crackled with sexual tension, but not all of it was from John and Gleason. There were still so many things that Samuel wanted to say to Cameron, not to mention the fact that as soon as they had a second to themselves, he wanted to wrap Cameron up in kisses and make him giddy with pleasure.

All of that was still a long way off, though, and as soon as the cab pulled into Manchester Square and stopped in front of number fourteen, the four of them piled out onto the pavement.

"Do we just knock on the door and see if Lady Selby answers?" Samuel asked, staring up at the stately building. Manchester Square was in a good neighborhood. As far as hiding places went, Lady Selby had chosen a comfortable one.

"It's a start," John said, marching up the steps to the door and knocking.

Gleason had already started around the corner of the building, no doubt looking for the entrance to the mews or the servants' door.

As it turned out, Gleason had the right idea. No one came to answer the door. As soon as it became apparent no one would be coming to answer it, John leapt down the steps and followed Gleason. Samuel gestured for Cameron to join him in following as well.

As they turned the corner leading to the back of the short row of houses, Samuel whispered to Cameron, "You and I have a great many more things to talk about. So don't go disappearing on me again before we've had a chance to discuss them."

Cameron eyed him warily. "I'm sorry for running off last night without telling you. I had to get away from that place, I just had to."

"I understand," Samuel said, placing a hand briefly on Cameron's arm.

There wasn't time for more. They found the back entrance to the house, and John knocked on the kitchen door. No one answered there either.

"What do we do now?" Cameron asked, frowning.

"We go in anyhow," Gleason said, picking up a large rock from the corner of the courtyard. He marched straight up to the kitchen door and used the rock to smash a window. Once he tossed the rock aside, he reached through the broken pane to unlock the door and let them all in. "Simple," he said with a smile.

"That's housebreaking," Cameron told him.

"It gets the job done," Gleason argued with a flat expression.

John didn't look as though he approved, but he

marched into the house all the same. Gleason went after him, and after exchanging a quick, guilty look, Samuel and Cameron followed.

The house was empty, but it had a feeling of being lived in all the same. The oven was still warm, and even though it was neat and tidy, a few pots and pans had been left out to dry and a few bowls and spoons rested on the counter, as though a meal had been prepared there recently. The rest of the house had the same not-quite-abandoned feeling as they made their way up the servants' stairs to the ground floor.

"Someone was here recently," Gleason said as they strode down the hall, poking their heads into various rooms—a parlor, a dining room, and a reading room. "Perhaps as recently as this morning."

"How do you know?" John snapped.

Gleason paused to smirk at him. "Because there's still a fire lit in the parlor."

John clenched his jaw, as if his attempt to challenge Gleason had failed. Gleason was right, though. The fire in the parlor had died down, but it was still lit. The house was warm too, though a bit of a chill was starting to take over.

John and Gleason started up the stairs to the first floor, and Samuel was about to follow when Cameron stumbled to a halt, flinched, and changed directions to enter the parlor. Samuel abandoned John and Gleason to their upstairs search and went after Cameron.

"What is it?" he asked as Cameron stooped to pick

something up on the far side of an armchair that was angled toward the fire.

When Cameron straightened, he had a small slip of paper in his hands. "It looks like someone dropped this and didn't see."

"What does it say?" Samuel strode to Cameron's side, glancing over his shoulder as Cameron opened the folded paper. It appeared to be a telegraph addressed to Lady Selby from her father in New York. Samuel didn't really care. He was distracted by the scent of Cameron's skin and the heat of his body as they stood so close. He didn't care what the paper said as long as it meant he could be right up next to Cameron.

"Do you suppose the papa in question who sent this is Lady Selby's father?" Cameron asked, turning to Samuel.

The gesture brought Cameron's face to within inches of Samuel's. Samuel's heart leapt in his chest at the temptation to kiss Cameron. He could have if he wanted to, and indeed, he didn't see how he could resist. Everything about Cameron fit so well with him. The man's body was perfectly shaped for molding against his, but more importantly, Samuel could see with sudden, stunning clarity that Cameron's softness and domesticity was a perfect foil for his ambition and frustration with society. He'd been such a fool to think that Cameron was anything other than exactly what he needed to tame his wild nature. And with Cameron, he might actually enjoy being tamed.

Instead of answering Cameron's question, he slipped an arm around Cameron's waist and leaned in for the kiss he so desperately craved. But before their lips could meet, a shout was heard from upstairs.

Samuel leapt away from Cameron in shock, staring out to the hall as his heart pounded. So help him, if he was interrupted while attempting to show his heart to Cameron one more time—

"Unhand me! Let me go! You have no right to manhandle me like this!"

Samuel's eyes popped wide as he recognized Archibald's voice. After the last week in Derby, he would recognize the sound of Archibald's peevish complaints anywhere. Samuel glanced to Cameron—who's face had gone pink and his eyes glassy—then hurried into the hall. Cameron followed him, and by the time they reached the hall, John and Gleason were practically dragging Archibald down the stairs.

"Let go of me," Archibald continued to shout. "You have no right to treat me this way." Archibald stumbled to a stop, gasping hard enough to cough when he reached the bottom of the stairs. "You two again?" He glared at Samuel and Cameron.

"Where are Lady Selby and Lord Stanley?" John demanded, shaking Archibald by the arm, where he held him. "Where have they gone?"

"Where do you think they've gone, you blithering dolt?" Archibald snapped. "And let go of me."

When John did let go of him, Archibald bolted for

the front door. Samuel stepped into his path, preventing the man from escaping once again. "Not this time," he said in what he hoped was a menacing voice. The whole thing had him too baffled and excited to sound completely threatening, though.

"She's gone," Archibald said, a desperate edge in his voice, turning back to the others. "She's already left."

"Just as the nursemaid said," Gleason added with a triumphant grin for John.

"Not now," John snapped at him, then turned back to Archibald. "What do you mean she's already left?"

"Just what I said." Archibald glared at John, then sent spiteful looks to the rest of them. "She must've booked her passage after your bitch of a sister kidnapped me from Hyde Park," he snapped at Samuel. "She managed to send a letter to me in Derby. I suppose she found out who it was that kidnapped me, and bless her, she was clever enough to address the letter to the housekeeper instead of Mrs. Thorne, so I actually received it."

"The one in your bag," Cameron said, almost as an afterthought. The pieces fit. That was how Cameron learned this address.

Archibald ignored the comment, or didn't hear it, and went on. "Annamarie said her father had wired the money for her passage, and since I'd left her anyhow, she was leaving on the first ship she could find."

"But you didn't leave her," Cameron said.

"She doesn't know that," Archibald snapped. "Because your bloody sister wouldn't allow me to send word to her about what had happened." He glared at Samuel.

"Sammy has no idea how much trouble she's caused," Samuel sighed.

"That would explain this, though." Cameron held up the telegram he'd found on the floor. John frowned, and when Cameron handed the telegram over, Cameron went on with, "It must have accompanied the money. It confirms Lady Selby's father will meet them in New York on March twelfth."

"She really is gone then," Archibald said, his shoulder sagging and his face losing all color.

"Not yet," Gleason said, pushing past them on his way to the door. "Mr. Oberlin, you said the ship is set to depart at three this afternoon?"

"That's what the timetable said," Cameron confirmed.

"It's not yet even one," Gleason said. "We have plenty of time to stop Lady Selby and Lord Stanley from boarding that ship."

"Then what are we waiting for?" John said, following Gleason out to the street as though the two were engaged in a race.

Two hours should have been more than enough time to travel through London and to reach the marina where Lady Selby's ship to New York was docked. Should have been, but between walking down to Oxford Street to hail a cab, finding one that would stop for five restless-looking men, then navigating through one of the busiest parts of London, then across another congested area of the city, then on to perhaps the most bustling part of the Thames, they encountered one delay after another.

"We would have gotten there faster if we'd walked," John grumbled when they finally were let out at the edge of the riverfront.

But as it turned out, they were dropped off at the wrong point. They did have to walk then—or rather, run. It was agonizing to be able to see the massive steam ship waiting in its berth along the river, but knowing they had a long distance to run before they could reach it.

"Blake had better be willing to lavish us all with praise once we've finished this whole business," Samuel told Cameron as they dodged dock workers, pedestrians, and peddlers in their rush to the ship. "Leaping into more insanity is not what I intended to do with my first day back in London after the madhouse of Derby."

"Lord Selby just wants to be reunited with his son," Cameron scolded him in return, jumping out of the way of a matchgirl as she inadvertently walked into their path.

"You're right," Samuel said with as much of a smile as he could manage, under the circumstances. "You're right about so many things." He paused to jump out of the way of a dockside tavern worker chucking a bucket of something Samuel would rather not have identified into the street, then went on with, "You see, Cameron, this is why I need you in my life. I need you to keep me honest and to remind me to be good."

Cameron glanced to him with wide eyes and raised eyebrows, but he didn't say anything.

They skidded to a halt at the entrance to the marina where the passenger ship was moored, then navigated their way around a confusing maze of partitions and queues for boarding passengers. The trouble was, the queues were all empty, and the ship's crew appeared to be packing away the gangplank and closing up what looked to Samuel's untrained eye like a cargo door near the back of the ship.

"We need to speak with a passenger on that ship," John called to one of the uniformed porters on the dock. "We need you to find Lady Selby and her son and take them off the ship."

The porter flinched and stared at John as though he'd grown another head. "No one's getting on or off that ship now," he said. "She's boarded and on her way out."

"She can't be," Archibald said, grasping the sides of his head. "Annamarie!" he shouted up to the line of passengers waving goodbye to those watching on land. "Annamarie, don't leave me!"

Samuel was struck by a sudden, awkward sense of pity for the man. As rotten as Archibald was, there could be no denying that he actually cared for Lady Selby and was heartbroken that she'd left without him.

The trouble was, she'd left without him. She'd taken Blake's son and boarded a ship for America, just as Samuel gathered she'd been threatening to do all along.

"We can't let her get away," John said, storming away

from the unhelpful porter and glaring up at the ship. "There has to be a way to stop her."

"Do you intend to lasso an ocean-going passenger ship, like an American cowboy, and stop it from putting out to sea singlehandedly?" Gleason scoffed at him.

"I intend to do something other than just stand here," John growled, marching toward what looked like the shipping company's office farther up the dock.

But Samuel could see the problem as plain as day. The ship was already moving out into the Thames. Lady Selby had gotten away, and there was nothing John could do about it.

CHAPTER 21

It seemed horribly unfair. Cameron stood gaping up at the massive ship, overwhelmed with sadness on Blake Williamson's behalf. All of the work they'd done and all of the effort they'd put into finding Lady Selby and Lord Stanley, and there it went, sailing away on the afternoon tide.

"We'll book passage on the next ship to New York," John growled as he and Gleason raced away to the row of buildings that lined the riverfront. "We'll go after her. I refuse to give up, just because the woman has run home to her father."

"Cameron, come on." Samuel nudged Cameron, then tugged his sleeve when Cameron continued to watch the ship.

"It just seems so wrong," he sighed, peeling himself away from the dock and jogging after John and Gleason. "Blake just wants his son back."

"And he'll get the lad, I'm sure," Samuel said in a reassuring voice. "John won't stop now, just because Lady Selby is taking the boy to America. And Blake and Niall won't give up either."

Cameron sent Samuel a grateful look. It was nice to be reminded that some families fought to stay together instead of tearing themselves apart over what amounted to small things. And it touched Cameron in a deep, though somewhat awkward, way that Samuel seemed to care so much about the matter now.

Samuel cared. The realization tucked itself against Cameron's heart like a memento from a particularly enjoyable concert or a handkerchief left behind by a lover. He'd been so certain that Samuel didn't truly care about anything but his own needs. Now, he knew better. It was still fresh and delicate, and Cameron wasn't sure if it was wishful thinking on his own part, but something had changed with Samuel. He could see it in the set of the man's shoulders as they caught up with John—who was making inquiries about the next ship headed to New York—and in the way he stole hopeful looks at Cameron as Archibald pushed John out of the way in an attempt to get the same answers faster. The sharp edges felt as though they had been worn off of Samuel, as if he was ready for something new and different.

"This is an outrage," Archibald shouted at the poor clerk behind the counter at the ticket window. "This simply cannot be true. There must be a ship heading to New York sooner than a month. A bloody month!"

"Calm down, Archibald," John growled at the man. "Transatlantic ships aren't like trains. One doesn't come along every few minutes."

"I have to go after her," Archibald insisted. "I have to explain to her that I didn't leave her willingly."

"What you have to do right now," John said, thumping a hand on the man's shoulder to hold him still, "is march straight up to your brother's house and explain yourself to him."

Archibald whipped around to gawp at John. "And why would I want to see so much as hide or hair of Edward anyhow? The man is a disgrace."

"I think he would argue that you're the disgrace," Samuel said, his eyes narrowed at Archibald.

"This coming from you?" Archibald sneered at him. "If the people of London and those who hand over money to hear your trite music only knew half of what I know about you—"

"Are you certain there isn't a ship departing for America sooner than one month?" Cameron asked the clerk behind the ticket window hurriedly. The sooner they got Archibald out of the country, the better. Especially if he had even the slightest inclination to talk about what had happened in Derby with anyone, particularly the press.

Judging by the suddenly tight way Samuel held himself and the furious twitch at the corner of John's mouth, both men realized the danger Archibald presented to them all, but Samuel in particular. The newspapers would fall all over themselves to print accusations that a black composer who had gained renown was also an invert who should be tried under the Labouchere Amendment.

"Ships don't sail in and out of London like trains," the clerk answered Cameron's question. "There's one departing from Liverpool next month, but that's as much as I know." He closed the ticket window, ending the discussion and the hope of an easy way to go after Lady Selby.

"You and I need to have a little talk," Gleason said, sidling up to Archibald's side and clamping a hand around his arm.

"I don't think I want to talk to you," Archibald said, trying to pull away. Gleason wouldn't let him go.

"Nonetheless, you and I are about to become the very best of friends." Gleason tugged him to the side, marching him away from the ticket office.

That left John, Samuel, and Cameron staring after them, at a bit of a loss.

"You don't think Gleason will hurt Archibald, will he?" Cameron asked, chewing his lip in consternation.

"Honestly, at this point, I don't care if he does or not," John said, rubbing a hand over his face. "Ian Archibald has caused more trouble for more people than I could ever have dreamed of."

"Then you obviously haven't met my sister," Samuel said in a grave voice.

"I have to agree," Cameron mumbled. "Archibald was

a kitten compared to your sister. And I think he really does love Lady Selby."

John sighed and shook his head. "There's no one more stubborn than a man trying to protect his lover." He sent Samuel a pointed look, then went on with, "I'm heading to Darlington Gardens to tell Blake and Niall where things stand. Are the two of you coming with me?" He started forward.

Cameron followed, Samuel at his side, but once they reached the street and John raised his hand to hail a cab, Samuel said, "To be honest, John, I'm so exhausted right now that I think I might collapse. But I need to borrow your assistant for the rest of the day, so he won't be going with you to Darlington Gardens either."

Cameron's brow shot up, and shivers curled through him as he looked to Samuel. They did have a lot to talk about. Cameron was almost afraid of how much they needed to say. He was afraid that, after everything they'd been through, the conversation that was about to take place would just be another in a long line of disappointments in his life.

John, however, looked as though something nice were about to happen instead. He grinned at Samuel and clapped him on the arm. "You two go have it out," he said.

A cab pulled up, thanks to John's signaling, but John stepped aside and offered it to Cameron and Samuel instead. The driver didn't look particularly pleased, but when Samuel gave his address and the man saw how much he stood to earn from the long ride, he accepted their passage.

Minutes later, Cameron found himself tucked uncomfortably into the back of the carriage, Samuel seated by his side. "I don't really know what to say," he admitted in a mumble. "And I'm quite done in myself, so there's no telling what words might come out of my mouth, if any."

"Then let me say what needs to be said first," Samuel said.

They were confined in a carriage, hidden away from the rest of the world, even though they drove through the heart of London in the middle of the afternoon, but Samuel reached for Cameron's hand and held it all the same.

"You cannot know what I felt when we returned to Thorne Hall last night and you were gone," Samuel began in a strained voice. There was a wealth of genuine emotion in his eyes that made Cameron's throat close up. "But more than that, you cannot know how I felt when Sammy and I caught Burberry cornering you in that closet. I would have torn the man limb from limb if he'd hurt you." Samuel's voice went hoarse.

"He wouldn't have," Cameron reassured him, his own voice strained. His heart was in a million places at once. More than anything, he wanted to believe that this was the intimate, lovers' conversation that he'd longed for so long to hear. But he could never tell with Samuel. There were so many things about the man that he didn't yet understand, even if he wanted to, even if his heart pined for him. "I won't let anyone treat me like that anymore," Cameron went on. "I'm not someone who can be pushed around for any reason."

"No, you aren't, my darling, amazing love," Samuel said, squeezing Cameron's hand.

Cameron's eyes went wide at the endearments, but he didn't know what to say.

"You are right," Samuel went on. "You've been right from the outset. You deserve to be treated better than I tried to treat you."

Cameron's mouth dropped open as his heart sped up. "You didn't treat me badly," he argued, ashamed of how breathless he sounded. "You were just doing what comes naturally to you."

"Maybe in the past that was what came naturally," Samuel said, "but this entire past week in Derby has left me so ashamed."

"Why?" Cameron blinked at him. "There's nothing wrong with the way you choose to live your life."

"There is," Samuel insisted. "Not because living on the fringes of society and enjoying everything that means is wrong, but because you made me see I've been doing it for the wrong reasons."

Cameron felt as though he were standing on the edge of a precipice, looking down into a great unknown. "And now you want to live that way for the right reasons?"

Samuel shook his head and shifted so that he could hold both of Cameron's hands in his. "I was angry because I was not accepted," he said. "I wanted to make fun of so-called polite society by doing something they would abhor right under their noses, then laughing at them for not seeing the truth right in front of them."

"That doesn't sound very nice," Cameron said, instantly regretting his choice of words. He felt like a green schoolboy who still thought the world was a kind place, which it most decidedly wasn't.

Samuel laughed, but not in a way that made Cameron feel bad. "It wasn't. And the only person I was hurting by acting out was myself. You made me see that I can still take what I want from the world, I can still experience pleasure in a way that would make sweet maidens and society gentlemen blanch in terror, but I can do it out of love and not spite."

Cameron grinned sheepishly. "It's always better to make love out of love and not spite."

"It most definitely is."

Samuel surprised him by leaning in, placing a hand on the back of Cameron's head, and pulling him forward for a kiss. It was so unexpected and so lovely that Cameron made a sound of surrender before he could think better of it. After that, it was too late to change his mind. He kissed Samuel back, sliding his tongue against Samuel's and giving his heart over to everything it wanted to feel and experience.

"I love you, Cameron Oberlin," Samuel said, so softly it was almost a whisper, as he ended their kiss.

Cameron gasped, hardly believing his ears. He'd

wanted to hear Samuel say something like that for so long, and now that he had, it was all Cameron could do to wrap his mind and heart around it.

"I didn't think I was capable of love," Samuel went on with a laugh, holding Cameron's face in both hands. "I didn't think I even wanted it until you came along. But you changed my mind thoroughly."

"I did?" Cameron cursed himself for sounding so vulnerable.

"Thoroughly," Samuel repeated with a smile. "You made me see that what I thought was a good time was actually a hollow facsimile of love. You taught me what a good man truly is and how he deports himself. Though I cannot give you credit for showing me how lovely domestic life can be," he said with a bit of humor, backing away.

"I can't?" Cameron asked.

"No," Samuel said, mischief glittering in his eyes. "I have to give your sister, Georgie, credit for that." His expression grew serious for a moment. "You didn't hear the things she threatened to do to me if I hurt you. She made my own sister look like a tamed canary in comparison."

Cameron laughed in spite of the swirl of raw emotion storming through him. "That sounds like Georgie. You know she refuses to speak to the rest of the family because of the way they cast me out, and she refuses to give them a single penny, even though they've come begging a few times."

Samuel's brow shot up. "You should refuse to help them as well."

Cameron blew out a breath and lowered his head. "They're my family. I can't stop at least trying to help them."

Samuel surged toward him again. "And that's why I love you, my darling. You have a heart that is ten times bigger than mine." He kissed Cameron again with such a fiery passion that Cameron began to wonder how much longer the ride to Samuel's house was and whether they would have time for a little mischief before getting there. Samuel inched back and said, "You are a better man than me, Cameron, but I want you to teach me how to love as wildly and openly as you do. I want to become a better man, the man you deserve."

Cameron could hardly draw breath. Everything Samuel was saying was exactly what he wanted to hear. "Do you truly mean it?" he asked with just a hint of doubt.

"I do," Samuel answered somberly. "And I know that I haven't given you reason to believe that I would make that sort of a change in my life, but I can assure you, I am more than ready for it. I think I have wanted to settle down and find peace for far longer than I have been aware of it. It was only when I met you that I recognized what that ache in me was."

Cameron's mouth twitched as a wave of mischief washed over him. "Is that what that ache was?" he asked, leaning into Samuel for another kiss and reaching for his trousers as he did.

Samuel groaned deep in his throat as Cameron kissed and fondled him. "You teach me how to be a good, sweet, domesticated man," he mumbled between kisses, "and I'll teach you how to be a wanton rake."

"I don't think it will take much teaching," Cameron answered, stealing a kiss before finishing with, "I think we're both just about there as it is."

Samuel laughed ironically. "I'm a little too close to being there for comfort, at the moment." He leaned back and looked out the window. "Thank God we're almost home."

Those words thrilled Cameron far more than he expected them to. Home. A home with Samuel. Not a lonely flat in Darlington Gardens by himself or a loveless marriage to a woman for the sake of having children. The home he had truly wanted all along was the sort that Samuel was taking him to—a place of contentment with a man he loved, no matter what the outer trappings looked like.

As it happened, the outer trappings of Samuel's house were far grander than Cameron could have imagined. The carriage pulled up in front of a stately, Georgian home in Mayfair. He and Samuel took a moment to straighten themselves out and to make sure they wouldn't be arrested on sight as they alighted from the carriage. Samuel paid the driver with an air of perfect banality, then walked up to his front door and knocked so that the butler could let him in, as though he were part of the society he claimed to revile so much.

"Thank you, Gerard," Samuel said with a twinkle in his eye as he handed over his coat and hat to his butler. "Oh, and Mr. Oberlin will be staying for a while," he added.

"Should I prepare a room for him?" Gerard asked with one eyebrow slightly raised.

"No need," Samuel said, taking Cameron's hand and leading him up the staircase.

Cameron blushed down to his toes. "Aren't you worried about the servants talking?" he whispered as Samuel picked up speed and whisked him around the landing at the top of the stairs and on to a bedroom.

"Don't you recognize Gerard from The Chameleon Club?" Samuel asked, his lips twitching. "He isn't going to say a thing."

Cameron glanced back at the stairs and smiled. Perhaps he did recognize Gerard after all.

A moment later, as Samuel tugged him through the door into his bedroom, Cameron didn't care where he knew Samuel's butler from. As soon as Samuel closed his bedroom door, he pinned Cameron against it, leaning into him and kissing him hard while making quick work of the buttons of Cameron's jacket.

"I thought you told John you were exhausted," Cameron said, suddenly panting wildly and desperate to get his clothes off.

"I am tired," Samuel said. "I'm tired of living my life

without love and without you. I'm tired of pretending that I'm someone I'm not in order to gain a place in a society I don't actually care for. And I'm tired of sleeping alone at night."

"I would be tired of those things too," Cameron said on a sigh, tugging at Samuel's tie to loosen it.

"I want you in my bed every night, Cameron," Samuel went on. "I want your body entwined with mine, and I want to be inside you."

"All right, if you insist," Cameron said with a breathy laugh.

Their efforts to undress each other picked up in intensity.

"But more than that," Samuel went on, "I want your love in my life. I want your hand in mine and your heart beating beside mine. I don't care what people say or whisper behind my back at concerts or public events. I want you there with me, sharing in every good thing that comes my way. I want to take care of you, and I want you to take care of me in all the ways that truly matter."

Every word that Samuel spoke was as good as a kiss, as far as Cameron was concerned. "I want that too," he said, shrugging out of his shirt and stepping out of his trousers as Samuel finished with all of the fastenings. "I want to be yours, and I want you to be mine. Forever."

"Done," Samuel said.

It was the last word either of them were capable of. Samuel shed the last of his clothes, then pressed Cameron against the door with another kiss. Their whole bodies were involved this time, and Cameron moaned with pleasure as Samuel's mouth slanted over his and Samuel's hands roved his body. He was far less subtle about what he wanted and reached straight for Samuel's cock, stroking it eagerly until Samuel groaned with pleasure.

"Keep up with that and we'll both be spent and passed out in no time," Samuel growled, pulling away from the door and taking Cameron with him.

"I don't see that it matters," Cameron panted, scrambling for the bed with Samuel and falling over it in a tangle of arms and legs. "We have all the time in the world to treat each other properly."

"And that we will," Samuel panted, rolling Cameron to his back.

It felt perfect to be so intimately entwined with Samuel. Cameron circled his arms around Samuel's back, digging his fingertips into Samuel's shoulders as they kissed like it was the only thing keeping them alive. Cameron didn't think he would ever get enough of Samuel's mouth on his own, or Samuel's cock sliding against his as they both undulated with pent-up passion. There was so much beauty in the way the two of them fit together and the way their hearts beat as one. Even if they did have much to learn about each other and how they would work together, Cameron knew they would work.

"I can't wait any longer," Samuel panted, raining kisses down Cameron's neck and across his shoulders and chest. "I have to be inside of you. It's the only place I want to be."

"I want that too," Cameron gasped, beaming up into Samuel's eyes and moving his legs apart to show just how much. "More than you could possibly know. I love you."

"God, I love you too." Samuel bent down to kiss him so hard Cameron thought his lips might bruise. He then reached for the table beside the bed, sending Cameron rolling awkwardly to the side, and pulled out a small jar of lubricant from a drawer. "Don't think less of me for having this on hand," he told Cameron with an almost playful grin.

Cameron grinned right back. "Think less of you? I'm so glad you have that I could cry."

"I definitely won't make you cry," Samuel said, unscrewing the top of the jar. "But I can't promise you won't scream."

Cameron laughed. It was silly and juvenile of them, but his heart had never felt lighter. There was something charming and delicious about bantering like ridiculous schoolboys as he rolled fully to his stomach and lifted his hips while Samuel made sure they were both slick and ready. It didn't matter how many times Cameron had done what they were doing or what the circumstances of those encounters had been, when Samuel slipped his fingers inside to make certain Cameron was stretched and ready, it felt new and wonderful. And when Samuel pushed inside of him, causing Cameron to cry out with pleasure at the sensation of fullness, it felt like bliss.

Samuel moved gently at first, careful enough to make certain Cameron was comfortable and enjoying himself. And, by God, did Cameron ever enjoy himself. It was as though the two of them were one at last, as if it were their souls instead of just their bodies coming together. It was everything he had ever wanted, and when Samuel started moving faster and harder, when he reached around to stroke Cameron's cock as he did, it was more than he could ever have dreamed.

As predicted, neither of them lasted long. Cameron spilled himself into Samuel's hand with a deep, beautiful moan and a series of shudders that he felt through his entire body.

"Cameron," Samuel gasped a moment later, then cried out, "Dear, God," as he jerked and tensed, then softened and curled over Cameron's back.

It was such a simple act, so basic and primal, and yet it filled Cameron with the deepest possible sense of contentment. He groaned happily as Samuel moved out of him, then collapsed by his side. It was far too hot, and the two of them were sweaty and messy, but Cameron didn't care. He snuggled against Samuel's side, resting his head against Samuel's shoulder as they caught their breaths. That was what life was, after all—messy and uncomfortable, but also beautiful and full of satisfaction when two people were in love.

"I am going to make you the happiest man in the world," Cameron hummed, kissing Samuel's shoulder and closing his eyes, as if he'd finally come home.

Samuel chuckled sleepily and rolled to fold Cameron into his arms completely. "Not if I make you even happier than I am," he said.

Cameron laughed at the ridiculous endearments, confident that there was much more silliness where that had come from, and that he would enjoy every moment of it for the rest of his life.

EPILOGUE

It took John Dandie a long time and an extraordinary amount of effort to track down the address in Croydon, but he was finally certain he had the right place. Better still, the landlady was willing to show him up to the flat in exchange for more money than she was likely to get from every tenant in the modest building for a month.

"Don't you tell him it was me who let you up here," she whispered as she unlocked the door. "That one's as likely as not to slit my throat while I sleep if he knew."

"I'll say I climbed up to the window," John told her with a cheeky wink.

The landlady blushed and guffawed, then let him into the flat. A little flirtation never hurt when it came to getting his way, even if he had no interest in ever seeing anything like that through.

Both he and the landlady looked this way and that before John slipped into the flat. The main room was dark, but he was pleased to see that the newly constructed building was equipped with electric lights. He found the switch and turned it, illuminating the flat with the eerie, incandescent glow that he didn't think he would ever get used to.

A moment later, he froze, his mouth dropping open at the sight that met him. It was as though he had stepped right out of England and all the way to the other side of the globe. The flat was decorated completely in the Japanese style. Delicate silk and lattice screens stood along one side of the room. A low table with flat, round cushions instead of chairs sat on woven mats near the center of the room. A single orchid decorated the table. The rest of the furnishings were sparse, giving the room a neat, crisp appearance. The walls were decorated with scrolls that stretched almost from floor to ceiling. John wondered if the Japanese letters on the scrolls were poetry, or a curse on anyone who entered the flat without permission.

The flat was two rooms, and even though his mission didn't require him to step into the bedroom, he did. The furnishings were every bit as foreign as in the main room, with a tall, plain wardrobe and a mattress on the floor with plain white, precisely arranged bedclothes covering it and a single length of black silk draped across the end. Something about that silk sent a shiver down John's spine, as did the artwork hanging from the wall facing the bed. At least, John hoped it was artwork. It was a single, extremely long length of black silk cord looped repeatedly over an iron bar about as long as John's arm. The bar had what appeared to be shackles at either end.

Prickles broke out across John's skin at the intriguing bit of art. A shiver that left him hard and unable to catch his breath. Perhaps this mission wasn't as clever an idea as he'd thought after all.

"I always knew you were inclined that way," Gleason's voice spoke softly from the bedroom door.

John gulped and whipped around to face the man, heart pounding. Gleason leaned against the doorframe, arms crossed, the most wicked look John had ever seen sparkling in his deep, blue eyes. His dark hair was tousled, as if he'd walked through the wind, but it only seemed to add to the impression John had that the man was the very devil. He wanted so desperately to find a snappy reply, to gain the upper edge over Gleason, but he had, in essence, broken into the man's flat and didn't really have a defense.

"I didn't hear you come in," was all John could think of to say.

Gleason straightened and dropped his arms, prowling slowly closer to John. "Not the first time someone has told me that," he said with a heated grin. He nodded past John to the curious artwork. "I have often been told I'm extraordinarily accomplished at tying knots as well," he said, the gleam in his eyes making John even harder.

"And since we always knew we'd end up here eventually...." He let his words trail off, but John absolutely heard the invitation in them.

"You spent time in Japan," John said, feeling like a nervous idiot. The plan was for him to slip in and out of Gleason's flat, delivering his gift, and not being seen. His secondary plan, if he had been caught, was to remain firm and haughty. Well, he had the firm part well in hand.

"I was stationed there in my long-ago naval days," Gleason confirmed. "And I stayed after because I had... connections there."

John had no idea what to say to that, particularly since he was certain from the way Gleason spoke that those connections were of a romantic sort. That was clearly the past now, and John was more concerned with the present. In more senses than one.

"I brought you something," he said, reaching into the inner pocket of his jacket.

Gleason's brow went up. "You broke into my flat to give me a gift?"

"Not a gift," John said, though it was absolutely a gift. "An offer."

"An offer is even better than a gift," Gleason said, his voice rough around the edges.

He stepped close enough to take the envelope John presented to him. Their fingers brushed. John felt as though he'd been struck by lightning. His gaze darted to the black cord and iron bar on the wall as Gleason opened the envelope, and he had to fake a cough to hide the way heat rose up his neck to his face.

Gleason's cool, seductive manner switched to surprise as he pulled the ticket from the envelope. "Passage from Liverpool to New York on the RMS *Umbria*?" He glanced coyly at John, his mouth curving into a slow smile. "John, are you trying to get rid of me?"

The way his name sounded on Gleason's lips had John clenching his body to keep from trembling. "Actually," he said, then had to clear his throat before he went on, "I was hoping you would come with me."

Gleason's smile brightened, and his eyes flashed with lust. "This is an interesting turn of events."

"No, I mean—" John huffed an impatient breath. He was supposed to have the upper hand in this conversation, not Gleason. It seemed that no matter what he did, Gleason always had an edge on him. What terrified John was that he liked it. "Blake and Niall are coming as well," he blurted before he could say or do something stupid. "This is the next ship departing England for America. We'll still be a few days behind Lady Selby, but not so much that she will have had time to disappear with Lord Stanley once they reach New York. They'll still have a fortnight head start, but I figured that the more men we had on our side, and clever men used to finding people at that, the more likely we'll be to catch up to Lady Selby and force her to return Blake's son."

He felt like a complete nob for blurting out the entire plan, but it was better than giving Gleason the idea that he was inviting the man to go away on a holiday with him.

"So you're telling me that you need a man like me to help you find something you've lost?" Gleason asked, his sensual lips trembling with mirth as he raked a glance over John. Before John could answer, he said, "I accept."

John writhed on his spot. "You'll come to New York?"

"I'll help you find what you've lost," Gleason said.

John knew full well they were talking about two different things, but he was so far on the back foot that he knew he wouldn't be able to rescue himself. He had to get out.

"Good," he said with a sharp nod. He marched past Gleason, out of the bedroom and back to the flat's main room. "I'll see you in three days in Liverpool then."

He made it all the way to the door before Gleason stopped him with, "John."

The single word was issued as a command. John turned to him with a perfectly banal lift of his eyebrows, as if asking a mild question.

"Should I bring the cord?" Gleason asked with a wicked grin.

John's heart ran riot in his chest, and he was in serious danger of unmanning himself. He scowled deeply at Gleason and marched to the door, grabbing the handle and wrenching it open. Before he fled into the hall, he shot back over his shoulder, "Fuck you."

As he dashed away, slamming the door behind him,

he could have sworn he heard Gleason say, "I certainly hope so."

I hope you've enjoyed Samuel and Cameron's story! Just a couple of quick author's notes....

I actually based the character of Samuel Percy, in part, off of real-life composer Samuel Coleridge-Taylor. Samuel Coleridge-Taylor was a very famous and celebrated black composer in Victorian England. He was the son of an Englishwoman and a doctor from Sierra Leone, but he was born and raised in London, and as an adult Coleridge-Taylor married a white Englishwoman. He was certainly one to break the stereotypes that we think of when we think Victorian England, and he (and his father) was absolutely proof that the entire Victorian era was a lot less whitewashed than we've been led to believe. But sadly, the incident in this book where Samuel is barred from entering the Royal Albert Hall because of his race, even though his symphony was being premiered, is based on an actual event from Coleridge-Taylor's life. So even though strides were being made, we still had a very long way to go.

. . .

JUST A LITTLE GAMBLE

ANOTHER NOTE I WANTED TO MAKE IS ABOUT telegraph boys. Sadly, back in the late 19th century, it was well known that telegraph boys delivered far more than telegrams. They were notorious for it, and very few of them were actually as old as Cameron was in this story when he took up the job. Doubly sadly, it was an easy way for attractive adolescents to make extra money for themselves and their families. The scandals involving prominent gentlemen of London society caught with telegraph boys sold a heck of a lot of papers in the 1890s, when newspaper readers suddenly developed a hunger for salacious stories involving men caught in violation of the Labouchere Amendment. The sudden public interest in these salacious stories might have helped the plight of telegraph boys in the short term, but they did a heck of a lot of damage to gay men, who could no longer easily fly under the radar of public notice, as they had for decades before. In fact, it became more dangerous to be a gay man in London from the 1890s up until World War One than it had been for half a century before that, as arrest records and court documents show. Just proof that even if we gain rights, it's far too easy for us to lose them again.

ARE YOU INTERESTED IN LEARNING MORE ABOUT THE continuing search for Blake's son and the trip to America to chase after Lady Selby? How do you think Blake's wide-eyed and impressionable valet, Xavier Lawrence is going to handle the big adventure, especially when he runs into gorgeous, sensual dancer Alexander Plushenko aboard ship? The only thing more thrilling than finding Zander is losing him and having to find him again. And you can find out more in *Just a Little Mischief*! Keep clicking to get started....

IF YOU ENJOYED THIS BOOK AND WOULD LIKE TO HEAR more from me, please sign up for my newsletter! When you sign up, you'll get a free, full-length novella, *A Passionate Deception*. Victorian identity theft has never been so exciting in this story of hope, tricks, and starting over. Part of my West Meets East series, *A Passionate Deception* can be read as a stand-alone. Pick up your free copy today by signing up to receive my newsletter (which I only send out when I have a new release)!

Sign up here: http://eepurl.com/cbaVMH

ARE YOU ON SOCIAL MEDIA? I AM! COME AND JOIN the fun on Facebook: http://www.facebook.com/merryfarmerreaders

I'M ALSO A HUGE FAN OF INSTAGRAM AND POST LOTS of original content there: https://www.instagram.com/merryfarmer/

. . .

AND NOW, GET STARTED ON JUST A LITTLE MISCHIEF...

London, St. James's Park – November 1890

It was a bad idea. Every bit of it. Xavier Lawrence turned up the color of his wool coat and tucked his hands under his arms as he walked with his friends along the perimeter of St. James's Park. There was a nip in the air, but it wasn't so much the cold that made him shiver and shrink in on himself, it was the dare his friends had proposed.

"Come on, Xavier," Adam nudged him, swaying close enough for Xavier to smell the alcohol on his breath. "You're new to London, but that doesn't mean you have to stay a virgin forever."

Adam and Nick snorted with laughter, practically falling all over themselves as they stumbled along the path.

"I'm not—oh, never mind," Xavier said, letting out an irritated breath. He could barely see the cloud of frost it made in the scattered lamplight of the park. St. James's Park was dark at night, which suited the men who roamed in the shadows on a night like that perfectly.

"How long has it been, eh?" Nick tittered—yes, tittered like one of the misses in the house where he served as a footman. "Surely not since you came down from West Riding, eh?"

"There's hardly been time," Xavier started to argue. "Lord Selby has been deeply occupied with family matters since we arrived and—"

He gave up explaining when Adam and Nick proved they hadn't been listening to anything since the words "deeply occupied" by guffawing and sniggering until they sagged against each other. Xavier didn't truly blame them for having too much to drink at The Cock and Bear earlier. All three of them were in service, and it was a rare night when their nights off coincided. It was even rarer that the three of them would be in London at the same time at all. Adam's and Nick's families traveled down frequently and spent more than just the season in their comfortable Mayfair townhomes, but Xavier hadn't been to London at all since becoming Blake's—that is, Lord Blake Williamson, the Duke of Selby's—valet years ago. Blake despised travel, and up until recently, he despised London. And Xavier still hadn't entirely resolved himself to referring to his august employer by his given name, but Blake insisted that was the way of The Brotherhood, but—

But Xavier was letting his mind wander too much to keep his thoughts away from the dare at hand.

"I remain unconvinced that this is a good idea," he hissed to Adam and Nick after a man in a dark coat with his hat pulled low wandered past them, glancing a little longer than he should have.

Adam made a sound of sloppy derision and pushed away from Nick to drape his arm over Xavier's shoulder. "St. James's is the best cruising location in London," he slurred, wafting fumes of alcohol in Xavier's direction. "Anyone can catch a bit of a bauble or a fit of a fumble or a tad of a tumble—oh dear, what was I saying?" He laughed, stumbling a bit as they walked, and dragging Xavier's shoulder down.

"What our esteemed friend is trying to say," Nick went on, sniffing and attempting to sound like his titled employer, "is that out there in the dark is a likely lad just waiting to thrust his pretty little hand down your trousers to get you off."

"And if you're lucky, not to mention in the proximity of an obliging shrub, he'll drop to his knees and suck you so hard you'll be like a wolf howling at the moon," Adam finished. He followed his statement with a howl of his own.

"Shush!" Xavier hissed, glancing around. "Are you trying to draw the coppers? They're probably everywhere in here, blackmailers too, just waiting to bring us all up on charges."

Indeed, there had been more than a few sensational arrests of "inverts and perverts" in St. James's Park reported in papers of late. Ever since the Cleveland Street Scandal a few years ago, newspapers couldn't get enough of salacious gossip stories about men caught with their trousers down. After years, decades, of relative obscurity, between the evils of the Labouchere Amendment and the public's thirst for titillation, what had once been the sort of thing one simply didn't talk about while carrying on regardless had turned into fuel for the fire of outrage that made newspapermen wealthy.

"We're just trying to initiate you into the joys and wonders of London," Nick said, dragging Xavier to a stop near one of the paths that crossed through the center of the park. "Don't you get tired of playing with your own willy all the time?"

"Yeah, let some other likely bloke play with it for a change," Adam added, far too loud for Xavier's comfort.

"Keep your voices down," Xavier scolded them again. He shook his head. There was only one way to shut the two nutters up. "Alright, I'm going in," he said, turning to start along the path.

"Are those the words of endearment your last bit of fun said?" Nick called after him.

Xavier turned to make a rude gesture at his friends—and they truly were his friends, but perhaps more so when they weren't in their cups—and hurried into the beckoning shadows of the park.

"I must be mad," he murmured to himself, tucking his hands into his coat pockets and trying not to look as conspicuous as he felt.

He reminded himself that he didn't actually have to find a man who would exchange a quick fumble for a few coins. He could cross the park and circle back, then tell Adam and Nick that he'd gone through with it. Paying for something like that felt dirty, even if that was what men like him, Adam, and Nick generally did in London. He'd never had any trouble finding a friend for a bit of fun at home, near Selby Manor. He'd always been rather popular with that set, though he wouldn't ever think of describing himself as fast. He was valet to a duke, after all. There were standards to maintain.

Standards which he felt even more keenly, now that Blake was in such a horrible, tragic spot. They'd just come to London less than a fortnight before—both as a way to hide Blake's daughters, Lady Margaret and Lady Jessica, from Lady Selby, and as so that they could track down Lady Selby and Blake's heir, Lord Stanley—and Xavier had been extra vigilant about not drawing notice to the family in any way, good or bad. He felt a great deal of personal responsibility toward Blake and the entire Williamson family. Not only had Blake hired him as valet knowing his proclivities, doing so had restored Xavier's flagging reputation with his family after his previous employer had sacked him. Sacked him for refusing an inappropriate advance, of all things. Even though Xavier had sworn to the man he would never tell a soul. The last thing Xavier wanted to do now that he was in London was bring more shame down on Blake's shoulders.

"Got a match?"

The friendly voice that issued from the shadows as Xavier walked past a spreading oak came as such a surprise that Xavier gasped and jerked to see who had spoken. He twisted, searching, and found a handsome young man with some of the most striking features he'd ever seen leaning against the oak's trunk, his hands in his pockets.

"I...er...are you addressing me, sir?" Xavier's heart sped up and his hands instantly went clammy.

The handsome man shrugged and pushed away from the tree. "I don't see anyone else."

Xavier swallowed. "Oh. Right." He craned his neck, looking this way and that, searching the darkness for his friends, policemen, his mother, anyone who might rain holy terror down on him for even thinking of talking to a handsome stranger. He focused back on the handsome man, who had strolled to stand so close to him that Xavier caught the scent of his shaving soap. The man didn't have a cigarette or a pipe or anything that would require a match. "Um, no," he said, bristling with anxiety. How was one supposed to do this at any rate? "I'm afraid I left my matches at home."

The handsome man shrugged and hooked his arm suddenly through Xavier's. "I guess we'll just have to go home and fetch them, then."

They started forward. Xavier thought he might fall over his own feet. Everything around them suddenly seemed threatening and full of eyes. He might as well have been walking through the park naked, he felt so conspicuous.

"Not a man of many words I see," the handsome man said.

"It's not that," Xavier mumbled, glancing this way and that. "It's just that I've only arrived in London recently, and my friends put me up to this, and I honestly have no idea what in God's name is going on."

The handsome man laughed. "If it makes you feel better, I don't generally do this myself." He slowed his pace, his arm losing some of its tension. In fact, Xavier hadn't realized how tense the man was until he relaxed a bit. "Stop glancing around," he whispered. "It looks suspicious. Pretend that we're old school chums or something like that."

Xavier nodded tightly, then stopped and stared at the man. "Hang on, you're American." He felt like a fool for not noticing the man's accent before. Then again, he'd been too stunned by everything he was doing to notice much of anything.

"Does that excite you?" the man asked.

Xavier's brow shot up to his hairline. In fact, it did, but the question was so blatant and titillating that he hardly knew what to do with himself.

The handsome man must have seen that he had Xavier completely off-guard. He glanced around quickly, then pulled him off the path and down to the shadows near the base of one of the bridges spanning the lake. Judging by a muffled sound coming from the other end of the bridge, someone was already plying their trade in the shadows.

The handsome man spun Xavier so that his back was against the foot of the bridge and started in on the buttons of his coat. "What do you like," he murmured, leaning in to whisper against Xavier's ear as he worked. "I can't say I know what the going rate for anything is these days, but I'm certain we could negotiate."

"I—oh!" Xavier let out a shaky cry as the man sucked on his earlobe. He had the horrible feeling that his boots were sinking into the mud of the lakeshore, but his cock was going in a different direction entirely.

Even more so when the handsome man finished with his coat and cupped his stiffening erection. He hummed as if impressed, "I see I have your attention."

"You have more than that," Xavier croaked. Flirting? He was flirting with the man? What was he thinking? It was near midnight in the middle of a royal park. He must have gone mad.

But the handsome man smelled divine, and he was gorgeous, and as he leaned in, Xavier could feel the heat of his well-formed body, even through their clothes. It was everything Xavier could do to maintain his dignity of bearing when the man unfastened his trousers and stroked his hand against his cock.

"What do you say?" the man murmured, kissing Xavier's neck. "A pound for a pound?"

Xavier's eyes popped open and he tensed. "That's an exorbitant sum for a fumble in the dark." He would have felt far more confident saying as much if his voice didn't crack and if he wasn't already leaking pre-come all over the man's hand.

"I told you I didn't know the going rate for these things," the man said, then shocked Xavier by slanting his mouth over his and devouring him with the single most sinful kiss Xavier had ever had.

WANT TO READ MORE?
PICK UP JUST A LITTLE MISCHIEF TODAY!

Click here for a complete list of other works by Merry Farmer.

ABOUT THE AUTHOR

I hope you have enjoyed *Just a Little Gamble*. If you'd like to be the first to learn about when new books in the series come out and more, please sign up for my newsletter here: http://eepurl.com/cbaVMH And remember, Read it, Review it, Share it! For a complete list of works by Merry Farmer with links, please visit http://wp.me/P5ttjb-14F.

Merry Farmer is an award-winning novelist who lives in suburban Philadelphia with her cats, Torpedo, her grumpy old man, and Justine, her hyperactive new baby. She has been writing since she was ten years old and realized one day that she didn't have to wait for the teacher to assign a creative writing project to write something. It was the best day of her life. She then went on to earn not one but two degrees in History so that she would always have something to write about. Her books have reached the Top 100 at Amazon, iBooks, and Barnes & Noble, and have been named finalists in the prestigious RONE and Rom Com Reader's Crown awards.

ACKNOWLEDGMENTS

I owe a huge debt of gratitude to my awesome beta-readers, Caroline Lee and Jolene Stewart, for their suggestions and advice. And double thanks to Julie Tague, for being a truly excellent editor and to Cindy Jackson for being an awesome assistant!

Click here for a complete list of other works by Merry Farmer.

Printed in Great Britain
by Amazon